Amelia Grey's Fireside DREAM

Abby Clements

Quercus

First published in Great Britain in 2013 by

Quercus
55 Baker Street
7th Floor, South Block
London W1U 8EW

A CIP catalogue record for this book is available
from the British Library

PB ISBN 978 1 78206 430 5
EBOOK ISBN 978 1 78206 431 2

10 9 8 7 6 5 4 3 2 1

Printed and bound in Great Britain by Clays Ltd, St Ives plc

Typeset by Ellipsis Books Limited, Glasgow

Abby Clements worked as a book editor before switching to writing. She lives in Crouch End with her partner and son in a home that (thankfully) needed less work than the one in this story. *Amelia Grey's Fireside Dream* is her third novel.

Also by Abby Clements

Meet
me
Under
the
Mistletoe

Vivien's
Heavenly
ICE
CREAM
SHOP

For anyone who's ever made a house a home

PART ONE

Summer

Chapter 1

The classroom slowly emptied, my students from 10E filing out into the school corridor in a hum of chatter, spirits high as the temperature outside soared. I walked from desk to desk collecting the copies of *The Great Gatsby* I'd handed out to them an hour before.

'Do you reckon anyone even opened these?' I asked Trey, who was lingering by his desk. At least a few of them had watched the film, so it had been possible to get some kind of discussion going.

'Dunno, Miss.' Trey shrugged, putting his exercise book away in his navy Nike rucksack. Behind him was the green sugar-paper display I'd put up at the start of term with examples of the class's creative writing: *If I were Prime Minister*;

Mo Farah for Mayor; *iPhones Allowed in Exams* . . . There was nothing from Trey there. Four years he'd been in my English class, and he still hadn't completed a piece of work without me sitting over him.

I checked the wall clock: 11 a.m., enough time to grab a coffee in the staffroom during break. Hopefully Carly would be around and I'd have a chance to catch up with her on the weekend. She'd been planning to see Alex again and I couldn't wait to hear how it had gone.

'Hand over your report book, then.' I held out my hand for it.

Trey made his way to the front of the classroom. His tie was loosely knotted and he wore a gold signet ring on his right hand. He towered over my five foot three frame these days.

I took the small book he passed me and signed it, before handing it back. 'You know how happy it's going to make me, the day we get you off report?'

Trey shrugged. 'I didn't do anything wrong this time.'

'So what happened?'

I sat down and pulled out a chair next to me.

'Nothing,' he said, with a shrug. 'I don't really want to talk about it, Miss.' He dragged the chair out anyway, the legs scraping on the floor, and slumped down in it. He let his rucksack fall to the floor.

I looked him in the eye, waiting for him to speak. Noise

drifted in through the open windows of the classroom, shouts and chatter as morning break got underway outside, the early burst of summer heat heightening the students' excitement levels. Trey's gaze dropped, his eyes shaded by thick eyelashes, and he shrugged his shoulders again.

'Go on.' I unlocked my desk drawer, taking out my wallet and phone – a precaution I'd started to take this term, after my bag was stolen during class time. 'I'm not in a hurry.' I put my things away in my handbag. Trey stayed silent.

'Like I said, I didn't do anything. Garrett walked in at a bad time. It looked like I hit Andy, but I never. Garrett's got it in for me anyway; he's been trying to get me expelled for ages.'

'I don't think that's true. If Mr Garrett thinks someone is being hurt, he can't stand there and watch it happen. He has to do something.'

'Like put me on report again. Andy and me were just messing about. Garrett wants me out. I don't even care any more, Miss.'

'Well, *I* do. You've got potential, Trey, and we can get you a few passes next year if you're willing to put the work in.'

'Potential,' he said, almost under his breath. '*What* potential . . . ?'

'Come on.' I gave him a gentle nudge. The faintest of smiles appeared at the corner of his mouth. For a moment he looked like the smart, cheeky kid he used to be, the one who'd joined my class in Year 7. 'You're bright. You're great with group work. You make us all laugh – when you're in a better mood than today. Now, just give me something on paper so that we can prove it to everyone else.'

'I know.' He scuffed the toe of his trainer against the table leg. 'I need to work harder.'

I tried to catch his eye. 'You can do it, you know. If you want support, I'm here. And your form tutor is too.'

He nodded silently, and bent to pick up his bag. 'Thanks, Miss.'

'Any time.' I turned to switch off the interactive whiteboard, and closed my laptop, checking the time before I did – five minutes, no time for a coffee. My chat with Carly would have to wait – but I could still manage a quick dash to the toilet before the next class arrived.

Trey got up. I watched him step out into the buzz of the corridor, his dark St Catherine's uniform quickly lost in the crowd by the metal lockers.

Maybe we can do it, I thought, picking up my handbag and heading for the toilet. Trey could still pull through his exams, come out with something. That glimmer of hope was why, after seven years of preparing classes and marking, sometimes barely seeing Jack, and often feeling a lot older than twenty-nine – with the wrinkles to boot – I was still teaching.

I reached into my handbag for my mobile – Jack usually messaged me about this time. I searched inside, but my hand touched nothing but a small notebook and the fabric lining. The bag felt light. *You're kidding me.*

My phone and my wallet were gone.

'A large one,' I said to Jack, as he brought a bottle of wine out that evening over dinner in our flat.

'Here you go.' He filled my glass, then came around to my side of the kitchen table and smoothed my dark brown hair – the short fringe never lay quite flat. 'Sounds like you could do with it after today.'

'Oh *yes*.' I shook my head, and gave a wry laugh. With his black curls and the trace of stubble on his jaw, Jack hadn't changed much since we'd met as students. One touch from him could still make me melt. 'I'm so annoyed, Jack. I feel like such an idiot.'

'You shouldn't have to deal with this stuff, Amelia. Simple as that. Did you cancel your cards?'

'Yeah, I sorted all that out at lunchtime. Luckily there was only a tenner in there in cash.'

'And your phone?'

'After the last one got nicked, I started taking my old Nokia into work. I've got my iPhone here.'

'Good. What about getting it back, though? You said you knew who took it?'

'I do. But it looks like Trey's gone. Lewis and I spoke to his form tutor, but he didn't turn up for afternoon registration. I'd be surprised if he turns up tomorrow. He's been looking for an excuse not to come back and maybe this is it.'

'You don't want to report it to the police?'

'Oh God, no. I mean, I'm furious with him, don't get me wrong. But at the same time, I know what he goes home to every night. It's a miracle he makes it into school at all. His brother left the school three years ago and went straight to prison. I don't want him going the same way.'

'You can't fix everything,' Jack said, 'but you're a good teacher.'

'Thanks. I think I needed to hear that today.' I smiled at him.

Dexter, our rescue tabby, wove his way through my chair legs, mewling gently. In our cramped kitchen, the three of us had got used to being at close quarters, and had learned how to work with and around each other. Dexter jumped up onto my lap and lay down, tilting his head towards me, inviting a stroke. A train passed by outside on its way to Dalston Junction, and the windows rattled a little in their frames. Another thing we'd all got used to.

Jack reached over to squeeze my hand. His touch – familiar, sure and steady – felt good.

'Summer holidays are just around the corner,' he said.

'Just think – in a couple of weeks it'll be lie-ins, picnics with Carly, ice creams, a chance to get perspective on it all.'

'You're right.' Jack, an eternal optimist, had the knack of reminding me what really mattered. 'Bring on the holidays.'

I left for St Catherine's at 6.30 a.m. the next day, driving through the pre-rush hour morning. Even the usually smoggy city air was light and fresh with summer on the way. The early start would give me some quiet time to prepare my classes before the chaos of the school day. I parked our silver Corsa and went upstairs to the staffroom on the second floor of the 1960s school block, immediately spotting Carly over by the window as I entered. Against the morning light, the silhouette of her curvy figure and springy, shoulder-length curls was unmistakeable.

'Hello stranger,' she called out, her smile wide. Silver bangles jangled on her wrists.

'Hi,' I replied, walking over and giving her a hug.

She boiled the kettle, got my mug out of the cupboard and automatically filled it with coffee, topping it up with milk from the fridge. We never needed to ask: late nights studying for our qualifications, and now years of teaching together, meant we knew each other's caffeine requirements pretty well. Long days in the classroom, then in and out of each other's shared flats in the evenings, planning lessons and chatting over coffee and toast. After qualifying, we'd both applied to St Catherine's and held our breath – we knew how unlikely it was that we'd both score jobs at the same place, but we did – and it had cemented our friendship for good.

'Heard about what happened to you yesterday, Amelia. That sucks.'

'It does a bit. Second time this term too. But worse things happen at sea, today's a new day . . . yadda yadda. Anyway, how are *you*?' I lowered my voice to a whisper; although there were only couple of other teachers already in, you never knew who might be listening. 'How was this weekend, seeing Alex?'

'It was amazing. We met for coffee and spent the day walking by the canal. We just chatted, walked his dog, got ice creams.'

'Nothing happened?'

'Nope.' Carly laughed. 'Nothing. And that's fine. We're still getting to know each other. It isn't right to move things on yet.'

'And is he planning to say anything to Jules?'

'Yes. At least he wants to. It's just a matter of finding the right time, which isn't now. A few more weeks.'

'After exams?'

'I think so. When Jules has officially left.'

I remembered how Carly had looked the day after she

met Alex, about a month ago. She'd come into the staffroom with a glow in her olive-skinned cheeks, something I hadn't seen since she broke up with Ethan. Having met Alex myself, I could understand why. He was gorgeous – tall, with salt-and-pepper hair, a lilting Irish accent and a wicked sense of humour.

The only issue was how he and Carly had met – at parents' evening. Alex's son was Jules Garrehy, one of Carly's A-level students, which meant they'd kept their friendship as just that, a friendship, so far.

'You must be going out of your mind,' I said.

'Yes, a bit.' Carly had a mischievous expression on her face. 'It's like he's this close,' she drew her fingers together so that they were almost touching, 'but off limits at the same time. It's frustrating. But then, I'm also happy.'

'Good. That you're happy, I mean. How do you think Jules is going to react?'

'Who knows?' Carly said, shaking her head. 'I've never been good at predicting teenage boys' behaviour. But Alex and Jules's mum have been separated for years now, and she has a new partner . . .'

'That's positive.' I took a sip of coffee. 'Although I suppose your mum or dad getting a new partner is one thing. That partner being one of your teachers probably changes the situation a bit.'

'True,' Carly said, biting her lip.

'Anyway, you're right not to hurry things. I'm the one being impatient. I just think you guys would be great together.'

'Thank you.' Carly's wide-set blue eyes lit up. 'So do I. I hope we get a chance. For now I guess I should just try and enjoy what's left of my twenties, being young, free and single.'

'Don't rub it in,' I said, laughing. 'A month, that's all I've got! Then I'm practically middle-aged.'

'Didn't we make a bucket list together, back on the teaching course?'

'God, you're right.' I smiled at the memory of Carly and me in the park, back when turning thirty seemed like something that would never happen to us. 'I probably still have it somewhere. I guess now's my last chance.'

'A few weeks of threesomes, tequila and abseiling, then?'

I laughed. 'Might kiss a policeman at Notting Hill Carnival. That was on there somewhere.'

Where had I expected to be at thirty? Married to Jack. Tick. Living in a flat where there was room to swing Dexter . . .

'It's only a number,' Carly said, 'and an excuse for a party. You're having one, right?'

'Yes.' Actually, I hadn't really thought about it. 'I'll keep you posted.'

'Listen, I'd better shoot off.' Carly gave me a hasty hug goodbye and grabbed a clear pencil case full of markers from the side. 'Got to rearrange the desks for a debate the kids are having in period one.'

'Oh yeah? What's today's topic?' Carly's sociology classes didn't always adhere to the curriculum as strictly as the headmaster would have liked, but her students adored her.

'"Women today have it easier than their mothers." Discuss.'

'No way,' I said, laughing. 'Things were a breeze back then.'

I thought of my mum, Rosie. When she was my age she was an air hostess with bright, bottle-blonde waves and a permanent tan, travelling the world. Grandma Niki and my grandpa looked after me – their brunette tomboy of a granddaughter – when Mum was away, down in their house in Streatham. One moment Mum was in Bali, the next in Tel Aviv, calling me up and filling me in on her adventures, occasionally taking me with her on longer trips. Mum's working life had seemed effortless and glamorous. OK, so apart from Dad's occasional visits she was practically a single parent – but Gran and Grandpa had helped out. And anyway, as far as I understood it, going it alone had really been her choice.

'It's Class 9F. So you can guarantee they'll think they know the answer.'

'Good luck. And let me know what they say.'

After lunch, I covered Isabel Humphries' Year 12s, as I had been doing for three months now, since she started her chemotherapy treatment. I handed out the sample exam paper I'd chosen for practice that morning, and the students, calmer and quieter than in my other classes, were writing in silence. As they worked, I caught up with some marking.

When the bell rang, signalling the end of the school day, the students filed up to my desk to hand in their answer sheets.

'Miss Grey,' said Eloise, a tall girl with hair tied back in a tight ponytail and foundation a shade darker than her skin. She dropped her voice to a whisper. 'Is it true that Mrs Humphries is dying, Miss?'

A crowd had built up around my desk, waiting to hear my answer. 'She's not very well, but she's getting the best treatment at the moment. Let's all keep our fingers crossed for her.'

'That means she's going to die,' Rob said, nudging Eloise in the side and then looking down at the ground. 'She's not coming back, is she? But she promised us, Miss. She said she'd help us prepare next year.'

I thought of the last time I'd seen Isabel Humphries, the

Head of English and the woman who'd mentored me since I was newly qualified. She'd come into the staffroom a month previously to meet me and check how her classes were doing. She had been thinner, her blonde hair patchy, and she'd looked older than her fifty-two years. But her voice and will were still strong and she was as matter-of-fact as ever, making sure I was following her lesson plans to the letter and doing enough exam practice to ensure her Year 12s would be ready for their A-levels the following year. When she'd got up to leave, she'd paused.

'You'll look after them for me, won't you?' she'd asked, her voice uncharacteristically soft.

'Of course I will,' I'd replied.

'Good. Because I trust you, Amelia.'

She hadn't told me then that the effects of the chemotherapy were so serious she'd decided not to return to work, but Lewis Garrett had let us know they'd be interviewing for a new Head of English.

'The best thing you can do for Mrs Humphries,' I said, looking at the small group of seventeen- and eighteen-year-olds milling by my desk, 'is work hard, and get the results you deserve. If Mrs Humphries isn't able to come back, then I'll be here to help you do that.'

'Cool,' Eloise said, her tone melancholy. 'You're all right, Miss Grey.' She turned to the other students. 'C'mon. Let's go.'

The teenagers left the room, subdued. I put their exam papers into my bag ready to mark at home that night.

Carly put her head round the door of my empty classroom. 'Fancy a drink, Amelia? Gorgeous hot evening out there. A few of us are heading over to the Kings Arms.'

'I'd love to.' I checked the time. 'But I promised Jack dinner tonight. Plus I've got a lot of marking to do.'

'You sure?' Carly asked, one eyebrow raised.

'Next time.'

Half an hour later, I was back at our flat. I turned the key in the lock and noticed a new graffittied tag along the top of our front door, in black marker pen. I'd have to get the paintbrushes out again.

Jack and I lived three floors up in an ex-local authority block a stone's throw from Broadway Market in east London. It was near to friends, handy for both our jobs, and over time we'd warmed to the area. At weekends we'd have coffee or brunch nearby, or go for a walk along the canal to Victoria Park. My best friend from university, Sunita, and her husband, Nico, were practically neighbours, and Carly was only a bus ride away. But the graffiti, and the constant noise, had started to wear both of us down and it felt like time to move on. We had put the flat on the market a couple of months before, but the response had been underwhelming – just one offer under the asking price so far. The search for somewhere new was proving just as tricky: while we'd had a mortgage agreed in principle, we'd yet to find a place we liked that was within our budget.

I put my bag down in the hallway and walked to the kitchen, passing framed stills from Jack's first feature-length animation project, *Pupz*, the story of a Labrador who has a litter of robot puppies. He'd studied animation at college, and after a couple of years interning at an animation studio he'd been given a permanent job and from there had started coming up with his own project ideas. *Pupz* had been Jack's career high to date – three years in the making and a hit at the box office in both Britain and the US. Since then, project commissions had slowed a bit, and at the start of the year he'd hit a creative block he hadn't quite worked past yet – but he was on the cusp of coming up with something good, I knew it.

I fed Dexter and sat down at the kitchen table to mark exam papers. It was eight when Jack arrived home after football. His T-shirt and hair were ruffled, and there was colour in his cheeks.

'Good game?' I asked.

'Yes. Great, thanks.' He came over to give me a kiss.

'Hey, sweaty,' I said, pushing him away playfully.

'All right, all right – I'll jump in the shower to freshen up.'

'Cool. I'll get dinner on the go.'

When Jack came out of the shower, we sat down to eat the pasta salad I'd prepared.

'Nico seems excited,' he said, starting to eat. 'He tells me he's been painting the nursery. They've gone for yellow, given they don't know the baby's sex yet.'

'This is what you guys talk about at football?' I asked, smiling.

'Not always. But this is kind of a big deal, isn't it?'

Sunita and Nico were more than just close friends of ours – they were the reason Jack and I were together. At Sunita's twenty-first birthday party, in our final year of uni at Manchester, she'd pointed Jack out to me, across the room, downing vodka jellies and shouting to a friend above the sound of the music. 'Check out Nico's friend from home,' she'd whispered. 'Hot, funny – and single.'

At that moment Jack had turned and looked at me, a smile in his brown eyes. After kissing a dozen frogs in the union bar, I knew him right away – Jack was the one.

Eight years on, Sunita and Nico's lives were changing.

'Four months, right?'

'Yeah, mid-September.'

'I'm seeing Suni tomorrow actually, with Carly. We're going for a few drinks at the Florence.'

'Big night out?' Jack joked.

'I wish,' I said, laughing. 'We're doing the quiz. But it'll be good to catch up with her.'

'Give her my love, will you?'

After dinner Jack and I migrated to the living room with bowls of ice cream, and Jack switched the TV on. When I'd finished my dessert I lay down so my head was resting on his lap, my feet hanging over the end of our sofa.

'You know what I noticed earlier?' I asked, as Jack idly played with my hair, one eye on the news. 'When I'm in the kitchen, I can touch both walls with my hands at the same time.'

'Uh-huh,' Jack murmured.

'And I've tried it before in the bathroom – I can do it there, too.'

'Nice trick,' he said, without looking down at me.

I wasn't showing off some kind of physical feat. Sadly, there was nothing elegant and long-limbed about me – I'm shorter than average, and look tiny next to Jack. But in this flat, I was starting to feel like an overgrown Alice.

'Do you think anyone's ever going to want to buy it?'

'Of course they will.' Jack lowered the volume on the TV, and I moved so I was sitting up on the sofa, facing him. 'We've had that one offer in already. I'm sure it's just a matter of time until we get a higher one.'

I looked around the room at our belongings crammed onto shelves and into corners – my sewing machine and teapot collection, a row of orange Penguin classics lined up against the skirtingboard, Jack's Mac and A2 portfolio of stills and animation storyboards. Boxes we'd never unpacked because there wasn't anywhere to store the contents, my set of Russian dolls balanced precariously on the mantelpiece next to our framed wedding photo.

'You're right,' I said. 'I'm being impatient. But looking round those places in Stoke Newington last weekend . . . they were so much nicer.'

'They were also out of our price range.'

The noise of men shouting drifted up from across the road, coarse and hostile.

'I know.' I thought regretfully of the gorgeous period features and bay windows, the friendly residential streets. All we really needed was a place with a second room big enough for me to set up my sewing machine and for Jack to work from home occasionally, but right now that seemed out of reach. Even if I got a promotion, and we made money on our current flat, we wouldn't get much more than we had now.

'It's not so bad living here with me, is it?' Jack said.

'It's not terrible, I'll admit. In fact, sometimes I almost like it.' I ran my hand over his jaw, pausing when my fingers met his lips. He pretended to bite them, making me laugh. He drew me towards him for a kiss.

That night the air was so dense and humid that even with all the windows open there wasn't any breeze. At pub kicking-out time, the chatter of drunken revellers dashed any hopes of sleep I'd had, and each time I changed position I felt more uncomfortable. Just after midnight, I got out of bed quietly – it was no small feat doing that when our double bed was wedged up against the wall, but I'd perfected a move and Jack barely stirred. A glass of water. That would help.

I went into the kitchen, filled a glass from the tap, and closed the window. On the wall was our house calendar, and I saw Jack had ringed a date in a few weeks' time and drawn a big red balloon next to it – my thirtieth birthday.

It reminded me of the list Carly had mentioned earlier that day – would I have kept it? I went into the living room and looked under the sofa, one of our few storage areas. I pulled out a blue shoebox and opened it, sifting through the teenage diaries and letters. There it was at the bottom, a sheet of lined pink paper folded in half.

Amelia's Things to Do Before She's 30

It was in Carly's writing, not mine. That summery day, after a jug of Pimms in Victoria Park, we'd talked through our goals and then written down each other's.

1. Swim with dolphins, I read. 2. Learn to rollerblade. I smiled. I'd done both of them – the first on our honeymoon in California, one of my favourite memories.

I scanned the other wishes – hopes of learning languages

and mastering Photoshop – to the bottom, the final point, number twenty. It wasn't the usual stuff of these lists, but it was a genuine dream I'd had since I was a little girl living in south London, where sirens were more common than birdsong. It was a place I'd read about in books and seen on TV, with green fields and roaring fires:

20 Live in the country.

Chapter 2

13B Addison Road

For Sale

One-bedroom flat in the dynamic environs of Broadway Market, Hackney. Double bedroom, modern living room, kitchen and bathroom. This ex-local authority property would make an ideal first purchase.

Saturday, 4 May

I woke up to the sound of the market traders setting up in the street outside. They chatted to each other, raising their voices over the scrape of metal on metal as they put their stalls together. Jack was still dozing by my side.

Sunlight filtered in through the metal blinds on our bedroom windows, and Dexter was mewing in my face, eyes wide. It couldn't have been much later than seven. I fed the cat, made a cup of coffee and got back under the sheets, propping myself up on cushions and switching on my iPad. My finger hovered in its familiar location, over the Rightmove app.

What was I really searching for? *Live in the country*, that was what I'd written down.

Perhaps we'd been restricting ourselves, only searching in London. It's not like either of us were looking for nightlife on our doorstep any more.

I changed the key terms, and widened my search area to take in areas outside the city. Jack stirred a little by my side, sleepily putting his hand on my leg and leaving it there. I smiled at the comfort of his touch, and instinctively covered his hand with mine. Maybe he was right: the summer break would give me some perspective and make everything seem rosier. But in the meantime, there was no harm in looking around, was there?

I dragged my finger across images of thatched cottages and Tudor-style buildings nestled in the green expanses of Kent and Surrey – gardens with rose bushes and jasmine, oak-beamed bathrooms with white fluffy towels, and kitchens bright with country-floral fabrics.

I clicked on one of the images to enlarge it. It showed a thatched cottage in Chilham – it looked like a lovely village, with a castle off the main square, a teashop and a pub – the White Horse. There was a train station nearby, so Jack and I would still be able to commute to our jobs. An extra hour or so on the train wouldn't seem like much if it meant waking up to birds singing, and being able to relax on deckchairs in a spacious garden in the summertime.

Jack snuggled closer to me, his face relaxed. He looked content. I hoped he wouldn't wake up. Here I was, dreaming out a future for the two of us, without having discussed it with him. He turned on his side and started to snore gently, and I looked back at the iPad and checked the details of two cottages in Kent, not far from where my mum had retired to recently.

It wouldn't take long to drive down and have a little look, would it?

'Kent?' Jack asked, over a breakfast of eggs Benedict later that morning.

'Yes, there were a couple of cottages that looked good. I thought it would give us an idea of what's out there.' I sipped at my orange juice.

'Not really,' Jack said, his brow creased. 'I feel like we're pretty settled in London.'

'I know. I did too. But you should see what our money could get us that bit further out. For the price of this flat we could have a whole house of our own. We'd be within commutable distance, so it wouldn't have to affect our work

– a bit of extra time on the train to read the paper or catch up on emails, that's all. And we'd have a little haven to go back to at the end of the day.'

Jack toyed with the eggs on his plate. 'But our friends are here in Hackney. Our lives are here.'

'We'd still see everyone – I'm sure they'd come and visit.' Over Jack's shoulder I caught sight of the calendar, the circled date that was silently nudging me along, insisting on change.

'I'm not against it, it just seems a bit sudden,' Jack said, putting down his fork. 'I know your work's been tough lately, but . . . Amelia, is this about you turning thirty?'

'No. No, of course it isn't.'

Jack raised an eyebrow.

'Really, I swear. We used to talk about it before we got married, don't you remember? Living somewhere more chilled-out, where we could go for long walks at the weekend. Get a dog.'

'I was thinking years down the line though. And anyway, that was before we got Dexter.' Jack glanced over at the worktop, where our tabby was currently prowling. 'He might have some strong feelings about that. I don't know, Amelia. My commute is long enough as it is.'

'But that's on the tube. The train would be far more peaceful, and I think they're upgrading the rail links in

Kent at the moment. You've been talking about wanting to work from home more – if we moved we'd have space for you to do that.'

I could see Jack was mulling the idea over.

'Imagine it, Jack. Our own cottage, with a garden. A *proper* living room, with an open fire! Somewhere we could toast chestnuts, marshmallows. Drinking wine with friends when they came to stay.'

For a moment it looked as if he might be softening to the idea.

This was my chance. I had to try. I took a deep breath.

'Jack, if you tell me now that you hate the idea, that nothing about it appeals to you, then I promise I'll forget all about it.'

Jack looked at me. I waited for him to tell me I was being impractical. A dreamer.

But slowly, a smile began to spread across his face.

'I don't see the harm in setting up a few viewings.'

That evening, Carly, Sunita and I were at our local, the Florence, tucked away at a table in the corner.

'That's John Travolta.' Sunita pushed her heavy-framed black glasses back on her nose. 'I'm sure of it.' She pointed animatedly at the cropped corner of a dark stubbled face on our quiz answer sheet.

'*Sure*, sure?' Carly said sceptically. 'Or sure like you were the last time, when we put down Justin Bieber and it turned out to be Tony Blair?'

'One hundred per—' Sunita stopped mid-sentence and put a hand on her baby bump, flinching a little. 'Yikes, it kicked me right up under the ribs that time.' Her expression swiftly changed to a smile.

'Want to feel?' she asked me and Carly. Putting down her pen, Carly rested her hand on the place where Sunita's growing baby was moving.

'Ha!' she said, her eyes lighting up as her hand moved. 'An elbow or something. How does it feel for you?'

'A bit weird, but lovely too. It makes it seem more real. I think even Nico believes it's happening now.'

I thought back to what Nico had been like when the three of us were at uni together. Always the first in the union bar and the last out, usually in fancy dress – a hula skirt or a Mexican wrestling mask, or with a stethoscope slung round his neck. Meeting Sunita had calmed him down a bit, but he was still a big kid at heart, something that being the owner of a Go-Kart track had allowed him to hang on to, and it still wasn't easy to picture him in charge of a small human being's welfare.

'Five months down the line, still four to go,' Carly said.

'It's gone so quickly,' I added. 'It feels like a few minutes ago that you guys announced it.'

'Back then I thought no one could be more shell-shocked

than we were,' Sunita said, 'until I saw the way you lot reacted. Never thought one split condom could affect my friends so much.'

'It was a bit of a wake-up call. I think we all feel like we have to be grown-ups now,' Carly added.

'Come off it. It's me and Nico who've had to sell on our Glastonbury tickets and keep the cash for our buggy fund, not you guys. You're all still free to party.'

Carly and I exchanged glances. 'Doesn't happen much any more though, does it?' I said.

Gareth, the pub landlord, took the microphone. 'Ladies and gents, that's the end of the picture round. Swap your sheets with the table next to you for marking.'

'Oh balls,' Carly said. 'We haven't even got them all down yet. Jessie J for this one, right?' She hurriedly scrawled the remaining five names on the lines in blue biro.

I smiled at the old men at the table adjacent to ours and swapped our sheet for theirs.

'No cheating,' a man in a flat cap warned me mock-sternly.

'I'm a teacher. Very trustworthy and experienced with a red pen.'

I took a sip of my beer and relaxed for a moment in the familiar buzz of the pub.

'How's school for you two at the moment?' Sunita asked.

'Two weeks till half term,' Carly and I answered in unison,

looking at each other and letting out a similarly weary laugh.

'Like that, is it?'

'It's not great,' I said. 'But things might change. I interviewed for the Head of English post, and given that most of the other teachers who applied haven't got much experience, I think I stand a good chance.'

'I'm sure you'd do a great job,' Sunita said warmly. She swept her black hair up into a topknot and tied it with a band. 'Let us know when you hear back.'

'What about you, Suni?' I asked. 'How's it been finishing up at work? Are they going to have to prise the laptop off you in the birthing centre?'

'No way. One more set of edits and I'm through,' she said. 'I've loved writing this latest book though. Even in the first trimester, when I was knackered, I was up late plotting it out.'

'Gory?' I asked, familiar with Sunita's crime novels. I'd got to read her first three books at proof stage, with Jack sneaking looks over my shoulder as I stayed up past midnight, swearing I'd stop after just one more chapter.

'The goriest yet,' she said, taking a sip of her spritzer. 'If I'm going to leave work for motherhood – at least for a while – I decided I should go out with a bang.'

'Excellent.'

Gareth read out the answers to the quiz, and I marked

the other group's sheet, adding a couple of smiley faces for the ones they'd got right.

'I told you it was Travolta!' Sunita announced triumphantly, as Gareth read out the answer for number five. 'I *rock* at pub quizzes.'

'Well done, Suni,' Carly said. 'Good to see that degree in criminal psychology isn't going to waste.'

Sunita sneered at her playfully, and we swapped our papers back with the table next to us.

I glanced around the pub where we'd spent so many evenings together, with its wood panelling, frosted glass and array of old-men regulars, and thought back to my conversation with Jack that morning. 'Do you ever imagine living anywhere else?' I asked.

'What, outside Hackney?' Sunita said, puzzled.

'Yes,' I said. 'Maybe even a bit further afield than that.'

'You don't mean . . . ?' Sunita said, eyes wide behind her glasses.

'You're not talking about . . . ?' Carly added.

'South of the river?' they said at the same time.

I laughed. 'Further.'

'Where?' Carly asked incredulously.

'It's just . . . I saw some beautiful country cottages online this morning, and I can't get the idea out of my head. Pretty houses with thatched roofs and beams, and gardens we could do so much with.'

'Gardens?' Carly said. 'You couldn't even manage to keep that cactus I gave you alive.'

'I did,' I protested. 'For a few months anyway. It was Jack who knocked the pot off the side and smashed it.'

'But apart from a garden,' Sunita said, 'what could the countryside give you that Hackney doesn't?'

'A really chilled-out location, a spare room that would work as a study, a really big living room . . .'

'A study, eh . . . ?' Carly said, raising an eyebrow.

'Yes,' I replied firmly.

'OK.' Carly shrugged. 'If you say so.'

'Look, don't get me wrong. I think it's great what Suni's doing.' It was a shame that just at that moment she was pulling her knickers out of her bum and wincing. 'But this isn't about starting a family. I spend enough time with kids as it is. I just want us to have a better standard of living.'

'You're really serious about this move?' Sunita asked, frown lines appearing between her strong dark eyebrows.

'Are you?' Carly said, looking hurt.

'We're just looking at a couple of places, that's all.'

The next weekend, after a busy week at work, Jack and I drove out to the countryside. The satnav directed us past green fields, and Jack and I listened to a rare groove playlist on my iPod. We'd already stopped at one cottage that morning – only to find that it was so near the motorway you could hear the traffic noise from the house. It had been an easy no.

'Nice to get away from the city for a day, isn't it?' I said.

'Yes, you can breathe out here, can't you? We're nearly there, I think,' Jack said, pressing a button on the navigation screen and looking at the map.

He turned off the A-road and down a country lane. As we caught sight of the house I drew in my breath.

'*You have now arrived at your destination,*' the female voice announced.

The cottage was nestled among green fields, with a few neighbouring houses scattered nearby. A well-tended front garden bloomed with forget-me-nots. Green wellies were lined up in the wooden porch as if resting after a long walk, and the front door window was stained glass. Sunlight glinted off the tiny coloured panes.

Jack pulled up in the gravel driveway and parked, turning the engine off. 'Wow,' he said.

'God, it's like something out of a film, isn't it?'

'It really is,' he said, peering out. 'I feel like a friendly flock of cartoon blue tits are going to lead us up the pathway.'

'Mr and Mrs Grey?' A voice from my passenger-side window

made me start. I turned to see a redheaded young man in a navy suit peering in.

'Yes, that's us.' I opened the door and got out to shake the man's hand. 'Amelia. And this is Jack. Nice to meet you.'

'Likewise. I'm Darren,' he said, shaking Jack's hand. His smile was warm, and distracted attention from his badly fitting suit. 'Welcome. Come inside, and I'll show you around Arcadia Cottage.'

Jack and I followed Darren towards the house, and he unlocked the front door.

'The owners, a young professional couple like yourselves, are out for the day – so there's plenty of time for you to have a good look around, if you're not in a hurry. It's worth it, believe me. This is a very special property.'

Jack's eyes went heavenwards and I gave him a discreet jab in the ribs. Just because Darren was an estate agent it didn't make him a liar – he looked like an OK guy to me. He opened the door to reveal a hallway with wooden floorboards polished to an immaculate finish. We could see through into the kitchen, which had large windows and wooden cabinets, copper pans hanging neatly above them. My gut feeling had been right. This place *was* special.

'See what I mean?' Darren said.

'It's really spacious, Jack,' I said, swinging my arms around me in the hallway. 'I thought a cottage might be small and poky inside, but it's not at all, is it?'

'Come and take a look at the other rooms,' Darren said, crossing the corridor. 'The kitchen is a great size, and was recently installed – the owners updated all the electrics and put in a new boiler when they moved in three years ago.'

Jack nodded approvingly. I peeked out of the kitchen window at the manicured garden I'd admired on the estate agents' website.

'And the garden is a gem. Go outside and take a look for yourselves.' Darren opened the back door, and motioned for us to pass. A stone path led through rose bushes to a neat green lawn. At the back of the garden was a wooden summer house shaded by a weeping willow. 'Feel free to explore – and do take a look in the summer house. It's a wonderful bonus.'

Jack and I went outside and walked up on to the lawn. After a few steps I turned round and looked back at the cottage: the grey stonework was every bit as attractive from the back.

'We could have barbecues out here, Jack,' I said. 'Picnics in the summer – we'd both have a chance to fine-tune our gardening skills.'

He gave me a look. 'Fine-tune?'

'Look, we just haven't had the opportunity yet, that's all. Come on. Tell me this isn't beautiful,' I said, stretching my arms out to take it all in. 'It even smells gorgeous – take a breath.' The lilac climbing up the trellis gave off a sweet aroma.

'OK, I admit, it smells nice.'

I smiled at this small victory.

'Are you certain this in our price bracket?' Jack asked.

'We'd be able to afford it, yes. Especially if I get that promotion.'

'Really quiet, isn't it?' Jack said.

'In a good way or a bad way?'

'Good, I think.'

We stood together for a moment beside the wooden summer house with its little desk and padded window seats. Strands of weeping willow swayed gently in the breeze.

This was it – this was the haven I'd been looking for, ever since I was young.

'Let's go in and see the rest of the place,' Jack said, taking my hand.

Darren met us in the kitchen. 'What did you think? Lovely out there, isn't it?' he said, his ginger eyebrows raised. 'But the best is yet to come.'

As he left the room, I picked up my pace to keep up, eager to see the rest of the house. Jack held me back gently and whispered in my ear, 'Try and play it a bit cool, eh?'

'How's this for an entertaining space?' the estate agent said, showing us into an elegant dining room. Jack's hand was clasped in mine, and I squeezed it hard, trying to hide my enthusiasm from Darren.

'It's cosy,' I said, fighting the urge to squeal. 'Is the fireplace original?' I let go of Jack's hand and crouched to peer at the attractive blue and white tiles.

'Yes, and it's in working order too. As you can see, the dining room leads directly through to the living room, and in the corner there's another original fireplace, similar to this one.'

'Imagine Christmas here,' I said quietly to Jack. 'Dinner at the table, and then wandering slowly through to relax by the fireside. How lovely would that be?'

'It's a practical layout,' Jack said calmly. Beneath his restrained expression, I could see a glimmer of excitement in his brown eyes. 'And the bedrooms?' he said, turning to Darren.

'Come upstairs. I don't think you'll be disappointed.'

We followed him up the staircase. There were two good-sized double bedrooms and a smaller third one, all with lovely views out over the garden or surrounding countryside. The bathroom, which we saw next, had been sympathetically decorated in the style of the cottage, and was dominated by a large white free-standing tub with claw feet.

'Room for both of us in there,' Jack whispered in my ear.

'Jack,' I said, nudging him in the ribs. I liked the idea though.

On the way back to the stairs, we passed a nook in the upstairs corridor. 'We could put Grandma Niki's side table here,' I said. Jack nodded, then gave me a smile that I hoped meant he could see what I could – that with our things in it, this place could really be a home for us.

Half an hour after we arrived, we were back in the lobby.

'Thanks for showing us around,' Jack said to Darren.

'It's a pleasure,' Darren replied. 'All the details are on this handout,' he said, passing me a printed sheet, 'but if you have any questions at all give me a call. Just to say, you might want to act fairly swiftly on this, if you're keen. I'm expecting quite a bit of interest.'

'OK.' I glanced at Jack anxiously, wanting the place even more desperately now. 'We'll be in touch soon. Let us know if there are any updates.'

We stepped out of the cottage and walked back to the car. We got in and closed the doors.

A couple of feet away, a black Jaguar slowed down and parked at the foot of the gravel pathway.

'Do you think they're here for a viewing too?' I asked.

'Maybe,' Jack said. 'But forget about that – what did you think of the place?'

I took a final look at the cottage, trying to fix it in my mind. The lovely grey stonework and lilac flowers, the traditional windows and immaculately maintained thatched roof. I pictured the rooms we'd walked through – what they'd look like with our furniture in them, our framed prints and photos up on the walls. We'd finally have a place that would do justice to the antique dresser and chairs I'd inherited from my grandparents, currently in storage because there was no space for them at Addison Road.

'I know it would mean a longer commute for both of us, we'd be further from our friends . . .'

'But?'

'But I love it, Jack,' I said, excitement bubbling up inside me. 'I can see us being really happy here.'

Jack fiddled with the car keys and looked away for a moment.

'And you?' I asked. My heart was in my throat as I waited for his reply.

Chapter 3

Only Half in Hackney

Saturday, 11 May

That evening, after we got back from viewing the cottage, I sank into a bubble bath. Candlelight flickered around me, and the room filled with the aroma of a Space NK candle Carly had given me for Christmas. I'd barely used it – a quick shower before I dashed out the door was normally all I had time for in the mornings. Our petite bathroom with its peach-coloured eighties fittings didn't match up to the elegant white tub we'd seen in the cottage – the one big enough for two. Here, the matching basin, bath and toilet and magnolia walls looked particularly uninspiring. When Jack and I had moved in, we'd intended to do the room up, but like so many other home improvements, we had never got round to it.

I thought back to my conversation in the car with Jack.

He'd talked about the cottage in a fairly detached way, but underneath I could tell he was starting to get excited. After two years our wedding seemed like a distant memory, and I thought we needed a new project. The best thing about Arcadia Cottage, of course, was that it was a project that was entirely manageable – it didn't really need much doing to it. We'd simply be adding personal touches here and there, in order to put our stamp on the place.

I smiled at the thought of the house and the way I'd felt in it, and how I'd sensed Jack felt too. It was a home. There were a couple of things we needed to check first, but I was confident Jack would want us to offer.

I squeezed out some Sanctuary body scrub, rubbing the apricot-coloured particles against the rough skin on my knees. If one day the paparazzi become interested in my knees (it happens, although granted not often to teachers in east London), I like to think I'll be ready.

I leaned back, my head cushioned on a towel, and visualized the cottage living room again. We could have the roaring fire I'd always dreamed of. Perhaps by Christmas we'd even be in there and ready for visitors, our presents wrapped and under the tree.

A knock came at the door, breaking my train of thought.

'Amelia,' Jack said, 'your mobile's ringing.'

I sat up and the water swooshed around me, some splashing onto the lino. 'Do you know who it is?'

'It's your mum.'

'Could you tell her I'll call her back in a minute?' I yelled through the door.

I washed off the grains that seemed to have adhered to every crack and crevice in my body and pulled a fluffy towel off the radiator to dry myself. I got another one for my hair and tied it up into a turban. As I pulled on a dressing gown I could hear Jack's voice through the door.

'Hi, oh hi, Rosie,' he said warmly. 'Yes, she's just in the bathroom at the moment. No, don't worry, you're not inter-rupting anything . . .'

A few minutes later I padded down the carpeted corridor in my slippers to where Jack was. I peeked into the front room and saw him sitting on the sofa, watching an episode of *Game of Thrones*. I crept up behind him and planted a kiss on his head.

'Hey,' he said playfully, turning round. 'You're dripping all over me,'

'You love it.' I kissed him on the lips this time.

'I do. I really must be a sucker,' he replied. 'Your mum said she was just calling for a chat.'

'How was she?'

'She sounded cheerful.'

'OK. Right, I'm going to put some clothes on and give her a quick ring.'

'Do you have to?' he asked, snaking a hand under my towel and touching the top of my leg.

'One phone call and I'm all yours,' I said.

I went into our bedroom and slipped on my pyjamas, chequered and so worn they were impossibly soft. They'd been a faithful companion of mine for so long that even Jack, who'd shown some resistance at first, had grown used to them.

I picked up my mobile from the bedside table, and pressed number two, speed-dial for my mum.

'Hi, Amelia,' she said as soon as I picked up. 'Nice bath?'

'Yes, thanks,' I said, sitting back on the bed. 'How are things?'

'Great, thanks, sweetie. Don't know why I was worried about retiring, it's been wonderful so far. Art class, aqua-aerobics, Pilates . . . my schedule's never been fuller. And Hazelton's such a welcoming village.'

'Glad to hear it. Seems like you're really settling in.' I thought about telling her about the house, but then stopped myself – it was early days, and I didn't want to jinx it.

'I am. I've made some good friends here. Will you and Jack come and visit soon, once the holidays have started?'

'Sure, Mum,' I said, feeling a pang of guilt that we hadn't popped in on her when we were viewing the cottages. 'What about the weekend after next?'

'Perfect,' Mum said, her voice lifting. 'I'll make you a birthday cake and we can have a little celebration.'

'There's really no need.'

'Darling, it's your *thirtieth*.'

'Honestly, it's fine. But, yes, it would be good to see you.'

We talked for a while, then said our goodbyes. I was about to get up and go back into the living room, when I thought of Dad.

His mobile sounded a dull tone, so I called his landline. His wife, Caitlin, picked up. 'Hi, Amelia. How are things?'

'OK, thanks. Good actually. Any chance Dad is around?'

'He's out at the moment I'm afraid, love. No mobile since . . . well, you know. I'm all on my own this evening.' She sounded tired and stressed. 'And Mirabel's off in town somewhere, left without even letting me know where . . . Honestly, I bet you never gave your parents this much of a headache.'

I thought of my half-sister Mirabel over in Ireland. A sixteen-year-old whirlwind of hormones and fury. Her texts and emails were erratic, and she'd rarely reply to my messages, but we stayed in touch on Facebook. Her recent batch of photos showed her out celebrating the end of exams, looking pretty hammered. I wondered how much Dad and Caitlin knew about what she got up to.

'I guess she's just letting loose a bit this summer – end of exams and everything. I was the same.'

'I bet you weren't,' Caitlin said. 'She's a wild horse that one.'

'Anyway, Caitlin,' I said, 'I was just calling on the off-chance—'

'If it's about the loan,' Caitlin said, 'I'm so sorry your dad hasn't got around to paying you back yet. I know he's been meaning to—'

'No, it wasn't about that. I was just calling to say hi, see how you both are.'

'Oh, good,' Caitlin said, sounding relieved. 'We're rubbing along, love. Looking out for the green shoots, like the rest of the country, eh?'

'Well, give my love to Dad and Mirabel, would you? Let them know I called.'

'Of course,' Caitlin said. 'I'm sure Joe'll be sorry he missed you.'

I put the phone down. I'd try him again in a week or so. I always got there in the end.

37 Birchwood Avenue, Streatham (1992)

I heard a car pull up outside. It was still dark, and even without checking my alarm clock I knew it was nowhere near time for school. I opened my pink curtains and peeked out onto the street, lit golden by street lamps. The car was red. I hadn't seen it before, and I couldn't see who was inside.

I climbed back under the covers and tried to get to sleep, but even with the duvet over my head I could hear Mum and Dad arguing in the corridor. In the corner of my room was my brand new dolls' house, a gift from Dad. I'd got it earlier that week, but I hadn't played with it much yet. I wanted to keep it all perfect until my friends came round to see it. Dad had been happy bringing it home and showing it to me, but my mum had been annoyed for some reason. She always seemed to be angry these days.

I heard Mum's voice getting louder now. I crept out of bed and went over to my door, then crouched beside it, listening. Dad's voice took over.

'You're making this impossible for me, Rosie,' he said. 'I've given you options, and you've thrown them all back in my face. It's like you've stopped caring.'

'Options,' Mum snapped back. 'Hardly, Joe.'

'You only think of yourself, and I'm tired of it.'

'Me?'

'We're both too young to be feeling like this,' Dad said. He sounded exhausted, his voice softer now. 'It seems like you need to be on your own for a while. I know you've always put yourself first, Rosie – used not to, but when we had Amelia things changed, for me anyway. I guess they never did for you. She needs to be our priority now, and watching us at each other's throats isn't going to help her.'

'You really think I don't care about this family?'

'I can't do this any more, Rosie. You're forcing my hand, and I resent you for it.'

The door slammed and a car engine started up. That was the last night the three of us were under the same roof.

A month later, the sign went up:

FOR SALE
Semi-detached family home with garden

*

At school that week the cottage was all I could think about. When my mobile buzzed at breaktime, and I saw Darren the estate agent's number flash up, my heart lifted.

'Hi, Amelia, it's Darren. From Grove and Co.'

'Hi,' I said, hoping that the nerves in my voice didn't give my interest away.

'You and Jack asked me to keep you updated on Arcadia Cottage, so I wanted to let you know that we've just received an offer for it.'

I moved away from the buzz of teachers chatting in the corner, and sat down in a quieter part of the staffroom. *Damn.* Those people in the Jaguar – it had to be. Should have known.

'Right,' I said, wondering how to play it. We would

probably be able to afford the cottage if we accepted the offer we already had on our flat – if those buyers were still around and interested.

'The vendor's currently considering the offer. Would you and Jack be interested in offering too?'

'Maybe,' I said, checking the wall clock – ten minutes till I had to get to my next class. Numbers raced through my head: the offer we'd had on our flat, survey and solicitors' fees, moving costs. 'Actually, yes, we're keen – really keen – but there are a few things we still need to work out. Could I let you know by tomorrow, Darren?'

'Sure – although tomorrow would be the latest. The vendors want this sale tied up as soon as possible.'

'Let me talk to Jack tonight,' I said, 'and we'll get right back to you.'

I put down the phone, feeling fiercely territorial. Someone wanted to get their hands on *our* cottage. Our new dream life. There was no way we could let them.

Back at the flat that evening, I sat on the sofa in a daze, thinking over our options. I'd called our estate agent and he seemed confident that the couple who'd offered on our flat would still want it – he said he'd check the next day. My cup of tea had gone stone cold by the time I heard Jack's key turn in the lock.

'Hey,' he called out. 'I picked up some food for us. Do you fancy Thai green curry tonight?'

It was my favourite meal, but right then I couldn't muster any appetite. I got to my feet and went out to the hallway to give Jack a kiss hello.

'You look weird,' Jack said.

'Do I?' I said, tidying my dark ponytail self-consciously.

'Yes. Your eyes are all sort of excitable.'

'We need to chat,' I said. 'About the house.'

'OK,' he said, still trying to read my expression. 'Let me put this stuff down and I'm all yours.'

Jack put the shopping bags down in the kitchen, and then turned to give me his full attention. 'What's up?'

'Darren called – there's an offer on the cottage. If we don't go in now, we'll lose it.'

'Right,' Jack said, taking a deep breath. 'And how long do we have to decide?'

'Tonight. That's it. Our estate agent's going to confirm tomorrow if the offer on this place still stands.'

'OK,' Jack said. 'It'll be tight though, won't it?'

'I'll get that loan back from my dad – that'll help,' I said. 'Think of it, Jack – we'd have all that wonderful space indoors and the garden in the summer to entertain people in. We've both said at different points that London living was wearing us out. Do we really want to spend the next ten years of our life here, without having tried out anything else?'

'I did get a great feeling when we were there.' He put a hand out to touch the wall of the living room and looked at the compact space. 'We've had some good times here though, haven't we?'

'Yes, we have. We've had some amazing times here, but moving on doesn't undo any of that.'

'I suppose.' Jack paused. 'It could be pretty exciting, couldn't it?' he said, his eyes meeting mine.

'I think so.' I tried to keep my excitement in check. 'What do you think? Shall we do it? Make an offer?'

'Yes,' Jack said, taking my hand and giving it a squeeze. 'I think we should.'

We stared at each other for a moment. This was the biggest 'Yes' in our relationship since I'd accepted Jack's offer of marriage on a windswept beach in Cornwall two and a half years previously.

'God, where do we start?' I laughed.

'By working out our budget?' Jack said. 'From what you were telling me it sounds like we might need to go in above the asking price if there's another buyer involved already.'

We sat up that evening, jotting down figures and making plans. When my eyelids started to droop, I climbed into bed beside Jack and took hold of his arm and squeezed it. He brought me close, and kissed me. We both felt it, I think. That our lives were just about to change.

*

At lunchtime the next day, I called our estate agent to accept the offer on our flat, then rang Darren, with Carly by my side for moral support.

'Think Kirstie Allsopp,' Carly mouthed elaborately at me as I greeted him. I tried my hardest to channel Kirstie, keeping the real me – trembling with nerves – under wraps.

'I'm pleased to say that Jack and I would like to make an offer on Arcadia Cottage.'

'Great.'

I took a deep breath, and spoke again 'Our offer is £350,000.'

'OK. I'll speak to the vendors now and be back in touch shortly.' Darren's voice was cool and professional, giving nothing away.

I put the phone down, excitement, anticipation and a little bit of blind terror bubbling up inside me.

'What?' Carly said, frustrated after hearing only half of the conversation.

'Oh, sorry – he's going to call us back. He has to speak to the vendors first.'

'We have to wait?' she said, her forehead creased.

'I thought you didn't want us to move?'

'I don't!' Carly said. 'But still, the suspense . . .'

'I'll meet you in the canteen in ten,' I said. 'I'm just going to call Jack and update him.'

Jack sounded as anxious as I felt when he answered his mobile, and I filled him in on the offer I'd made.

'I'll call you the moment I hear anything,' I reassured him. 'I guess it might be later today. I didn't ask.' I should have asked, I realized. 'In the meantime you get back to work – without that we'll struggle to pay the mortgage wherever we're living.'

'The moment you hear anything?' he asked.

'The very second. I'm not going to decide anything without you.'

'I hope it works out,' he said. 'You know what? Since last night I've been getting really excited about this. I can see us there and—'

'We've done what we can, and it's out of our hands now. I'm sure we'll hear back soon.'

'OK,' Jack said. 'Thanks for making the call.'

I walked towards the canteen to meet Carly, my stubbornly silent phone in my pocket, willing it to ring.

'At the end of term we've got a class trip to see *Romeo and Juliet* at the Globe theatre,' I announced to 10E. 'Could you all take one of the forms on my table and get it signed by your parents or guardians?'

'Day off!' Shanice shouted from the back of the class. 'Whooop! Thanks, Miss Grey.'

'Glad to see you so excited, Shanice.' I was distracted by an eraser whizzing past my nose. 'Who threw that?'

A dozen blank faces in the first few rows looked at me innocently.

'We'll be doing some classwork related to the performance in the coming year, so it's not optional. This is an amazing opportunity for you to see one of Shakespeare's plays performed in the way it would have been during his time.'

'Boring,' came a voice from the back.

'Rupesh,' I said, 'you're welcome to stay here and take down the class displays if you'd prefer that?'

'Nah,' he replied. 'I'll probably go. Hey, Miss. Is Trey going?'

'Yeah, what happened to Trey?' Shanice chimed in.

I glanced over at his empty desk unconsciously. 'Your guess is as good as mine right now. But if any of you see him, please tell him to get in touch.'

'I seen him, Miss,' said Andy, from over by the window. His pale golden hair was close-cropped, the skin on his cheeks reddened slightly with acne.

'You have?'

'Yeah. He lives on the same estate as me. I tried to talk to him, but his brother Sean told me to stay away, that Trey was with him now, he wasn't coming back to school.'

Sean. Not the best result.

'I know his brother thinks I grassed him up for hitting

me,' Andy said, 'but I never did – we were only messing around. Garrett saw what he wanted to see.'

'Garrett's a knobhead!' another boy shouted out.

'Paul,' I swung to face the student who'd shouted out, 'why don't we go and visit the head after class. If you feel that strongly you might want to say it to his face?'

'Aw, no, Miss, not again,' Paul said. Laughter broke out across the classroom.

'Right.' I took a deep breath and let it out slowly. 'Now, if no one else has a burning urge to be sent to the Head, let's get on with the lesson. In groups of four, consider the question on the board: *1984 – what aspects of Orwell's novel can we see in our modern world?*'

With the scrape of chairs, the students arranged themselves into groups with a few muttered complaints about who they'd been put with. 'I'll take that, thank you,' I said to Paul, who was googling the question on his iPhone. I took the phone and put it in my pocket.

'Nah . . .'

I gave him my steeliest look and he fell quiet.

The class fed back their answers and I was heartened to see that some of the students did at least seem familiar with the text I'd set them. The bell went.

'See you all tomorrow,' I called out. 'Paul, wait behind, please. Let's go to Mr Garrett's office now and I'll let him decide, after he's heard the full story, whether he thinks you deserve your phone back.'

We walked together down the corridor. 'You got a husband, Miss?' Paul asked chirpily.

'Why do you ask?'

'Because you're pretty.'

'Don't think you can charm me, Paul Reilly,' I said, feeling a faint glow nonetheless.

'I saw your ring, anyway,' he said with a wink.

I knocked on Lewis's office door.

'Come in.'

'Hi, Mr Garrett. I've got Paul Reilly here, who wants to let you know what he did in my class today.'

'Paul,' Lewis said, taking off his reading glasses and putting them to one side on his desk. 'Welcome back. *Again*.'

'I've got his phone in the confiscation locker. Just let me know what you decide.'

'Sure,' Lewis said. 'Oh, and Ms Grey, before you go – are you free for a meeting tomorrow lunchtime? There's something I was hoping to talk to you about.'

'Of course,' I said. Perhaps this was it. The news I'd been waiting for about the Head of English job. 'I'll see you here at one.'

Lewis gave me a nod, revealing his scanty combover, and I closed the door.

*

I went to my car shortly afterwards, and loaded my bag and books onto the back seat. My mobile buzzed in my pocket.

I scrambled to answer it. The cottage. I checked the number and clocked the dialling code – Kent. It had to be Darren. I sat in the driver's seat trying to steady my nerves. Our whole future could rest on this yes or no.

'Amelia!' Mum – of course.

'Hi,' I said. Her caller ID hadn't shown up this time. 'Where are you calling from?'

'A friend's house,' she said. 'I've been thinking, about your birthday. Is there anything in particular you'd like? Are you still into sewing? I could look into one of those craft courses . . .'

I heard a beep – another call was coming through. 'Lovely, yes. Sorry, Mum, I'll call you back.' I switched calls before she could reply. Forget manners, this was too important.

'Have you heard anything?'

Jack, I realized, feeling slightly disappointed. 'Not yet. I'll let you know when I do. *STOP THAT!*' I shouted through the open car window. The football that had been thrown against my car bonnet rolled gently to the ground, leaving a slight indentation in the metal.

'Sorry, Miss,' said one of my Year 7 girls, scurrying over to collect it.

'No ball games in the car park, Cassie. You know that.'

'I just called a second ago and the line was engaged, so I thought—'

'I was on the phone to Mum.'

'Oh. OK, I'll wait to hear then.'

'See you at home.'

I started the engine and drove out of the car park and on to the main road, the familiar route home, listening to a Strokes CD Jack had left in the stereo. Caught up in a traffic jam on Hackney High Street, I pressed the button to wind down the window and let in some fresh air. Instead the car filled with fumes and the smell of a nearby kebab shop. Coughing, I pressed to wind it back up again. A different life was out there for us – we'd both glimpsed it. I crossed my fingers on the steering wheel. Please let us get the cottage, I prayed. Please.

Maybe our offer wasn't high enough, I thought to myself. If it was the Jaguar people they wouldn't be short of a few quid. I didn't want to lose the cottage.

I parked outside the flat and climbed the exterior stairs to our floor. The faint smell of urine that could normally be ignored was brought out by the heat of the summer's day. I let myself in. We were lucky – really lucky. We had our own place – something most people our age didn't – and we had each other.

Dexter arched his back and I bent down to stroke him.

'Hello, Dex. Did you miss me?' He pressed his head against my hand.

My phone rang. As I reached for it, I reminded myself to breathe.

'Amelia, hi. It's Darren.'

Breathe, I told myself.

'I'm pleased to say that the owner has decided to accept your offer. Arcadia Cottage is yours.'

I leaned against the wall of the kitchen and tried to take it in. 'That's fantastic news.'

Chapter 4

Arcadia Cottage

For Sale

Seventeenth-century cottage with thatched roof in the picturesque
village of Chilham, Kent. Three bedrooms, all original features,
beamed ceilings – excellent condition. Large garden with a summer
house. Must be seen, early viewings advised. Contact Grove & Co.

Thursday, 16 May

Jack came back from work that night full of excitement
after my call. 'We did it,' he said, looking bright but dazed.
'We're moving to the countryside!' He beamed, his initial
hesitancy now only a distant memory.

I hugged him and we did a happy jig right there in our
hallway. He pulled back a little.

'Now what do we do?' It was as if he'd suddenly sobered up.

'The same things we did when we bought this place, I suppose. Only this time we have the sale of our flat to arrange too.'

'Oh, yes. Right.'

'The survey might show up a few things given the age of the cottage.'

'This is nuts, isn't it?' Jack said.

'A bit, yes. But it feels right.'

'I love you.' He kissed me and we stood there in the hall for a minute, holding on to each other, unable to wipe the smiles off our faces.

The next day I couldn't stop thinking about what we were about to do. My mind buzzed with excitement and memories of Arcadia Cottage. It was going to be ours.

The bell rang for lunchtime, and after the Year 8 class I was covering had filed out, I made my way down to the headteacher's office. I knocked once, and Lewis answered the door swiftly.

'Amelia,' he said, ushering me into his office. 'Thanks for coming.'

I took a seat at his desk, and he sat down opposite me. 'Good to be here without having to bring a student, for once.'

'Ha ha,' Lewis said uneasily. 'Yes. Paul Reilly shared his

choice language with me the other day, but the prospect of two weeks' worth of detentions seemed to quieten him down a bit.'

'Right,' I said. 'Thanks for handling that. Any word from Trey Donoghue's parents about his whereabouts, by the way?'

'I'm afraid not. I spoke to his Head of Year this morning. We can't get hold of his parents, and his social worker seems to think he's living with his brother Sean at the moment, which isn't great news,' Lewis said, his tone one of weary resignation.

'Are Social Services doing anything about it?' I asked. 'Trey's only fifteen, he needs to be here in school – and Sean's only just got out of prison.'

'I understand your concern, but it's up to Social Services at this stage.'

I pictured Trey, wide-eyed and handsome beneath his tough facade. I should have worked harder to keep him here, I thought.

'Listen, Amelia. I wanted to have a word about something else today.'

I took a deep breath, trying to stay calm. This news could make such a difference to my life.

'You know how much I value you as a teacher, and you've made some great progress with all of the classes you've been teaching this year.'

'Thank you.' I was grateful for the unexpected praise. I'd been focusing so much on getting through the days that it had been a while since I'd found the time to be proud of what I'd achieved.

Lewis shuffled papers on the desk into a tidier pile, not meeting my eyes.

'There are going to be some changes at St Catherine's – and when we return after the summer break some aspects of the school are going to be run slightly differently.'

'OK,' I said. 'I guess we've all been expecting that.'

It wasn't as though we could carry on the way we were. The details of the last OFSTED inspection still echoed in the halls of the school, and were embedded in all our minds. In spite of our hard work, our commitment, the talent of some of our pupils, there was a word that had reduced that to nothing – *failing*.

'Thank you for your application for the role as Head of English.'

I could do it. I knew I could. I could help steer St Catherine's back on course.

'But I'm afraid we've decided to appoint an external candidate. Graham Kilfern has achieved some fantastic results over at William Greaves School,' Lewis said, 'and I think he could really turn things around here.'

'Sorry?' I croaked.

'Graham Kilfern. He will be our new Head of English, starting from September.'

That was it. I hadn't even had a look-in.

'OK, right,' I said, trying to swallow my hurt pride. 'I look forward to meeting him.'

'I know this is likely to be disappointing for you, Amelia,' Lewis continued. 'As I said, we really value everything you do here. But we felt that in order to show our commitment to changing the fortunes of St Catherine's we needed to recruit externally in this case.'

My chest felt tight. I'd worked hard preparing for that interview – surely I was well enough qualified to at least have been worthy of serious consideration?

'How will the new appointment affect me?'

Lewis closed the folder he'd barely looked at and moved it aside on his desk, leaning forward on his elbows. 'There are a couple of things that will affect you and the other members of staff. As I said, we respect how you teach, and we want you to be able to continue doing that in the way you have been up till now. But there are certain classes, particularly those students heading for exams, where we have not yet seen the attainment we had hoped for – and Mr Kilfern has expressed a wish to take those over and teach them directly.'

'My exam classes are going?' I choked out.

'No, no,' Lewis said. 'Your A-level class seem to be

performing well, and we're happy to leave things as they are. But I think we both know that there have been some issues with 10E, and a fresh approach could benefit all the students there. And all Mrs Humphries' classes will naturally transfer to Mr Kilfern.'

I felt the breath go out of me. 10E, the class I'd nurtured since the day they arrived at the school – the chaotic group of teenagers I'd thought I might be able to bring in line over the next year. It was true that the results weren't brilliant – but with fewer assistants for those with special needs, and only a handful of students who had English as a first language, I felt we were doing OK. They were improving.

'But . . . I have plans for 10E. And I promised Isabel's Year 12s I'd see them through.'

'I'm sorry, Amelia. It's not a decision I've made lightly. It's for the good of the school as a whole. You'll be taking on two of the new Year 7 classes instead.'

I sat there, mute and numb. I didn't want to start again with Year 7s – I wanted to see my own classes through, and fulfil my commitment to Isabel's class.

I'd done it before – walked out of this room with my tail between my legs only to get home, cry on Jack's shoulder and realize what I should have said. Rerun the conversation with him and said all the right things. I took a deep breath, and opened my mouth to speak.

'So if there's nothing else, I think we're finished for today,' Lewis said. 'There isn't anything else, is there?'

I paused. 'No. There's nothing else.'

Ladies toilets. Now.

I texted Carly.

She arrived a couple of minutes later, as I was reapplying my lipstick.

'Are you OK?' she said, placing her hand on my arm. 'Your hand is shaking.'

I saw it then – my right hand trembling as I held the tube of No.7 lip colour.

'Not really,' I said, putting it away in my handbag.

'What's up?'

I tidied my hair in the mirror and pressed my lips together to even out the colour. 'It's this place, Carls. You give and you give – and you get nothing back. Garrett just told me there's a new Head of English starting.'

'They didn't . . . ?' Carly said, leaning against the basin and looking at me straight on. 'They wouldn't . . . ?'

'They wanted to get in someone external. But it's not just that: they're moving my exam classes over to this new guy – the ones that it's most important I see through, anyway.'

'That's terrible,' Carly said, shaking her head.

'It's crap. I feel really undermined.'

'I'm not surprised. There comes a point where you need to put yourself first.' She put her hand on my arm.

'I don't have any choice right now but to accept what Lewis is proposing – well, telling me,' I corrected myself.

'Don't you?' Carly said, tilting her head. 'The last thing I want is for you to leave, but there are other schools around.'

'I can't resign.' I shook my head. 'Not now. I mean . . . we're buying this cottage. I'm not sure we'd even get the mortgage approved without my job.'

'You're a great teacher, Amelia. You'd find something else. Hopefully somewhere they'd look after you a little better than here.'

I let the thought settle. 'I can't.' I bit my lip. 'I really can't. But just in case I change my mind,' I said, 'the notice date – it's the end of May, isn't it?'

Carly nodded.

On Saturday morning Jack was babysitting his nephew Oscar round at his sister's house, and I was emailing the surveyors to arrange for them to look at Arcadia Cottage. We would need to get going quickly if we wanted to keep things on track for our agreed completion date with our buyers – mid-August.

With the offer on our flat lower than we'd been hoping for, and with the costs of moving we'd worked out, Jack and I were going to need every penny we could get. I was going to have to call in my dad's loan. I rang him on his landline, and Caitlin picked up again.

'You're in luck, love,' she said warmly, but with that same hint of strain in her voice. 'He's just walked in through the door. *Joe!*' she yelled. 'It's your daughter here on the phone for you. The well-behaved one.'

'Hi, sweetheart,' Dad said. His voice carried a faint Irish accent now, after years in Dublin.

'How's it going, Dad?'

'Fine, thanks. Just been out in town, met a few friends for a drink. Needed one after the job I had this morning – really demanding customer, and the electrics he'd done himself were a mess. Pouring down out there though. I'm soaked. How are you doing?'

'Good, thanks,' I said. 'Actually, I've got some exciting news. Jack and I have just had an offer accepted on a cottage – we're moving to Kent.'

'To the countryside, eh? That's great, Amelia.'

'We're really looking forward to it. This cottage is perfect, Dad. You know how I always used to dream about living in the country, when I was into *Anne of Green Gables* and all that.'

'Did you? Yes, rings a bell. That's nice. *Caitlin!*' he called. 'Couldn't make me a tea while you're at it, could you? Chilled to the bone over here.'

'Anyway, Dad.' I paused, trying to find a good way to

phrase it. 'I was wondering if you might be able to repay some of the money we lent you. It's just—'

'Costs a fortune moving house, doesn't it? Solicitors' fees and all that. Yes, sure love. I'll be right on it. You'll see the cash within the month.'

'Thanks, Dad,' I said, sighing with relief. That five grand meant we could finally stop losing sleep over paying the solicitors, and it would help towards the stamp duty.

'No worries, sweetheart.'

'How's Mirabel doing?'

'Don't ask, Amelia. That girl. She's refusing to go to sixth form, says she doesn't care what results she gets. I mean, I know she's seen her dad make a good living without much of an education, but I'm always telling her it's not me, it's your sister you should be looking at for a good example.'

'I don't know about that,' I said, laughing.

'Seriously, though. Teaching college, a steady job for . . . what? Ten years is it now?'

'Seven,' I said, thinking back to the conversation I'd had with Lewis, how little that time had suddenly seemed to matter.

'She could do with a good dose of your self-discipline, really. Nothing Caitlin and I say seems to be getting through to her at all. And this guy she's going out with—'

'Mirabel's got a boyfriend?'

'Boyfriend, girlfriend . . . I don't know. With jeans that tight it's hard to tell.'

'Dad!' I said, smiling.

'Anyway, love, I'd better go. Kettle's boiled and I'm gasping. Good to talk to you, though. Love you, sweetheart.'

'Me too, Dad.'

I hung up and put my phone down on the bed.

I looked round at our bedroom – overflowing laundry basket, Saturday papers on the side table, my bra hooked over the end of the bed, and Jack's stinking football boots up on the windowsill.

The place was in a complete state. I grabbed the laundry basket and tipped the contents into the washing machine. Pulling on marigolds and switching on the radio, I got to work doing the washing-up and then scrubbed the kitchen surfaces. While I was working, the prospect of school on Monday, and at some point having to tell my classes I wouldn't be teaching them any more, seemed to fade slightly. Dexter watched me, his head following my movements as if I were a tennis ball at Wimbledon.

I mopped the floors, then cleaned the oven and the bathroom cabinets until they gleamed. The hours flew by, and it startled me when I saw Jack in the doorway, mid-afternoon.

'Wow,' he said, looking around the flat in disbelief. 'What have you done to this place?'

'Hi,' I said, giving him a kiss. 'Just thought it could do with a tidy-up.'

'OK,' he said. I knew he could see right through me. He'd known me long enough to see that periods of emotional upset tallied with spotless surfaces.

'Thanks for doing it,' he added. 'How about we get out of here and go to the pub?'

'Sure,' I said. I grabbed my wallet and followed him back out of the front door and down the stairs.

We walked over the footbridge, crossing the canal. On the other side, cars passed with loud music blaring on the hot summer's day.

In the Florence, Jack ordered a couple of pints at the bar.

'Thanks,' I said, taking a sip of the cool beer.

I noticed Jack had caught the sun a little bit: his forearms and face were tanned. 'It's nice to be out just the two of us, isn't it?'

'Yes. I'm so confused, Jack. On the one hand I'm really excited about the cottage, our new life together – and on the other I feel like my professional life has hit a real wall.'

Jack took my hands in his. 'You know I'll support you, whatever you decide to do.'

'Thanks.' It didn't fix things, but it did make me feel stronger.

'Have you thought about looking at the schools near the new cottage?'

'Yes. I had a quick look online this morning, just to see what was there.'

'And?'

'They look nice,' I said. 'I mean, small and local – a different world from here.'

'But maybe a change wouldn't be such a bad thing?' Jack ventured.

'I guess so. I'll do some more research next week. Now, let's talk about you for once,' I said. 'How's work at the moment?'

'Really good, actually. The funders liked the storyboard we put together for *LoveKatz*. You know, the one I told you about? Cats meet robots, and battle to form a new world order?'

'How could I forget? That's fantastic.'

'Hope we get it,' he said, drinking more of his beer. 'Morale is low at the studio, and we need a fresh project. It'll probably mean some long hours, getting the full pitch ready – don't know how that will be with the new commute, but maybe I'll be able to do some stuff on the train first thing in the morning.'

Jack wasn't exactly the earliest riser, or the brightest when he did get up. Seemed like we'd both be making a few changes in our lives.

'You'll manage.' I said. 'I know you will.'

'In other news, it's just two weeks,' Jack said, a mischievous glint in his eye, 'until the big—'

'Don't say it,' I said, smiling and covering my ears and starting to hum loudly. 'I don't want to hear it.'

'Three-O,' he mouthed.

'Argh! I hate it that you are, and will always be, younger than me.'

'It's only six months. I can't get too cocky really. Now, what are we going to do to celebrate?'

'I don't know,' I said, wrinkling my nose. 'Maybe have a few people here? Reserve a corner of the pub?'

'Cool. Leave it with me.' Jack winked. 'I'll make sure you have a great night.'

'You sound a bit saucy when you say that, you know.'

'Good,' he said, leaning across the table to kiss me.

I took a day off school on Friday. OK, I took a sickie. In all my time teaching I'd never once done it – and while I felt guilty at first, by the time I'd driven to the outskirts of London that guilt was replaced by a feeling of liberation.

On Monday evening I'd sat down at our kitchen table with my iPad and scanned the *TES* online site for job ads. Then, finding nothing, I'd looked again at the schools close to Arcadia Cottage. There were no secondary schools in Chilham itself but a few nearby, including a couple in Canterbury. I browsed the pages and tried to picture myself working in one of them. They all looked so *calm*.

While I couldn't see any vacancies advertised, I reasoned

that perhaps they'd be open to me coming in in person to discuss opportunities. I took a note of the headteachers' email addresses and drafted an email introducing myself and outlining my experience.

By Wednesday I'd received two replies inviting me in. Carly was right – there were other schools out there, and they might actually suit me better.

I couldn't resist driving up to Chilham on my way over to the schools. The village was just as quaint as I'd remembered it, with a bustling local tea shop and Tudor buildings overlooking the central square. I felt a tingle of excitement – with any luck, this place could be our new home.

I drove on towards the first school, Woodlands Secondary, on the outskirts of Canterbury, and parked. The three-storey Victorian building was surrounded by green space, with a generous playground and a basketball court. Straightening my white blouse, I opened the school gate and walked through – there was no metal-detection arch here. As I passed through the corridor I could hear chatter and bustle in the classrooms, but it was calm and upbeat, with no shouting. I peeked through a window and enviously watched as a teacher spoke with two dozen pairs of eyes on her attentively, the students' books open on their desk.

I knocked on the headteacher's door, and got a cheerful reply almost immediately. 'Come in.'

Standing by her shelves with a book in her hands was a

woman of around fifty with pale gold hair, wearing a smart navy suit.

'Hi,' I said.

'Hello, you must be Amelia Grey.' She walked towards me with her hand outstretched. 'I'm Charlotte Jacobs.'

'Pleased to meet you.'

'You caught me doing a little bit of office reorganization,' Charlotte said, blowing some dust off the top of the book and putting it back on the shelf tidily. 'Been meaning to sort out these shelves for ages. Thanks for your email, and for popping by.'

'Thanks for having me. It seems like a lovely school you have here.'

'Oh, you've caught us on a good day,' Charlotte said with a smile, taking a seat opposite me. 'We had sports day yesterday and I think it wore them all out.'

'Well, as I said, I'm moving to the area, and I was hoping you might keep me in mind if you have any vacancies.'

'Yes – I was really pleased to hear from you. I've had a look at your CV and I think we could learn so much from having someone with your experience here, Amelia.'

My heart lifted – did that mean there was a chance?'

'I'm afraid we don't have anything for you at the moment,' Charlotte continued, 'but I have a feeling that come spring we might. Shall we stay in touch on that?'

*

'How did it go today?' Jack asked me when I got back to the flat that evening.

'The schools were gorgeous – both of them. The first one, Woodlands Secondary, was my favourite, really friendly and welcoming. But there's nothing available at the moment. The Head at Woodlands said she thought there might be an opening in the spring, so they're going to keep my details on file. I knew it was unlikely that anything would be available for September, but I don't know – I still hoped, I guess.'

'Something will come up.'

'I registered with the local supply agency and they seemed positive about my chances of getting regular work locally.'

'Great.'

'Sort of.' I was leaning against the kitchen worktop as Jack and I spoke. 'Jack, how can I give in my notice at school when I've got no job to go to? It seems insane. Maybe I should just stick it out.'

'Are you sure you really want to?' Jack said. 'It's hard seeing you like this – so unhappy at work.'

'I think you're probably right – I'm not sure I can stick this out for another term, not with what Lewis is proposing.'

'You have to do what's right for you.'

'And the mortgage?' I asked.

'It's already been approved, hasn't it? I'm sure we could

find a way to pay it, particularly if you can get some supply work.'

'Yes, but aren't we obliged to tell them if our work situation changes?'

'Look, don't think about this now. Make the decision you need to make, and we'll work it out.'

'Lewis,' I said in his office on Monday, keeping my voice level and calm. 'Your decision about the class changes when the new Head of English arrives – is there no flexibility on that at all?'

'I'm afraid not,' Lewis confirmed.

'OK,' I said. I could do it. I could do this. 'In that case, I'd like to hand in my notice.'

Lewis looked at me, brow furrowed, surprised.

Oh God. That was a completely mad thing to do. Well, I'd done it now – there was no other way out than forward.

'I feel that changing teachers so close to some of these students' exams isn't going to help them. We're the only consistent thing in some of their lives.'

Seven years of early starts and late nights marking, of anxious weekends preparing and parents' evenings dealing with demanding families. Seven years – for what? I had a new life in the country almost within my grasp. Why was I holding back from taking that opportunity with both hands? I felt a rush of adrenalin.

'I'll continue working to the end of term, of course. But you'll need to look for a teacher to fill my place after that.'

Lewis's jaw dropped the tiniest fraction, a barely discernible movement. 'I'm really sorry to hear that, Amelia,' he said. 'Isn't there any other way we can resolve this?'

'It doesn't sound like it. I'll put my resignation in writing for you.' I picked up my jacket and left the room.

I walked down the corridor and into the staffroom in a daze. Carly caught me by the elbow as I opened my locker. 'Are you OK? You look really pale.'

'I've done it,' I whispered to her. 'I've just resigned.'

'Really?' She turned me round so that we were walking away from the other teachers and towards a quiet corner of the room. 'That's amazing. Although God only knows how I'll cope without you. How did Garrett react?'

'I think he's in shock.'

'I'm not surprised. He's going to be stuffed trying to find a teacher with your experience before September. But that's his problem. How are you feeling about it?'

'Maybe I'm in shock too. What I've just done makes no financial or professional sense, really. We've got the cottage to think about too. I'll need to ring the mortgage company and update them—'

'But how do you feel?' Carly repeated.

'I feel excited.'

'Good things are just around the corner for you,' Carly said. 'I know it.'

The next fortnight seemed to pass in a blur. I went through the motions in my classes, struggling to get my head around the fact that they'd have a new teacher come September, and I'd be . . . well, for the first time in my life I didn't know what I'd be doing.

On Saturday I was woken by our doorbell ringing. When I peered through the spyhole I could see our postman standing on the doormat next to a delivery man. I opened the door to them.

'I couldn't get this one through the letter box,' the postman said, passing me the Jiffy bag and then a stack of envelopes.

'And these are for you too,' the delivery man said, handing over a bouquet of red, pink and white roses. 'Happy birthday. I'm guessing that's what it might be?'

'It is,' I said. 'And thank you.'

I closed the door and went back into the flat. 'Look what—' I started to say, and then spotted Jack in the kitchen. He'd laid the table for us, with a bunch of stargazer lilies in the middle, and was cooking pancakes at the stove. My hand went to my mouth.

'This is lovely,' I said, going over and squeezing him around the waist.

'Well, you deserve it,' he said. 'Although it looks like someone might have outdone me.' He pointed to the gifts I'd just received.

'The flowers will be from Mum, I'm sure,' I said, checking the gift card.

To Amelia – on your thirtieth. Have a very happy day.
Love from Mum x

'And the package?' Jack asked, flipping a pancake up into the air and catching it effortlessly.

'I'm not sure.' The handwriting looked very much like Dad's, but his gifts didn't usually arrive until a day or two after my birthday. I ripped open the Jiffy bag.

Inside was a black velvet jewellery box. I flicked it open and two delicate silver drop earrings caught the morning sunlight.

'Wow,' Jack said, putting the pancake onto a plate and turning to look. I knew what he was thinking: Dad still hadn't paid us back the money he owed us – but this was different.

I checked for a card inside the package and found a small one, with a ballerina picture on the front.

To Bellissima Amelia on your big b'day.
Have fun and bottoms up! Lots of love, Dad x

I held up the earrings and felt a lump come to my throat. They were absolutely gorgeous.

'You ready?' Jack asked later that evening, scanning my turquoise dress and the earrings Dad had sent me, which fell elegantly almost to my shoulders.

I nodded and then, looking in the hallway mirror, added a white flower to my hair. 'Now, done.'

'You look gorgeous,' Jack said, kissing me. 'And not a day over twenty-nine.'

I punched him gently on the arm, and he led me out the front door.

We arrived at the Florence, and I expected at least to see Carly and Sunita, but I could only spot a few familiar faces milling around the bar: regulars at the pub, not my friends.

'You did tell people it was here, didn't you?' I asked Jack nervously.

'Oh crap, I completely forgot.' Jack slapped a hand to his forehead. I saw the ghost of a smile appear at the corner of his mouth. 'Come out here and take a look,' he said, leading me out of a door at the back.

I could hear the buzz from the beer garden as soon as we opened the door – and when I looked out the place had been transformed. The trellis was strung with white fairy lights and paper lanterns in green and orange, and each of the wooden tables up on the decking was covered with

Mexican striped tablecloths. It was a warm summer's night, and there was a clear sky overhead; the stars shone through the city smog.

A colourful banner was strung up on the wooden fence

Happy 30th Amelia!

'Did you do all this?' I said, turning to look at Jack.

He shrugged. 'I might have. With a little help from the fairies.' He nodded over at Sunita and Carly, who were looking at us from the far side of the garden.

Sunita brought over a tray of cupcakes decorated with green icing, candles burning on the central three cakes, and greeted me with a kiss. 'Happy birthday, sweetheart. The green's meant to represent the countryside,' she explained. 'I didn't realize it was going to look gross. I think I put too much food colouring in.'

A chorus of 'Happy Birthday' started up and I blew out the candles and took a cake for myself. Like everything Sunita made, it was delicious. 'They taste far better than they look,' I said.

I passed the tray to Jack and Nico.

'You'll come down the Go-Kart track next week, won't you?' Nico said to Jack, taking a cake from me with a smile. 'I'm going to close it to the public so it's open just for friends – a sort of baby shower.'

'A baby shower?' Jack said.

'Yes. Well, with me and Suni not married yet I never got to have a stag, so I thought we could have one now instead. You're up for it, aren't you?'

'I know,' Sunita said, nodding over at them, 'any excuse for these guys, eh? Can I get you some Prosecco?'

'Thanks.' I walked with her to the bar.

'He's already been on the sambuca, and he's supposed to be working early tomorrow,' she said. 'Watch he doesn't drag your husband into that.'

'I should have known I could count on you guys to get the party started.' I laughed.

'Yes,' Sunita said. 'Although Nico's drinking my units tonight.'

Carly made her way over to us. Sunita put a glass of fizz in my hand.

'Got you a little pressie,' Suni said, passing me a gift bag. I opened the parcels carefully – a delicate cream and china blue blouse from Reiss and a matching necklace.

'Thanks, Suni,' I said, giving her a hug.

'Clothes shopping for other people is a whole lot more fun than trying to find something I can squeeze into.'

'And a little something from me too,' Carly said, passing me a carefully wrapped blue package.

Inside was a pretty scrapbook, and an illustrated book on vintage-style interior decoration I'd been going on about to her.

'I thought the scrapbook might be useful for mood boards

and things, when you're planning how to do up the house.'

'That's a lovely idea,' I said, giving her a hug in thanks. Flicking through the decorating book, I felt a rush of excitement – I couldn't wait to get started adding the touches and polishes that would really make the cottage ours.

'St Catherine's won't be the same,' Carly said. 'I still can't believe you're really going.'

'We'll only be an hour away, and we'll have plenty of room for you both to stay over. You can give yourselves a weekend trip to the countryside.'

'So much change going on at the moment,' Carly said. 'Why do you all insist on changing your lives so much? I was quite happy with things the way they were.'

'Byeee!' I called out to the last of the revellers at our party, as Jack and I made an exit just after midnight. It had been a brilliant evening and send-off, catching up with old friends and making plans for them to come and visit.

A little worse for the wear, we made our way home, recounting conversations we'd had with people during the night.

'And in September—' Jack said.

'We're going to be all settled in our new home!' I said excitedly. I didn't mind at all that when we got home that night it would be to a flat full of cardboard boxes. We were taking steps towards a new life together.

'I can't wait,' Jack said, smiling. 'I thought you were nuts at first, but I have to hand it to you, this was a good idea.'

'Glad you agree. And when I've got a job again it'll seem like an even better one.' I gave him a smile. Yes, things would be stretched for a while, but there was no going back – since I'd given in my resignation I'd felt free, light. I might have just turned thirty, but I felt younger than ever.

When we got home, Jack took out his mobile phone and put it on the side as we got ready for bed.

I noticed the answerphone icon on his screen. 'You've got a message,' I said, pulling my pyjamas on and realizing I had the trousers on back to front.

'Really?' he said. 'I haven't checked it all evening actually. Probably work.'

As he rang through to check his message, I put on my pyjama shirt and did the buttons up slowly. I still felt a glow from the evening we'd had. I was so touched by the presents Sunita and Carly had picked out for me. All in all, entering my thirties felt pretty good so far.

'Shit,' Jack said, his eyes flicking up to look at me as he listened to the message all the way through. 'Shit, crap, bollocks,' he added.

'What? What is it?' I said, startled.

He put the phone down. 'That was the bank. A message from this afternoon. It's not good news.'

'I guessed that,' I said, my heart racing. 'What's going on?'

'There's a problem.'

My breath caught in my throat. This could not be happening. We were moving. To the country. And someone else was moving into our flat. It was all organized, it was all ready.

Jack looked at me. 'They've reconsidered our mortgage application in light of your resignation. It's been rejected.'

Chapter 5

Limbo

Sunday, 9 June

With a mug of tea in one hand and a couple of paracetamol in the other to soothe my hangover, I looked around at our kitchen – its crummy peeling cabinets, tired grey lino flooring, and tiny windows looking out onto the train track – and fought back tears.

How had our countryside dream disappeared just like that, in an instant? One moment we were all set to move into a cottage where I knew we could have been really happy, and now we were back at square one, stuck here.

What choices did Jack and I have now that the cottage had fallen through? Pull out of the sale of our place and stay in Hackney, even though I no longer had my job at the school keeping me there? Let down our buyers and risk not finding new ones?

Jack and I had spent a restless night in bed. My mind had been whirring – why couldn't I have just stuck it out one more term? Could we have got away with not telling the bank about me leaving my job? Our cottage, the home that was destined for us, was now out of our reach, and in two months we'd be handing over our flat too. If we didn't make a decision soon, we could end up homeless.

I couldn't sit around moping today though, and that was probably a good thing. I'd arranged to meet Sunita in Oxford Street at ten, so I had to pull myself together. She needed help with doing some baby shopping and had promised me waffles at the cafe in John Lewis afterwards. There's very little I won't do for a waffle.

I downed the pills with the dregs of my tea and then washed up my mug. Some fresh air would do me good. In our bedroom I put on a loose, orange silk top and slim black jeans with bronze pumps and slipped my phone and wallet into my handbag. I took a quick look at myself in the mirror. My hair was a bit of a mess – with the frenzy of the last few weeks at work I hadn't had it cut for a couple of months, and there were dark shadows under my eyes from the unsettled night.

I got a bus and then the tube into town, and found Sunita waiting for me at the doorway of the department store. 'Morning,' she said. 'God, Amelia, you look dreadful.'

'Thanks.' I frowned.

'Sorry. But you do look tired. You didn't even seem that drunk last night.'

'It's not that,' I said, blowing air out of my cheeks. 'It's the cottage. Everything's fallen through, Suni.'

We walked through the fragrance department and I filled her in on what had happened when Jack and I got home the previous night.

'That's terrible. What a massive bummer.'

'I know. I should have seen it coming. I think I was just fooling myself that it would all work out – I'd get a new job, or they'd take a chance on us.'

'Not sure mortgage lenders are big on taking chances on people any more,' Suni said. 'I'm so sorry, hon. Are you sure you're still up for today?'

'Yes, it's fine. It's good to have something else to focus on.' I took a breath to steady my nerves. Talking about the cottage had brought all that emotion back, and I really didn't want to cry.

'It's good to have some company. Nico's not really been the best at helping get us organized.' There was a trace of strain on her face.

The two of us spent several hours idling around the baby department on the third floor, picking out woodland animal nursery decorations, a baby monitor, a car seat and a Moses basket. Plus an activity mat and some bootees I couldn't resist getting Suni as a gift.

At about three, my stomach started to growl. 'Suni, not that I'm not having fun, but didn't you say something about waffles?'

'Waffles!' she said, a light going on in her eyes. 'Of course. God, how has it come to this, that I'm more focused on expensive travel systems than carbohydrates and cream with you? Sorry. Let's go to the cafe before I lose my mind completely.'

A quarter of an hour later we were in a window seat overlooking the crowds on Oxford Street, with two plates of waffles, whipped cream and strawberries between us.

'Thanks for coming today, Amelia. It wouldn't have been as much fun without you.'

'No worries. What are friends for?' I said with a smile. 'I'm happy to help out with this stuff, but not sure how much use I'll be on the night feeds.'

'True,' Sunita said. 'Hopefully Nico will be more of a support then. I'm hoping something will click when the baby's here.'

'Nerves?'

'I think so. He's excited. But yes, nervous too. He had a nightmare about delivering the baby himself in Sainsbury's, and since then he's paled a bit whenever we talk about the birth.'

'I bet he'll be brilliant on the day.'

'We'll see. What about Jack? Is he still clucky?'

'Yes,' I said, breaking off a chunk of waffle with my fork and adding a bit of cream and a slice of strawberry to it. 'You should see him when he talks about you two. But you know Jack – I'm sure next month he'll have moved on to something else.'

'And that's what you want? For him to forget about it?'

'To be honest, yes.'

'Do you think you might change your mind, in a couple of years, say?'

'It's possible,' I said, with a shrug. 'But I can't really imagine it. I like things the way they are. Anyway, right now we've got enough to think about without bringing another human being into the equation. We need to find somewhere to live, for starters.'

'OK. Let's think about your flat first. Could you negotiate a later move date with the buyers, give yourselves time to work out a plan?'

'Possibly,' I said. 'I'll look into it next week. I just can't forget about the cottage, though – the garden, the space, the fireside. It's so peaceful out there – you can hear your heart beat. I really wanted this. Both of us did.'

'I'm sure you'll find somewhere else.'

'It won't be the same,' I said sulkily.

Sunita raised an eyebrow.

'Sorry,' I said. 'Did I just regress to ten years old?'

'Listen. I know a good short-term cure. Hot chocolate

with whipped cream. You'll keep a pregnant woman company, won't you?'

I got back from the centre of town later that evening, and found Jack working on a storyboard at the kitchen table.

'How was your day with Sunita?' he asked. 'Did you get everything she needed?'

'It was good, thanks. You're really interested in hearing about all the baby stuff?'

'Yes, why wouldn't I be?'

'A baby monitor and some other bits and pieces,' I said. I located a pile of takeaway menus by the doormat, and pulled out one for a local curry house. 'Fancy a takeaway tonight?'

'Yes, sure. Sounds good.'

'How was your day today, anyway?'

'Busy. I've been working on this storyboard, but I can't get it quite right. I can't stop thinking about the cottage.'

'Yep,' I said, nodding in acknowledgement. 'That makes two of us.'

'What do you think we should do now? I feel we've already said goodbye to this place.'

'Me too. If we do stay here, I'll need to think about work right away, line up another job in London for the start of term in September.'

'Staying's not our only option,' Jack said. 'We can still move, we just have a more limited budget now, that's all.'

I paused. 'I suppose we could keep looking . . . see if there's anything we could get with a mortgage based on just your salary. And somewhere we can live over the summer without relying on a joint income.'

'Let's do that. I bet there are some bargains out there.'

I felt less sure than Jack seemed. 'We'll be OK, won't we?'

'Of course we will.'

The next day at school I looked around for Carly in the staffroom but couldn't see her anywhere. I checked my phone for messages and saw one from her.

Toilets, now?

I walked down the corridor and pushed the door to the staff toilets open. Carly was leaning against the far wall, her eyes puffy and red from crying.

'Carly, what's happened?'

'It's Alex,' she said. Her tears came fast, and she put her hands up to her eyes to brush them away.

'Come here,' I said, bringing her into my arms for a hug. She held on to me tight, like a baby koala, sobbing into my shoulder.

'What is it? What's he done?' I said after a moment, pulling back.

'It's not what he's done. Well, it is, but I can understand it. He finally told Jules about us and he freaked out.'

'I thought he was going to wait until the end of term?'

'Yes, me too. But apparently one of Jules's friends saw us out together and he started to get suspicious. He's furious that his dad's been lying to him even though – well, you know . . . nothing's even *happened* between us. Alex feels awful – he wants us to stop seeing each other.'

'I'm sorry, Carly. God, I really thought this would be OK.'

'Well, it definitely isn't. We should have been straight with Jules from the start. I've got a class with him this afternoon. This has all turned into a nightmare. I'm just praying that Garrett doesn't get to hear about it – that really would be the icing on the cake.'

'He won't,' I reassured her. 'No one ever tells him anything, definitely not the students. You know that.'

'I just thought . . .' Carly said, tears still in her voice. 'I thought that a bit of time was all we needed.'

When the weekend rolled around I was pleased to get out of the flat. Jack drove us down to Mum's village, Hazelton, about half an hour away from Canterbury. The motorway made way for green fields, oast houses and handwritten signs advertising fresh eggs.

I saw my mum waiting in the window of her small terraced house, waving eagerly. She came out of the house and on to the pavement, bounding up to us, in her blue shirt dress and ballerina pumps. 'Great to see you,' she said as we got out of the car, giving us both a kiss and a hug. She smelled of the hairdresser, expensive shampoo.

'Amelia. My daughter. So grown up. Thirty!' She turned to Jack to share her mystification that I wasn't still a newborn. He nodded and smiled, as if he too was surprised that I'd grown out of my romper suit.

'You look well.' She smiled. I glanced down at my faded H&M skirt and flip-flops. My hair still needed a cut. That was a mother's love for you, I guess.

'Now come inside, you two, I've been so excited about you coming down.'

We went into the house and walked through to the open-plan living and dining room.

'The house has changed a bit since you were last here, hasn't it?' she said.

It looked homier now, with floral curtains, cushions on the sofa, and candles and a bowl of pot pourri on the coffee table.

'Come and sit down. Tell me, how's everything going?'

I settled down on the sofa next to Jack, and Mum sat down opposite us in an armchair.

'OK,' I said. 'It's been a busy few weeks.'

'Oh yes?'

'Actually, I've resigned from my job.'

'Really?' Mum's eyebrows shot up. 'I thought you loved teaching?'

'I do. But things at the school have changed.'

Jack put his hand gently on my leg, comforting.

'Jack and I were also hoping to move out into the country – not far from here, actually. We found a cottage we really liked in Chilham.'

'Chilham? Beautiful village. Why didn't you say something?'

'We were waiting until it was all confirmed. It didn't work out, unfortunately.' I tried to keep the emotion out of my voice. We were moving on now.

'Oh, what a shame,' Mum said, putting her hands together in her lap. 'That's bad luck.'

'I'm sure we'll find somewhere else,' Jack said. 'Although we've got to be a bit more modest in our expectations now. Our budget's dropped a lot.'

'If you're interested in places round here,' Mum said, 'and you know I'd love it if you were nearby – then I can always ask around for you.'

'Thanks.'

'How was your birthday, anyway?' Mum said, perhaps sensing that I wanted to change the subject. 'Did you do anything to celebrate?'

'Oh, it was great, thanks. Jack threw me a little party at the local pub. All our friends were there.'

'Lovely,' Mum said brightly. 'Any word from your dad?'

'Yes, he sent me some earrings.'

'That's nice. Right, I think it's about time I put the kettle on.'

Mum got up, then paused. 'When you said you were interested in buying round here, would you consider Hazelton itself?'

Jack and I looked at each other. Living on my mum's doorstep hadn't exactly been in our plan. But then again, did we even have a plan any more?

'What did you have in mind?' I asked.

She sat down, her face animated.

'There's a wonderful cottage not far from here – needs work, but I reckon you could get it for a snip. The owner's elderly and her family want to have her a bit closer to them.'

'I don't think the satnav can find it,' I said, pushing various buttons as our guide told us again and again to take a U-turn when possible. Twenty minutes and three wrong turnings after leaving Mum's, we were taking a detour on our way back to London so that we could get a look at the cottage she'd mentioned.

'Mum said it was by a dirt track though. How about over there?' I pointed to a hedgerow with a path next to it.

'Are you sure? It doesn't look like there's anything down

there. I don't want to end up driving on to someone's farm like we did in that last village.'

'I'm pretty sure. Look.' I pointed to the outline of a building just visible through the leaves.

'OK, let's give this one a go.'

Jack turned up a wide muddy path and a cottage that fitted Mum's description came into view. It was isolated, with no other houses for miles around, and had a thatched roof and an apple tree in the front garden. The walls were covered in wisteria, the last of the fading blooms lilac against the grey stone. If you squinted, it didn't look a world away from the house we'd fallen in love with.

'Brambledown Cottage,' I read from the plate at the entrance to the driveway. 'This is it.'

'Looks good,' Jack said. 'It's pretty similar to the other place, isn't it? A bit shabbier maybe, but it's the same size, the same style of porch. Actually, it's good how the house and garden aren't overlooked by any neighbours. I think that's an advantage over the other house.'

I hadn't expected much – Mum and I had quite different tastes – but perhaps this really was an option for us. I peered at the downstairs window and caught sight of a woman's silhouette. She turned to face us. She was pale and elderly, her white hair up in a loose bun, and her eyes seemed to look out the car but somehow not see it – they were glazed, unfocused.

'Shall we get out and take a look?' Jack asked.

'I don't think so,' I said, nodding over to the old lady, who was still motionless, staring at us. 'Looks like the owner's still living there. We don't want to scare the life out of her by poking around. There isn't even a For Sale sign up yet. Let's get in touch with the estate agents and organize a proper viewing.'

'OK,' Jack said, turning on the engine again and cranking the car into gear. 'We'll come back. Definitely worth a viewing though, isn't it?'

'Yes,' I said, buckling my seatbelt up. 'Being so close to Mum – well, it's not what we planned, but this place does seem pretty much exactly what we're looking for.'

The cottage, with its serene setting, had brought something back into my life and perhaps Jack's too – hope.

The following Saturday Jack shook me awake gently, and I buried my face in the pillow, groaning. My head throbbed, and I could barely breathe out of my nose. My skin prickled, both hot and cold at the same time, and there was a film of sweat on my face and chest.

'Are you OK?' Jack said, putting a glass of water on the bedside table for me.

'No,' I said, wiping a sweaty strand of hair away from my face. 'I'm ill.'

Every year, when June rolled around, my excitement at

the empty weeks ahead was tempered by a bout of summer flu. A year's worth of stress would catch up with me, engulfing me in a fog of tissues. I'd naively thought that this year, with just a month left until I left St Catherine's for good, might be different.

'*Drugs*,' I moaned, before drifting back into a foggy doze.

Jack returned a few minutes later with a mug of Lemsip. 'Here you go.'

I took it from him gratefully, and managed to sit up in bed.

'Should I cancel the viewing?' he asked, checking his watch. 'It doesn't feel right going to see the place without you.'

'No,' I said. 'There's no point both of us missing it.' I took a tissue from a box on the side and blew my nose. 'This cottage could be just the place for us. Why don't you have a look, take a few photos? You can tell me about it this evening.'

'If you're sure?' Jack said.

'I'm sure,' I said. 'There's no way I'd last the journey, let alone be able to drag myself round the place. If you like it, we can go back and see it together when I'm better.'

'OK,' he said. 'I'll be back by six. You've got enough to keep you entertained till then?'

'Yes,' I said. 'Don't worry. I might ring Carly, see if she fancies coming over.'

'Feel better soon,' Jack said, giving me a kiss on the head, his hand gently touching my arm, refreshingly cool against my hot skin. 'And if you get any worse, call me and I'll be right back.'

'I'll be fine,' I said. 'Used to St Catherine's flu by now.'

When I heard the front door close and Jack leave the flat, I pulled the duvet up around me and texted Carly.

Hi, C. I'm ill. Fancy sofa, box set of New Girl and some After Eights? You'll be the best friend ever if you come and keep me company Xx

Carly's reply came a moment later.

You're lucky I'm so single. Best offer I've had in ages. See you in fifteen xx

There weren't many people I'd let see me in my ratty dressing gown and PJs, hair up in a scruffy topknot, but Carly was one of them. We were sitting on my sofa, halfway through a second episode of New Girl and a good way through the box of chocolates I'd opened.

'Pretty selfish of me really, getting you round here,' I said. 'You'll probably get ill now too.'

'Don't worry about it,' she said, putting another chocolate in her mouth. 'Only a matter of time; I get it every year as well. Anyway, who knows how many more opportunities we'll get to do this? I'm not going to take you for granted.'

'Ah, that's nice. Although I'm not holding my breath on moving soon. By the way, any news from Alex? I mean, Jules is on his way to uni in September, isn't he? Surely that could open the door to you two trying things again?'

'Nothing,' Carly said. 'I've got Jules giving me the silent treatment in class, and Alex not replying to my texts. I feel like an idiot for ever thinking something positive might come of this. Maybe I should be out on dates and meeting someone new.'

'Don't give up, Carls. You said before that you thought he was worth it.'

'He is,' Carly said, shaking her head and letting out a weary laugh. 'And I'm crazy about him. But this is family. Since the divorce he's wanted to give Jules security and keep their relationship strong. I don't want to be the person to undermine that.'

'Maybe Jules will come round to the idea,' I said, taking another tissue from the box and blowing my nose. 'With time.'

'I don't know. He seems pretty set at the moment. You're so lucky with Jack,' Carly said. 'It's all so straightforward. You love him, he loves you, you want the same things. Neither of you has kids with anyone else. Your wedding was a dream.'

'Thank you.' My eyes drifted unconsciously to the wedding photo on the mantelpiece: Jack and me in front of a vintage car by Clifton Suspension Bridge in Bristol, close to where he grew up. 'It's not always been smooth sailing, believe me. But I can't complain. Jack's great.'

'I thought, back then, that you were tying yourselves down too soon,' Carly said. 'But maybe it was me who was late to the party. I didn't mind waiting for Alex at first, but now I feel gripped by this fear – if this doesn't work out, is that it for me? Do I really have time to find someone else?'

'You're insane,' I said. 'A – it will probably work out, and B – if not, of course you have time.'

'Sorry,' Carly said. 'I'm really hormonal right now. And having a teenager in charge of my love life isn't helping at all.'

Later that evening Jack opened the bedroom door with a creak, waking me up from what felt like a drug-induced coma. Before Carly left she'd given me a hefty dose of Night Nurse, and I must have gone out for the count. I didn't even remember her leaving, but she had obviously switched off the lights and TV before she did, because the flat was silent now.

'Hey, Amelia,' Jack said, climbing on to the bed beside me.

'You're back.' I could make out through bleary eyes that it was my husband who was beside me, but his face looked strangely wobbly, and the bright light in the hallway behind him hurt my eyes.

'I am. I brought you a creme egg. Not easy to find out of season, but I happen to know that they have unique restorative powers.'

I brightened immediately, and raised myself up to a seated position in bed to receive it from him. I unwrapped the foil from my surprise. 'You're an angel.' As I bit into the chocolate shell, I pieced the day together again and remembered where Jack had been.

'The cottage,' I said. 'What's it like? Is it beautiful like the other one? With a big garden?'

'The garden's enormous,' Jack said. 'Like your mum said, the house definitely needs some work, but it's got heaps of character – even more original features than the other one – and it looks like we could snap it up cheaply. The asking price is sixty grand less than for Arcadia Cottage, and Shannon, the agent, hinted that they'd probably accept an offer under the asking price. If they did, we would have money left in our budget to do it up.'

'Sounds good,' I said, still battling through feelings of slight delirium in an effort to concentrate on what Jack was saying. 'What was it like inside?'

'The layout was quite similar to the first cottage,' he said. 'You have to use your imagination a bit more, as the owner's been living there for more than fifty years, and at the moment it's full of her stuff. The kitchen's a bit outdated, but we could do that up. Even with the money we lost on the last survey and solicitors' fees, I think we'll have enough to do the work. This place just needs a bit of a tidy-up.'

'Can I see the photos?' I asked, intrigued. Jack got out his iPhone and showed me some dark interior shots – the bathroom looked quite old-fashioned but had lovely oak beams, and the bedroom was spacious. I could see there was a window with a great view out on to the surrounding fields.

'It looks nice,' I said. 'In a few days I should be well enough to go for a viewing.'

'We might need to move fairly quickly,' Jack said, shifting position on the bed to face me. 'It was an open house today – there were three other couples looking around.'

'OK, sure. I'll go and see it as soon as I'm better.'

The next weekend I drove down to Hazelton on my own, as Jack had to work. Instead of stopping at my mum's house I drove through the local high street, with its clock tower, independent shops and lively village green, and carried on until I reached Brambledown Cottage.

When I arrived there was a woman in her twenties, with highlighted hair pinned back in a bun, waiting for me at the gate. I parked and got out of the car.

'Hi, you must be Shannon,' I said. 'I'm Amelia.' We shook hands.

'Thanks for coming, Amelia. Jack mentioned how important it was that you see the place too and of course we completely understand that. We've had interest from two other couples but I've encouraged the vendors to hold back on any decisions until you've had a chance to see the place for yourself.'

'Thanks. I appreciate that.'

Shannon went up to the wooden front door and knocked on it once, firmly.

I looked at the front garden – by the apple tree the grass was overgrown, and by the front path there were two flowerpots lying on their side, broken, with soil spilling out of them. It would all need a tidy-up, but there was potential – and with the low price the cottage was on the market for, Jack and I were expecting to have to do a bit of work.

There was no answer, so Shannon tried the door again, knocking harder this time. 'She's an old lady,' she said, by means of explanation.

Five minutes later we were still waiting on the doorstep. 'I'm really sorry about this. Let me ring her son and see what's going on – he said a viewing today would be fine.'

Shannon stepped away from the door, mobile to her ear.

I saw movement in the living room, and took a step closer. There was the same woman I'd seen before, standing, silently, in what looked like a silk dressing gown. She looked up and our eyes met. She put a hand to her chest as if seeing me had frightened her.

I glanced over at Shannon but she was deep in conversation on the phone.

The wooden door swung open, and the woman stared at me accusingly – elegant and tall, with her white hair pinned up haphazardly and a wild look in her eyes.

'Hello,' she said, her gaze softening. 'You came. Come inside.'

I walked into the hallway, noticing the original wooden staircase and getting a brief glimpse into the kitchen.

'Sarah,' she said.

'No, I'm Amelia,' I said, offering her my hand.

The woman shook her head, confused.

'I've come with Shannon, the estate agent,' I said, motioning back outside to where Shannon was standing. She'd hung up the phone and was walking towards us.

'Mrs McGuire,' Shannon said from the doorstep, 'I'm here to show this lady around your property. Is that still OK with you? Your son said it—'

'Round my property?' the woman said, angry and confused. 'Absolutely not. What are you planning? To take things? From a defenceless old woman? I won't have it.'

'No, Mrs McGuire,' Shannon said, shaking her head and smiling.

'Are you laughing at me?'

I backed away quietly until I was standing next to Shannon just outside the doorway.

'No, certainly not. Not at all I just wanted to show Amelia round the cottage, because she's interested in buying it. You know, like we did with those couples the other day?'

'Buying it?' the old woman snapped. 'How ridiculous. It's not for sale. I won't have strangers in my house.'

Shaking her head, she slammed the front door shut with such force that I took a step back.

'Oh dear,' Shannon said. 'I'm so sorry about this. She was absolutely fine last time, but her family did warn me that she wasn't well.'

'She seemed frightened by us.'

'Just confused, I think.' She held up her mobile phone 'Her son David said he's down in Sussex today, otherwise he'd come here himself and let us in.'

'Oh,' I said with a pang of disappointment. 'I suppose it can't really be helped . . . but I have come all this way. Is there anything we could have a look at – the garden maybe?'

'Yes. I don't think we should risk going in, but there's a low fence round the side that means we'll be able to get a pretty good look.'

She led me through a narrow alleyway to the back of the house. The heady scent of honeysuckle crept into my nostrils. The wooden fence, heavy with white climbing hydrangea, had bowed in a section, so that we could have walked right into the garden if we wanted. I peered through the gap.

The garden was wild and untended, stretching back for what seemed like miles, with nothing but fields behind it. An oak tree stood at the far end. Blasts of colour came from within the wild grasses – hollyhocks and wild poppies were flourishing in the untended land, and there were two tall sunflowers by the opposite fence. In a sunny spot to my left there was a large patch of lavender next to a rose bush – I wondered if in the past the garden had looked quite different from how it was now.

Taking in the sweet smells, and the distant birdsong, the betting shop and railway tracks we looked out on from Addison Road felt a world away.

'Needs a bit of TLC, obviously,' Shannon said, pointing out the thick weeds. The grass in some areas had grown to waist height. Only the paved area by the house was under any kind of control.

'But it's beautiful, isn't it?' I said, taking a lungful of country air. Yes, the space needed taming, but the garden had potential we'd never find in a city flat – a place where I might be able to discover my green-fingered streak. I picked a poppy from the ground by my feet and held it up. 'I think it could be lovely.'

Rather than go straight home, I called my mum to see what she was up to.

'What a lovely surprise,' she said. 'I'm just at the post

office. Why don't you come into the village and we can go for a stroll, get some ice creams on the green?'

'Sure,' I said. 'I'll be right over. I'll meet you on the high street.'

I drove to the village, about fifteen minutes' away, and parked in a side street off the main road. The high street, lively on the sunny day, was a mixture of modern boutiques and cafes, a mini-market, and a jeweller's and antiques shop that looked as if they'd been there for centuries. I peered in through the window of the antiques shop and spotted a fireplace and some attractive standard lamps in there – I made a mental note to tell Jack about it. If we did go for the cottage, this might be just the place to pick up some bargains to furnish it with.

I crossed the road and spotted Mum right away, standing on the pavement waiting for me in a turquoise wrap dress and ballet pumps. We hugged hello.

'So, what did you think of the cottage?' she asked, as we made our way over to the village green.

'The viewing was a non-starter, unfortunately,' I said. 'The old lady who lives there refused to let me go in and look around.'

'Oh no – what a shame. You didn't get to see any of it?'

'I only had a peek inside, and then there was what I could see through the window – not much really. But we did go round the back to the garden, which was incredible – really big. Did you say you'd been in there?'

'No, I haven't – I've just seen the outside, like you. But people round here say it's a diamond in the rough. It's been neglected for a while, and if you'd met the owner I'm sure you'll have seen why. But a young couple like you and Jack, well, I'm sure you could work wonders with it. Add tons of value.'

We reached the bandstand and took a seat on the steps.

'It would be mad to offer on it, wouldn't it, without having seen it properly?' I said.

'Oh, I don't know. Sometimes in life you just have to take a leap of faith, don't you? And you said you were restricted in your budget. It's not every day that a cottage like that comes up.'

'The agent did mention there'd been other interest. I can't see she'll hold them back from offering much longer, and it'll be a while till I can get back here again.'

'What did you feel when you were there?' Mum asked.

'I don't know. I liked it, I think. I mean, I was a bit thrown by the situation – the old lady being so bewildered by my being there. But the cottage was certainly charming, and I love the idea of a garden we could really put some work into.'

'Talk to Jack tonight. I'm sure the right response will come to you.'

'I hope so,' I said. 'It's such a big decision, isn't it?'

'Yes,' Mum said. 'I felt the same when I bought my place – but I've never looked back. Hazelton's a great place. Really friendly.'

'This seems like a lovely spot,' I said, looking out over the lawn that divided the high street in two. Mums were pushing buggies and school kids played in the central area, and there was an ice cream stand just to our left.

'99 with a flake?' my mum asked.

'Yes, please. Now, that's my kind of decision.'

I arrived back in Hackney in the early evening. Jack had left me a note to say he was at a cafe down by the canal, with Sunita and Nico. I put on a cardigan and went down to meet them.

'Call this work?' I said to Jack, when I saw the cold beer in his hand. He got up and gave me a hug.

'I was working all day, I swear,' he said, laughing. 'They forced me out.'

'We did, it's true,' Nico said. 'You know how hard it is to persuade your husband about these things.'

I shook my head and kissed them all hello and took a seat beside them. Early evening sunlight flickered on the canal, and the sun was setting behind what remained of the Olympic park.

'So, what's the verdict?' Jack said. 'What did you think of the place?'

'I'm really confused,' I said. 'Long story, but I didn't get to look inside – but from what I could see it had lots of charm, and Mum says she'd heard it's got tons of potential and thinks that at that price it's a steal.'

'You didn't get to see any of it?' Sunita said.

'I only had the briefest of looks inside, before the owner made it clear she wanted me out. I saw the garden though, which was beautiful. Stretches back for ever.

'Ah, the envy,' she said. 'Fond as I am of our metre-square concrete slab, I'd do anything for a bit of lawn, especially when this one comes.' She put a hand gently on her stomach.

'I got a – I don't know. I think I got a good feeling about it though.'

'What's the deal with the buyers of your place?' Nico asked.

'They wanted to move in mid-August,' Jack said, 'but we persuaded them to give us a couple more weeks. If our offer's accepted, we could push everything through in two months. What do you think, Amelia?'

The truth was, I wasn't sure what I wanted any more. It seemed like after years of everything playing out pretty much as I expected it to, things were now taking on a life of their own. But I could picture me and Jack in Hazelton, in that cottage. I really liked what I'd seen of the village.

'You know what? I think we should go for it.' I said, a smile breaking out on my face. 'We can just about afford it, we can add value to it, and it'll be an adventure.'

Sunita smiled at me encouragingly.

'Let's call both agents on Monday, Jack. And right now, I think I definitely need a drink.'

'That wasn't bad, Miss,' Shanice said. 'It was hardly that boring at all.' She was walking with me through the exit of the Globe Theatre, with the rest of the group bounding ahead. July was drawing to a close, along with the school term and my time at St Catherine's.

'I kind of liked it too, although I didn't understand all of it,' Paul said, shrugging. 'And it was lame having to stand up the whole time.'

'You would have been standing up in Shakespeare's time,' I said. 'Unless you'd been rich, of course.'

'Of course I would have been rich, Miss,' Paul replied with a grin.

The group reached a stretch of grass outside Tate Modern.

'What about here, Miss?' Shanice shouted over.

'Yes, let's take a seat, everybody. Did you all bring something to eat?'

My students sat down in loose groups, and got food and drink out of their rucksacks. A couple of them gathered around Shanice, and peered over to see what they were doing.

'Don't look, Miss,' she said with a smile.

A moment later, she brought over a cake covered in white icing with red and blue lettering on it, and the other students gathered round me.

I felt tears spring to my eyes as I read the message:

Good Luck! We'll miss you. 10E

The next day at school, the end-of-term atmosphere was impossible to miss. The volume in each of my classes was louder, the students were more excitable, but the biggest change was in the staffroom – all the teachers who during term had struggled through, with frown lines growing increasingly deep between their brows, now had smiles on their faces and colour back in their cheeks.

I was starting to feel lighter too. Part of it was finishing school, but the other part was that moving to Kent seemed as though it was really going to happen. Our offer on Brambledown Cottage had been accepted, we'd had our survey done, and now our solicitors were ironing out the contractual details. With any luck, we'd complete in August and pick up our keys at the start of September. Yes – we were taking a risk, given that I hadn't seen properly inside the cottage, but it felt right.

I sought out Trey's form tutor, Mrs McKenna, and passed

her the package I'd put together. 'I know we don't know yet about next term, but in case he does come back, I don't want him falling behind. So this is the course material we've been studying, plus the things that he might have missed and some websites that will help him catch up.'

There was also a letter, saying that whatever was going on, I hoped he'd come back to school.

'Thanks,' she said, taking it. 'I'll send it out to his case-worker. We're all hoping to see him again soon, so hopefully she'll make some progress getting through to him.

I went over to my locker and cleared it, putting notebooks and stationery into a bag and separating out a couple of books to return to the library.

'Looks strange like that, doesn't it? All empty,' Carly said, appearing by my side and handing me a coffee she'd just made.

'Thanks,' I said, taking it. 'Yes, it does. Hard to believe this is probably the last coffee we'll ever have together in the staffroom.'

'Seven years of teaching – and learning. Oh, and despairing,' she said, laughing.

'I'll miss this,' I said, giving her arm a squeeze. 'I'll miss you.'

'Tell me about it.' She smiled. 'You're going off to a coun-tryside adventure and I'm just going to be stuck here on my lonesome.'

She made a sad face and pouted. Thankfully her days of being genuinely down over things with Alex seemed to be drawing to a close. She'd resolved not to wait around, and had even been on a couple of internet dates. Nothing had come of them, but she'd vowed to get on and move forward, and she wasn't wasting any time.

'You'll be OK,' I said. 'You'll find someone else to be a coffee-slave for soon enough. And I get the feeling I might still see you around.'

'Damn right,' she said. 'Just you try and stop me coming to visit.'

'It's been a journey,' I said, and gave her a big hug.

I walked out into the car park that afternoon and loaded my car with the things from my locker and classroom that I'd accumulated over the years. It was just a couple of boxes, not as much as I'd expected. The students grouped together by the school gates on the warm day, free at last to enjoy the summer and do whatever they wanted, and yet none of them in any hurry to leave the school premises. They, like me, had mixed feelings about letting their schooldays go.

'Take with us, or box for charity?' Jack said, holding up a grey Manchester University hoodie.

'Don't you dare put that in the charity bag,' I said, smiling and taking it from him. I felt the soft cotton against my face and put it on over my pyjamas. 'Look, it fits perfectly still.'

'It looks cute on you, actually,' he said, drawing me into his arms and kissing me. 'Although I don't feel we're making a whole lot of progress on this decluttering mission.'

I glanced around the living room, where we were boxing up our belongings ready for the move to Hazelton. After a couple of hiccups, where our solicitor said they'd had trouble getting the vendor's signature, we were finally ready to exchange. In two weeks another couple would be making this flat in Addison Road their new home, and we'd be moving to Hazelton. My mum couldn't have been more excited at the news that Jack and I would be living so close to her.

But trying to reduce our belongings and ensure we were only taking things with us that we would really use wasn't proving easy.

'Not even one teapot?' Jack said, holding up one of my collection. Admittedly it wasn't the prettiest – a souvenir from Scarborough, with a tacky picture on the side. But it had been one of my first, and a reminder of a trip I'd taken there with my grandparents. It wasn't going anywhere.

'No way,' I said firmly. 'Don't even think it. All the teapots are coming with us. We have space. It's your comic book collection that needs reducing, if you ask me.'

'Comic books?' he said, holding up an early edition of

Sin City from a towering pile we'd taken out of one of the cupboards. 'I swear you only do it to wind me up. They're *graphic novels*, Amelia.' He smiled. 'And they are most definitely not going anywhere.'

Dexter leapt out of an empty box he'd been hiding in and balanced for a moment on the side, then, as the box tipped, the flap made a little ramp for him to descend on to the carpet. He came over to us, and wound his way round Jack's legs.

'Don't worry, Dexter,' he said, bending to pick him up. 'I'm fairly confident you'll make the cut.'

'We're really doing it, aren't we?' I said, grinning.

'We certainly are.'

PART TWO

Autumn

Chapter 6

Brambledown Cottage

Welcome to Hazelton
Population: 3,000
Twinned with Chinon, France
Winner of best kept British village 1999

Saturday, 7 September

'What time are the removal men coming again?' I asked Jack, peering out of the window at the street below. The leaves on the plane trees that lined the road had changed from green to yellow and gold, a few gently fluttering down to the pavement. A light rain was falling.

'Midday, so any time now.' Jack joined me. 'Actually, look.' He pointed to a large lorry parking up outside the betting shop. 'That's probably them.'

'Right, so this is it,' I said, taking a deep breath.

'All set for our new life,' Jack said, squeezing my hand. 'No second thoughts?'

'None. I can't wait.'

We let the removal men in, and all four of us went up and down the stairs of our block with the boxes. When the lorry was full, Jack and I went back up to the flat to do a final check. We dipped in and out of the rooms that we'd spent the first two years of our married life in, and met again at the front door, the same sorrowful expression on both our faces.

'I guess this is the last time we'll ever walk out of this place,' Jack said.

I thought of our first day in the flat . . .

'Welcome to our castle,' Jack had said, throwing open the front door to Addison Road and leading me through into the flat.

It was bare – but I loved it. I scurried, full of excitement, through each room, reminding myself where everything was. It didn't take long – in around three minutes I was back in Jack's arms. 'Our own place,' I said, kissing him. 'We're here, Jack.'

He smiled, a flicker of light in his brown eyes. 'Next step – furniture.' He laughed.

'We've got a bed; what more could you possibly want?' I

said cheekily. The bed, which the removal men would be delivering later that day along with the other things from our old rented flat, was a cheap futon, but it would do for now.

Jack squeezed my hand tight. 'I can't wait to marry you,' he said.

'Me neither.'

Dexter wove between my legs, bringing me back to the present.

'We won't forget you, Dex. Don't worry,' I said, scooping him up into my arms.

Jack passed me the plastic box we used to take him to the vet, and together we persuaded him to go inside.

'We're going to make new memories, you know,' Jack said, reading my mind. 'Even better ones.'

I kissed him, and smiled, ready now to leave our London life behind.

'Come on, sweetheart,' Jack said, ruffling my hair. 'It's time to go.'

We drove behind the lorry, stopping off at our rented garage to pick up the antique furniture Grandma Niki and Grandpa had left me. We loaded the side table, drinks cabinet and wardrobes into the van – I was happy we'd finally have somewhere to put them.

As we drew closer to the cottage, the busy streets of East

London seemed no more than a distant memory. I gazed out of the car window, thinking about what the cottage would be like inside, and how we'd settle into the village. By the time we arrived in Hazelton, I was chewing my nails at the prospect of our new start.

The agent, Shannon, met us by the front door and passed us the keys. 'Hi,' she said, with a smile she was clearly forcing. 'Here are the keys. Welcome to your new home.'

'Thank you,' Jack said.

'Is everything OK?' I asked.

'I'm sorry about all the stuff still in there,' Shannon said, 'but I'm sure you can work around it. The living room and bedroom are full of Mrs McGuire's furniture, so only part of the house has been professionally cleaned. Her family have been trying to reason with her, but she hasn't been exactly cooperative about moving out.'

'What?' I said. 'Is there nothing you can do? We need to move in today.'

'It's been a bit of a nightmare, I'm afraid,' Shannon s aid, tugging at her highlighted hair distractedly. 'Believe me, I've been trying. But the owner's refusing to listen to anyone.'

I turned to look at our removal men, who were already unloading boxes from the back of the lorry.

'We need the cottage cleared,' I said. 'Isn't that usually the deal?'

'I'm sorry,' Shannon said feebly.

'When will it be sorted?' Jack asked.

'They've promised me her things will be gone by the end of the week. The house is yours now, and you can move your things in but, as I say, you may just have to work around what's in there.'

'We'll make do,' I said to Jack. 'At least we can move in.'

'You haven't seen inside yet, have you?' Shannon said, turning to me. 'After all that palaver at the viewing. Well, with a bit of vision, I'm sure you'll be very happy living here.'

Shannon left, and got into her car.

'Vision?' I asked Jack nervously, once we were inside the porch. A feeling of dread built up inside me. 'Jack, what did she mean by that?'

'We said we were willing to do some work, Amelia, didn't we?'

In the cottage hallway, the early evening sunlight was filtering through windows that were thick with dirt. To our right was a wooden staircase with dark wood banisters, some spindles missing, some broken. The removal men were putting most of our things in the garage – just a few essential boxes and the bed would be moving in with us today.

The dust, the grime, I thought, as I ran my finger over the dado rail – it was all superficial. A few days and it would be clean – hopefully sorted by the owner, but if not, then with some work from us. The hallway whispered from the past through original flooring, tiles and skirting boards.

'Let's look at the living room first,' Jack said, leading me through to a room on the left. 'We can put Dexter in there while we get settled.' He carried the cat box with him. 'Like I told you, the owner has been living here since the nineteen sixties. For the past few years she wasn't able to get up the stairs on her own, so she was using the living room as a bedroom. The layout's a bit weird at the moment but we can change that easily enough.'

I peeked round the doorway, my heart in my throat, hoping to see a reception room as cosy and welcoming as the one we'd fallen for in Arcadia Cottage. But despite the dark timber beams and posts, and the original windows, my hopes were dashed – with a bed in the middle of it, and clothes on rails all around, the room was dingy.

'Look, I know what you're thinking,' Jack said, putting his arm around my waist. 'But honestly, there's so much potential here – have you seen the windows?' He pointed to the windows at the front of the house, criss-crossed with iron latticework, but it was hard to make them out, obscured as they were by someone else's belongings.

'They look original,' I said, stepping into the room to get a better look. 'Cleaned up they should be nice – although,' I tapped the wood round the edge, and a piece fell away, 'we're going to have to replace these frames, don't you think?'

'Maybe, yes. Here, check this out – the fireplace.' Jack crossed the room and touched it. 'Beautiful tiles,' he added. The ceramic tiles, in dark red and blue, did look pretty underneath their coating of soot. 'And it works, apparently.' He pulled out the tray under the fire, letting loose a cloud of black dust.

'Nice,' I said, but I felt as if I was clutching at straws. Some appealing tiles in a room that would need to be all but gutted before it was inhabitable. I silently prayed things would improve when we saw the other rooms.

'What do you think, Dex?' Jack asked, opening his box. Dexter cowered towards the back of the box and refused to come out. 'He'll get used to it soon enough.

'Come and look at the kitchen – you'll love it,' Jack said confidently.

Whatever it was like, it couldn't be worse than our cramped space in Addison Road, I reasoned. But one glance inside told me otherwise – the 1970s units, the peeling lino on the floor, every surface covered in old plates and clutter. The one saving grace was a dark red Aga tucked away in an alcove, an authentic rural touch in what otherwise looked like a bric-a-brac sale.

'I mean, we'll probably need to change the cabinets,' Jack said.

'Probably? They're awful.'

I looked from the china ornaments of owls, to boxes overflowing with pans and crockery, and paintings stacked up against the walls.

The floor was covered with dark green lino panels, curling up at the edges as it reached the cabinets – seventies-style pale green units that no longer stood exactly in line with each other so that there were gaps between some of them. The covering on the doors had started to peel up and bubble in places, and the large fridge, once white, presumably, was now a nicotine yellow.

'Definitely time for an upgrade,' Jack said, opening one of the cabinets and peering in, then stepping back as if a smell had put him off.

The counters, thick with grime, were cluttered with notebook pages and recipe books. I saw a loose handwritten sheet and picked it up to take a closer look.

Ellie's Extraordinary Apple and Blackberry Crumble

INGREDIENTS:

Five apples from our tree
Blackberries from the garden

I put it to one side, under a mug with owls on it, next to one that said 'World's Best Mum'. I was finding it difficult to see past all the *stuff*. Being stuck inside with it was making me feel claustrophobic.

We continued round the ground floor. The downstairs toilet had a tiny shower room installed in the corner with a seat in it and ageing pipework hanging off the wall. 'It looks like this hasn't been touched for years,' I said. 'We'll need plumbers in to replace a lot of this pipework.' I remembered the notes on the survey that I'd read – the surveyor had mentioned that a lot of things were in need of updating, but I hadn't expected it to be quite this bad.

'Come and see the cellar.' Jack led me down the stairs. 'This'll be great for storage,' he said, apparently oblivious to the smell of damp that I found overwhelming.

'Maybe we could take a look at the garden?' I said, pausing midway on the staircase. Getting outside for a bit would help me get things in perspective. We walked through the kitchen towards the back door – the area by the door was clear, at least.

Jack found the key on our new key ring, and opened the back door on to the garden. 'Let's go outside and get some fresh air.'

'Good idea.' I was longing to leave the stuffy, claustrophobic atmosphere. I'd sometimes teased Mum for the way she liked to hang on to mementoes and souvenirs – but I'd never seen the home of a real hoarder before. It was starting to look very much like we'd managed to buy one.

Once outside though, I was able to forget the chaos of the house. Summer had faded, and with it had gone the brightest greens and the red sprinkling of poppies, so the garden looked different from the last time I'd seen it. But the leaves on the oak tree had turned a pale burnt umber and gold. Even though dead leaves had formed a mulch on the patio, there was something beautiful in the light that fell on the overgrown grass.

'It's gorgeous, isn't it?'

'Yes,' Jack said. 'So much space.'

'Oh dear, there's going to be a lot for Dexter to kill out here, isn't there?' I said, with a wry smile. Our tabby was an expert bird and mouse killer, and even in the urban sprawl he'd managed to bring in some grotesquely beheaded prey most weeks.

'He's going to be a proper country cat,' Jack said. 'But while he gets his bearings, we should do that butter on the paws trick, shouldn't we? Make sure he doesn't head up the motorway trying to get back to our flat.'

'Do you think? He doesn't even seem to want to leave his box at the moment.'

'He'll adjust. Let's go upstairs. We'll have plenty of time to explore the garden over the next few weeks.'

I didn't want to go back indoors. I wanted to stride out into the long grass and feel it against my hands, lose myself out there in the undergrowth and trees. Forget about the stress of moving for a moment.

'Come on,' Jack said.

I followed him and we closed the kitchen door behind us. The steps up to the second floor were tired and rickety, the wood wearing thin in places. 'Some of these steps probably need replacing,' Jack said. 'We might even want to take the whole staircase out. It'll be fine, though. We just need to find someone who does really authentic restoration.'

'We've factored all this into the fifteen thousand pounds we put aside, right?' I said. The pots of money I'd thought we were going to make on buying a cheaper place seemed to be disappearing before my eyes – a new fitted kitchen, a revamped downstairs bathroom, restored window frames . . .

'Yes,' Jack said, 'and the five thousand your dad owes us.'

'Yes,' I replied, feeling slightly guilty about it. 'I'm sure that will come through soon.' I'd persuaded Jack it would be fine to take the money out of our joint account, that Dad would pay us back before the summer.

'OK.' Jack took my hand and led me along the upstairs corridor. I flicked a switch on the wall, but no light came on. With the doors closed, blocking the daylight, it was difficult to see our way around. I found another switch, pressed it, and this time the corridor lit up in pale golden light. Framed black and white photos hung on the walls, and wooden shelves spilled over with glass jars filled with embroidery thread in every conceivable colour.

'Do you remember me saying that she used to be a dress-maker?' Jack said. 'Apparently she collected sheep's wool from the barbed wire fence down by the stream, and dyed and spun it.'

'That's nice, and I'd probably appreciate it more in another situation. But right now, I'd rather she'd taken her stuff with her. It's as if she's still living here. It's creepy.'

'It won't be for long, Amelia,' Jack said. 'I'm sure they'll sort it out soon enough.'

But the truth was, I wasn't frustrated with the owner, I was annoyed with myself, and perhaps also, just a little bit, with Jack.

'And the master bedroom,' he said, opening the door directly in front of us. 'Ta-da!' In Jack's blurry iPhone photos, it had looked OK. As with most of the rooms in the house, there were timber beams, painted black, above us. The ceiling sloped down at the side, and there were two windows, low down, with heavy dark blue velvet drapes that hung to the floor. Beneath the boxes and bags that lay cluttering the floor was a tatty navy-blue carpet, and the magnolia paintwork looked nicotine-stained in places. Even with the heavy old-fashioned drapes, the two windows made this one of the lightest rooms in the house. But I didn't want to sleep here tonight, or any night.

'Come over here – there's a great view of the garden.' We went to the window, and I tried to pull myself together. Jack and I were a team, and we had to stand united on this, one of the biggest moves we'd ever made. He pulled back the curtains and I looked out on to the wild garden below, and saw that at the foot of it there was a wide stream, glinting in the sunlight. A field with sheep in it lay just beyond. 'This is what we'll be waking up to,' he said. 'No noisy neighbours, no trains rattling by, no late-night fights in the street waking us up.'

I smiled, and squeezed his hand. 'It's quite a view, isn't it?'

'Unbeatable.'

Across the landing was the bathroom. I thought of the white claw-foot tub and period basin and taps at Arcadia Cottage and wondered if this room would look the same. When I entered the room, I fought back bitter disappointment. A primrose-yellow sixties-style bath, toilet and basin were oddly clustered in one corner, on a blue lino floor. Large flower prints were papered on the walls and tatty blue curtains hung by the small window. The pipes were boxed away in wood, which only served to draw more attention to them.

'Bit dated,' I said.

'It needs a bit of a makeover, yes,' Jack said, as if it were nothing, the job of a quiet afternoon.

I longed for the free-standing tub, for a bathroom that was an escape, not this depressing place.

'There's another room across the way,' Jack said, leaving the bathroom and opening the door across the landing. He couldn't open it the whole way as the room was filled with sewing machines, a dummy and other dressmaking equipment. 'A study, or whatever we want really.'

I poked my head around the door to get a better look inside. 'Nice little window, and it's a good size,' I said. 'It would be ideal as a study.'

There was one more room, almost as big as the master bedroom, that would be for guests – once we'd cleared the cobwebs and given it all a lick of paint, that was.

A ladder led from the landing up to the attic space and the trapdoor was open. 'Have you been up there?'

'Not yet. Fancy it?' he challenged me.

'Maybe later,' I said. 'I think I've had enough adventure for one day. Shall we have a drink to celebrate?'

'Sure,' Jack said. We made our way back down the wooden stairs.

'What do you think?' he asked.

'There are things I like.' I forced a smile. I couldn't blame Jack. I could have insisted on viewing this place if I'd wanted to. I'd decided to go with my gut feeling, and it had brought us here.

Downstairs in the kitchen, I got out the bottle of champagne I'd kept in my bag and poured it into two mugs, the only receptacles I could find.

'To a new start,' I said, raising my mug.

Jack chinked his mug against mine. 'You are happy to be here, aren't you?' he asked.

'Of course I am,' I lied. We'd only been here a few hours and already I missed our flat, the soft, worn carpet under my feet. It was starting to dawn on me that Carly and Sunita wouldn't be able to drop by any more. We'd chosen this change – I had chosen it. But now I wondered if we'd made an awful mistake.

'It's just – it's different, isn't it? And there's quite a lot to do.'

'We can do it,' Jack said.

'We, meaning . . . ?'

'We meaning *we*,' Jack said.

'But Jack, realistically, with all the preparation you're doing for this pitch? Let alone if you get the commission. The hours you were working on *Pupz*, weekends too – you didn't have a spare minute.'

'I'll find time to help,' Jack said. 'I'll make time.'

I bit my lip, wondering whether to say anything or not.

'I wish you'd told me this was a major project. It's nothing like the other place.'

'I told you it needed work. You agreed for us to offer on it without having seen inside – I didn't force you.'

'I wasn't thinking straight.'

'Do you regret it? Is that what you're saying?'

I fought back tears. 'No. It's just not really how I expected it to be, that's all.'

Chapter 7

The Garden

On the Mood Board

Patio, wooden summer house with gingham-covered window seats, a rope swing in an oak tree. Deckchairs. Daffodils, bluebells, poppies, sunshine on green leaves.

Monday, 9 September

On Monday I was woken up by the sounds of rain falling gently against the windows and Jack scrabbling around in the dark.

'Are you OK?' I said, still half-asleep and disorientated. I was lying in our familiar bed, but facing in the wrong direction, and stuck on an island in the middle of heaps of clutter.

'I'm looking for my suit,' Jack said. The previous evening

came back to me – the way I'd spoken to him. I'd been tired out – but that was no real excuse. I hadn't been fair on him.

'We've got a meeting today with some of the animation funders. I need to wear a suit for it.'

'Our clothes are in that box over there,' I said, pointing towards the doorway.

'Nope, tried that one already. It's your stuff.'

I pulled on my dressing gown and joined Jack in his search, opening our boxes until I found his charcoal suit. 'Here you go,' I said, handing it over. Finding anything in the chaos of the cottage felt like a victory of sorts. We'd spent yesterday picking up essential supplies and food from Hazelton village, and hadn't made much of a dent in the cleaning or unpacking.

'Thanks, Amelia. You should go back to sleep.'

I put a hand on his arm. 'I'm sorry, about last night.'

He pulled me closer and kissed me on my forehead. 'It's OK. I can understand how you're feeling, I think. It will get better. I promise.'

After he left, I went downstairs to make some breakfast. Furry slippers protected my feet from the splintered floorboards and the dust that still covered much of the house.

In the kitchen, I took the kettle and mugs out of our emergency supply box, and put some water on to boil. As I looked out of the window, two blue tits came to rest on the sill. 'Poor birds,' I said out loud, thinking of Dexter. Out of his box now, he was prowling along the worktop looking at them menacingly. 'You don't know what you've got coming to you.'

A good night's sleep had restored some perspective. But this place didn't feel like home yet. The kitchen was still a mess, crowded with another woman's clutter.

I drank my tea, got out some country cottage magazines and the interior design book Carly had given me, and flicked through them for inspiration. There were some really nice ideas in there – how to create a light, bright and functional kitchen. I took out my sketchbook.

I sat at the kitchen table and noted down the ideas and colour schemes that appealed to me – bright reds and plenty of wood. I tore pictures out of one of the magazines and glued them down until a picture began to form. The first thing to tackle, I thought as I stirred milk and a teaspoon of sugar into a fresh cup of tea, was the kitchen units. They all needed to go.

I went back to the sketchbook, and ideas came thick and fast – a traditional-style country kitchen, with florals and wooden worktops. Yes, the kitchen cabinets would be expensive to replace – one of our biggest costs on the whole project, most likely – but the right ones could really transform the room. I wasn't quite sure what to do about the lino flooring.

A knock came at the front door, startling me. I pulled my dressing gown around me and swiftly checked my appearance in the hallway mirror. My hair was tousled and untidy, and as I hurriedly tried to flatten it, another knock came.

I opened the heavy wooden door. There on the doorstep was a man about my age, with light brown hair, grey-green eyes and a dusting of stubble. He was dressed in faded jeans and a pale blue shirt, the sleeves rolled up.

'Hi,' he said, smiling warmly, a dimple appearing in one of his cheeks.

I pulled my dressing gown more tightly around me, feeling self-conscious. 'Hi,' I said in reply.

'You must be Amelia.' His voice was soft and lilting, with just the trace of a local accent.

Was it too late to pretend to be someone else, only to reappear as a more presentable version of myself?

'Yes, that's me,' I said. 'Can I help you with anything?'

'I'm hoping it'll be the other way round,' the man said, smiling again. 'I should introduce myself. I'm Callum. Eleanor's . . . Mrs McGuire's grandson.' He put out his hand and I shook it. His hand was strong and in the moment that our skin touched I felt it was slightly rough.

'Oh, hi,' I said, relieved. 'Come in.'

'Are you sure? I don't want to intrude,' he said, looking at my dressing gown.

'It's fine, honestly. Give me a minute and I'll be right back.'

Callum stood in the hallway and I dashed upstairs to put some clothes on. I grabbed the first things I could find – a pair of jeans, a bra and my old university hoodie. I pulled my hair up into a ponytail.

'Let's go through into the kitchen,' I said, coming back down the rickety staircase. 'Can I get you a cup of tea?'

'I'm fine, but thanks,' Callum said, his voice softening. 'Listen, I feel bad about what's happened. We all wanted the house to be ready for you and your husband to move into. But Gran – well, she had other ideas,' he said, shaking his head with a faint smile. 'Out of the blue this week she says she wants to keep hold of everything, even though the bungalow she's moved into is half the size of this place. It's been a bit of a nightmare.'

'Oh dear.' The chaotic state of the house was beginning to make more sense.

'Anyway, none of that is your problem, but my dad feels terrible, and we wanted to explain. There's enough for you to be getting on with without having to work around Gran's stuff.'

'It's not been ideal,' I admitted.

'You must have wanted to turn round and walk right back out again,' Callum said. I noticed how the corners of his eyes crinkled a little as he smiled. 'But listen. I've found a storage space not far from here, and Gran's allowing us to move what's here into it for now. According to Dad, they talked this all through months ago, but with her Alzheimer's what she says isn't always written in stone.'

'Right,' I said, feeling bad about my earlier snap judgements. 'Now I can see how things got a bit complicated.'

'Gran's coping. Just about. But she's not getting any better, and that's part of the reason we want her a bit closer to us all. Where was I going with this . . . ?' He gave a weary laugh. 'I'm rambling, aren't I?'

Looking into his eyes, I shook my head. 'Don't worry. Carry on.'

'Me and my cousin Spencer will be back in a couple of hours with a lorry to clear everything out. If that's OK with you?'

'That would be fine. Brilliant, in fact,' I said, a weight lifting. With any luck, Jack would come home to a lovely clear house and we could start unpacking. I could have cheered.

'OK, great,' Callum said. 'Thanks for being so patient. I'm not sure all Londoners would have been.'

'Is it that obvious?'

'A bit. You sound . . .'

'Like I'm in *Eastenders*?'

'Hardly, no . . . but you've got a trace of an accent. Anyway, why the move?'

'We wanted a change. Actually, this is going to sound stupid, but living in the country was one of the things I'd promised myself I'd do before I was thirty. I didn't quite manage that – but we're here now.'

'I admire that,' Callum said. 'A lot of people get stuck in their comfort zone, don't they? And you're clearly up for a challenge. I don't think Gran has done anything to this place for about forty years.'

'Yes.' For some reason I didn't want to admit to Callum that it was more of a challenge than I really wanted.

'Good luck with it. This place has history, and it's beautiful underneath. It certainly didn't always look like this.'

'Did you come here a lot?

'All the time,' he said. 'Dad used to bring me and my sister to see Gran and Granddad every weekend for Sunday dinner. We've always lived close by.'

'With all those memories, no wonder it's been difficult for your gran to move.'

'Yes, that's right. There's a lot she's not ready to say goodbye to. And the truth is, we're not ready to say goodbye to her.'

He looked over towards the kitchen. 'What are you going to do about these monstrosities?' he asked more brightly, pointing to the kitchen cabinets. 'I mean, unless you like them, that is?' He raised his eyebrows as if he wouldn't be able to believe anyone could.

'Hmm, yes. There's retro and then there's . . . well, these cabinets.' I smiled. 'They are definitely going to go.' I showed him my sketchbook, with ideas for the new kind of furniture I wanted to install. 'This is what I'm thinking of doing.'

'Nice,' Callum said. 'The kitchen's always been the centre of this house. This is where we'd come when we were little, and watch while Granny Ellie baked. She was big on baking. Still is, although since she started forgetting things, her cakes are getting a little hit and miss.'

'I love to bake too,' I said. 'I'm glad to hear I'll be continuing a Brambledown Cottage tradition.'

'Oh yeah,' Callum said. 'Definitely.' He stepped forward to look out of the kitchen window. 'Wow, it's a mess out there, isn't it? Great garden though – you'll see when you get the lawnmower on it. Me and my sister Alice used to play for hours out there. There's a little stream at the back. You must have seen that, right?' Callum glanced back at me, and as our eyes met I felt suddenly self-conscious.

'Actually, I haven't yet,' I said. 'I've only had a peek through the fence. There was a lot to do when we arrived on Saturday.'

'Oh, we have to go down there then,' Callum said, his eyes lighting up.

'Now?' I said, glancing at my sock-clad feet.

'No time like the present. This is your house now – don't you want to get to know it?'

'Yes, I suppose so,' I said. 'What about your cousin?'

Callum glanced vaguely in the direction of his watch. 'Oh, it's fine – we've got time. Come on. Get some wellies. It'll be wet in the grass after the rain last night, but like I said, this cottage is your place now. You have to at least explore the grounds.'

'Now, wellies,' I said, with a smile. 'Strangely, they are one of the few things I'm going to be able to locate.' I'd shoved them in the coat cupboard when we'd first arrived. I went out there now and fished them out of a cardboard box of outdoorsy things that we'd barely touched the whole time we'd lived in London.

I pulled them on over the bedsocks I was still wearing, and Callum turned the handle of the back door. 'Hang on,' I called out. 'I'll get you the key for that.'

He jiggled at the latch until the door opened easily. 'The tricks of the house,' he said with a smile. 'Years of practice.'

'Wow. We're going to need to up the security levels around here.'

'Oh, Hazelton's a hotbed of crime.' He laughed. 'Right, you all set?'

I nodded.

Together we walked over the paved area, and then stepped

out into the long grass of the garden. Thick, wet clumps of grass clung to my wellies and dampened the cuffs of my jeans, but I didn't care – out here in the fresh air, I felt free.

In the garden most of the wildflowers had faded back, and brambles and blackberries were spreading up the fence to the right of the house. The patch of lavender was still there, the soft purple standing out among the golds and greens.

'Those blackberries are delicious,' Callum said. He went over and plucked a few from their thorny stems. 'Here, try them.'

I took the ripe fruit from his hands, stained with juice, and ate one. It was sweet, with just a hint of tartness. I put another one in my mouth. 'They're perfect.'

'Here, you've got some . . .' Callum reached out a hand and brushed away some red juice from my chin.

Feeling myself blush, I scrubbed at the spot with my hand.

'Follow me,' he said, clearing the grasses ahead of us.

'You could get lost out here.'

'Absolutely. Alice and I used to hide when our mum called us in for tea, and sometimes she just gave up searching.'

'You sound like you were terrors.'

'She'd joke that we kept her young.'

'Does she still live in Hazelton?'

'In spirit,' he said, with a smile. 'She died ten years ago.'

'Oh, I'm sorry.'

'Don't be.' Callum shrugged. 'Part of life, isn't it? And she had a full one. It's good to be here again, actually – it brings her back. See that oak tree?' He pointed to an oak about ten feet to my left, with winding, thick branches stretching out against the pure blue sky.

'Yes, looks good for climbing.'

'Exactly. It's perfect. Mum used to climb up there with us. When you have kids they are going to love playing out here.'

I spotted a shuttlecock in the grass and picked it up. It was weathered and grey but still mainly intact. 'One of yours?' I asked.

Callum took it with a smile. 'Could be,' he said. 'Although it's been a good few years since Alice and I played any badminton out here. You wouldn't believe what it looked like then – big flat lawn, well-tended flowerbeds . . . Like I said, it's been years since Gran did anything with it, or let any of us touch it for that matter.'

'She wouldn't let anyone help?'

'She's not big on being helped out,' Callum said with a shrug. 'You've probably picked up on that by now. Anyway, look – we're nearly there.'

Pulling my sleeves down over my hands, I swiped away some brambles that were cutting into our path at chest level. I heard a soft sound, the gentle, soothing trickle of water over rocks.

'See it?' Callum said, pointing just ahead of where we were standing.

There at the bottom of the garden, where ferns grew lush and thick, just before the garden turned into fields, was a stream about a metre across, with rocks and pebbles lining either side.

'Water gets much higher than this when the rain's heavy.'

I bent down and looked at it, sunlight reflecting off the ripples. 'Must be lovely to dangle your feet in on a hot day.'

'Oh yes. With the trees down at this end, it's always shady and cool. Mum liked it down here. She could keep half an eye on the two of us playing, with her head in a book at the same time.'

'Bliss.'

This summer there hadn't been time for a holiday, not even our usual trip to a music festival. Sitting by the stream and reading, letting a sunny afternoon drift by, sounded idyllic.

'Thanks for bringing me down here,' I said to Callum. 'It feels special. I hope we can get the garden back to how you remember it. Although who knows when we'll get round to that with so much to do on the cottage.'

'I'd be happy to get it started, if you're looking for someone.

Spencer and I are both after a bit of outdoors work. Or we could give you a few tips if you want to do it yourself.'

'You're a gardener?'

Callum smiled. 'I'm a whatever-turns-up man. Or I have been for the last few years, anyway.'

'As it happens, a whatever-turns-up man is exactly what we're looking for. When would you be able to start?'

'Whenever you like – next week?'

'Sounds good. I'll just need to have a chat with Jack first, work out our budget – which I wish was infinite, but sadly isn't.'

'Sure. In terms of getting starting, we'd need to cut the grass first, bring the place into submission a bit, and then you could decide how you'd like the new garden to look. Do you have any ideas?'

'Not really.' I shrugged. 'But I'd like to keep some of the wildness, I think. Not too tidy, with flowerbeds – I loved the poppies and sunflowers that were here back in July.'

'We could run a loose pathway through, with paving stones,' Callum said, pointing, 'and have a wildflower garden to the left, then perhaps a trellis for the honeysuckle up nearer the house.'

'Great. I can't wait to get started. Isn't it going to be weird for you, though, to see us updating the place? Taking out some of the old fittings?'

'Are you joking?' Callum said. 'I can't wait to see what

you do. We've been nagging Gran to let us change the cabinets and give the place a clear-out for years. In fact, I'll happily join in with a sledgehammer.'

Callum and his cousin Spencer, a twenty-something version of him in baggy jeans and a T-shirt, spent the morning moving boxes and bags and loading them into a van, chatting loudly and laughing together. I made my way past them and into the kitchen. I'd gathered a basket full of blackberries and some apples from the front garden. In the pocket of my apron were bunches of lavender – I bound them with string and hung them up high over the Aga.

Under a mug by the window, I found the crumble recipe that Eleanor had left and looked over the ingredients. We had all of them in the small box of supplies we'd brought with us. There wasn't much I could do in the house until Callum and Spencer had cleared it, and baking always soothed me. I washed the fruit under the tap in the stainless-steel sink.

My gaze fell on a spiral-bound notepad. On the first page was a shopping list, with groceries – *vegetables, flour, butter* – written in curved black script.

Curious, I dried my hands and turned the page.

There, the words were curved and larger.

I didnt want to do it. I had to.

I shut the notepad and put it back where I'd found it. These weren't my things to be looking through.

'Hi, Amelia,' Jack said, arriving home and putting his bag down in the hallway. 'How did it go today?'

'Good,' I said. 'Really good actually.'

'*Really* good?' Jack echoed. 'You've changed your tune.'

'Come with me and you'll see what I mean.' I took him by the hand, ignoring his slightly startled expression as I led him through to the living room.

'Wow,' he said. The bare bones of the cottage – the blank canvas we'd be working on – were now visible. The room was clear and full of warm evening light. There was no rickety old bed, no piles of clothes and trinkets. Callum and Spencer had carried off the whole lot in a couple of hours, spiriting it away in a rented lorry and then coming back to scrub and clean every surface. Yes, there were broken floorboards, and the window frames were rotten in places. But it looked like it could be a living room now, one day.

'Wow, what a difference, eh?' Jack said. 'Did you do this?'

'God, no,' I said, shaking my head. 'The owner's grandson, Callum, and his cousin came around. They took all Mrs McGuire's things away and put them in storage. Callum was really apologetic.'

'OK,' Jack said.

'She's losing her memory – that's why she wouldn't let go.'

'Oh, I see. Poor woman. Well, that's good that they were able to sort everything out today.'

'They were brilliant. Come and take a look upstairs.'

I grandly threw open the door to our bedroom, and the brass handle came loose in my hand. 'Oops.' I put it down on the floor and led Jack forward into the room. 'Don't let that put you off.' The owner's sewing equipment and bric-a-brac had all gone and the room was clear and clean. Only a couple of our boxes stood in the middle of the floor.

I snaked an arm around Jack's hips. 'It's our place now, Jack. Really, all ours.'

After Jack and I had excitedly discussed our ideas for the bedroom, I got the crumble out of the Aga and scooped us both out generous portions. I added some vanilla ice cream to each bowl and passed one to Jack.

'This is incredible,' Jack said, taking a forkful.

'All home-grown. I used a recipe I found in here before the guys cleared it. I think it must be Callum's grandmother's.'

'Well, it gets a big thumbs-up from me.'

'I've asked Callum and his cousin to come and help us out with the garden, get things kick-started out there. I know we didn't put aside much for it, but their rates are reasonable, and I reckon they could do a lot in a couple of weeks. Is that OK with you?'

'Sure,' Jack said. 'Although I think we'll need to keep it fairly limited. I don't suppose you've heard anything from your dad?'

'I haven't heard from him, no,' I said, 'but I haven't checked my balance for a while. He might have paid some money into the account. Anyway – enough about that. How was it, your first day commuting from here?'

'I'm sure it will get better.'

'Oh, that doesn't sound good.'

'It wasn't great. The train was delayed, then diverted, so I ended up arriving at London Bridge over forty minutes later than I planned to.'

'That's really bad luck.'

'I wish bad luck was all it was. There was a sign up in the station about some upgrade work they're doing. You know the high-speed rail link that we're hoping will add value?'

'Yep.'

'I guess we should have thought more about the impact of the works in the short term. It seems as if trains may be running slow or rerouted during the months that the work is going on.' He looked tired, and the strain showed a little around his eyes.

'Only a hiccup,' I said.

'Exactly,' Jack said, forcing a smile. 'That's what I thought. Anyway, we need to think about how you're going to get around now, too.'

'Interesting you should say that. I mentioned to Callum today that we were thinking about getting a second car but couldn't really afford it. He says he has an old banger we can use – for the time being, that is. He's been meaning to sell it but can't quite bring himself to, I think. I'd just need to sort the insurance.'

'That sounds like a good solution,' Jack said.

'Great. I'll tell him yes, in that case.'

Chapter 8

The Kitchen

On the Mood Board

Traditional wooden cabinets, dried wild flowers in antique glass bottles on the windowsill, retro appliances: Smeg fridge (red). Gingham? Cath Kidston-inspired florals. Shabby-chic dresser (white), teapots, copper pans. Fitted kitchens from Moben catalogue – Note: dream kitchen! Wooden table and chairs with hand-sewn seat cushions. Aga with pan cooking on top.

Tuesday, 10 September

From the bathroom window, I saw Spencer pull up in his truck and Callum park alongside him in a battered green Morris Minor. So, this was the car he'd mentioned to me. I was excited at the prospect at being able to get around easily on my own. I rinsed my mouth out, put my toothbrush down by the yellow sink and went downstairs.

I saw an envelope on the doormat, addressed to me and Jack. It looked like Suni's handwriting. Inside was a card with a quote from one of our favourite books, *I Capture the Castle*: 'I Write This Sitting in the Kitchen Sink . . .'

I opened it and read her message.

Hope you've found somewhere more comfortable to sit in your new house. Happy New Home! Love from Suni and Nico x

I smiled, and looked around for somewhere to put it. With no furniture I opted for a windowsill by the stairs. Her baby was due any day now. I hoped she was doing OK.

I opened the door.

'Hi,' Spencer said cheerfully, from over by the van. Callum was unloading garden equipment and waved hello. 'Your chariot's arrived.' He laughed, pointing back at the car. 'Shall we just go through to the back and get started?' He looked apologetically at his muddy wellies. 'I can take these off before I go inside?'

'No, it's fine. You can get in round the back – the fence is down. Not that it would really matter anyway; the cottage is going to get a lot dirtier over the next few weeks, when we get started on the work.'

'Morning,' Callum said, joining us, rake in hand. 'Here are the car keys. She's all yours.'

'Thanks so much. It's really kind of you – and it's going to be a complete lifesaver. I don't know how we thought we'd cope out here with just the one car between us.'

'No worries. I'm glad she'll be in safe hands. Right, shall we go out there and have a chat about what you'd like to do?'

'Sure,' I said, leading the way.

We stepped over the broken fencing and out into the garden. 'So, I've been thinking and I really liked the idea of the wildflower garden. Let's keep the ferns at the back by the stream, and all the wisteria on the house at the moment.'

'What else do you like . . . flowers? Any particular colours?' Callum asked.

'Hmm, I'm not really an expert. But I like bluebells and daffodils.'

'Great, good starting point. OK, how about we get some bulbs? Bluebells I can get from my own garden, and I can pick up some narcissi and daffodils – we could have them up here, so that you can see them from your kitchen window. You'll have to wait for them, of course, but that's the joy in gardening.' He smiled. 'You need a bit of patience. We could put in some late-flowering plants like clematis and Japanese anemones, so you have something to look at now.'

'That sounds perfect.'

'Anything else you'd like? Dream big and we'll see what we can do.'

'I know what I'd really love,' I said, 'but we could never afford it.'

'What's that?'

'A summer house out here.' I remembered the one at Arcadia cottage, with its cosy window seats and bookshelves.

'And that's not in your budget at the moment?'

'No, no way.'

'Dreams are important,' Callum said. 'Why don't we leave a patch of the garden clear for that, near a grassed area, and then, in the future – who knows?'

'That's a good idea, yes.'

'Great. Well, we'll be clearing the place today, and then tomorrow or the day after I'll get down to the garden centre so we can get started.'

'It's going to be a busy day for you,' I said. 'Sounds like you'll be needing some tea and biscuits.'

I went inside put the kettle on. As I waited for it to boil, I looked through the window and watched Callum and Spencer discussing where to start.

I put some biscuits on a plate and took that and the mugs outside for them.

'Thanks,' Spencer said, descending on the biscuit plate.

'If you need anything just give me a shout.'

'What are you working on today?' Callum asked, brushing a strand of sandy hair out of his eyes as he followed me back indoors.

'The kitchen. I'm going to pick out some new fitted units, and get some wooden shelving installed.'

'So it's farewell to those old gems?' he said, pointing to the green cabinets. 'Or should I say good riddance?'

'More like the latter, I think.'

'It's about time. You know what, Amelia, I have a feeling if you take this flooring up there might be something better underneath. Do you mind if I . . .' He bent to inspect a corner that was peeling back.

'Go for it. Whatever we do, this is coming up,' I said, scuffing a toe against it.

He peeled back a tile and beneath the gummy layer of glue it looked like there was stone. 'It's the original flagstones,' he said.

'Really?' I bent down to join him and take a closer look.

'It'll all need a really good scrub, but I imagine the whole floor is like this.'

My skin tingled with the excitement of the find. 'That would look stunning: the original flagstones, maybe a rug under the table to warm things up a bit.' I glanced around the kitchen, seeing it in a different light.

'No idea why Granny Ellie covered them up,' Callum said, shaking his head. 'I guess it was trendy or something.'

'How's is your gran? Is she settling into her new place all right?'

'Not too bad,' Callum said, getting to his feet. 'She's getting used to it, at least, although she's been in a terrible mood since we moved her. The main thing is she's somewhere we can all look in and keep an eye on her, which puts our minds at rest, especially Dad's.'

'I can imagine,' I said.

'I should get started on the garden.' Callum picked up his tools. 'I can't let Spence have all of the fun out there.'

As Callum and Spencer worked outside, I texted Sunita from the kitchen.

> Thanks for the lovely card, Suni. How are you doing?
> Not long now x

Her reply came back a moment later.

> Glad you liked it. All good. I feel enormous but very ready to meet the baby now. I think Nico might be starting to freak out, though – he was out drinking till 3 a.m. last night. I'm trying not to be worried about that Xx

I thought of Nico's excitement whenever I'd heard him talk about the pregnancy. Surely this was just a temporary hiccup, his way of working through things. I replied,

> Nico will be fine, Suni. Try not to worry. You are a strong, brave woman. Keep me posted on everything and call me if you ever want to chat xx

That morning I browsed websites looking for the perfect fitted kitchen, my pulse racing as I imagined how it would transform the cottage. My favourite had wooden cabinets with a traditional feel, the option of an additional brunch bar, and gorgeous cream counters. I pasted the links into an email and sent it over to Jack with a note – *What do you think of these?*

A short while later, as I was fixing lunch, and reply pinged back. I dashed over to check it:

Hello, A. These kitchens look great. And I hate to put a dampener on things . . . but have you seen the prices? Can we really afford them? Jx

I put down my plate with a pang of disappointment. Couldn't he see how worthwhile it was spending a bit more? I typed a message back.

Just this one thing, Jack? I think it's worth splashing out. The kitchen is so important to both of us. Imagine the fun we'll have cooking in here. Don't you think it's worth getting something a bit special? Ax

Jack replied a moment later.

I'm not completely against it, just think we need to be realistic x

If we could just get that money back from my dad, we wouldn't have to worry. I went back to my laptop and typed in my online banking details. I scrolled through the recent deposits – beside my final salary payment from St Catherine's was one from Dad.

I smiled to myself. OK, so it was a couple of months later than we'd agreed, but he'd come through. I was about to message Jack when I saw the amount: four hundred pounds. It was only a fraction of what he owed us.

There had to be a note explaining when the rest would come, but there was nothing in my inbox from him.

I picked up my mobile, took a deep breath and called him.

'He-llo,' he answered, in a sing-song voice.

'Dad, hi. It's me.'

'Hi, Amelia. Great to hear from you. I was just saying to Caitlin, it's been a while since I heard from that elder daughter of mine. Are you coming over to pay us a visit?'

'Not right now. We're kind of busy at the moment, what with the cottage and everything.'

'This new house of yours, eh? Congratulations. A quick trip to Ireland, though – I'm talking about a weekend here. Your sister would love to see you too. I know I said I'd come and visit, but with things so busy with work, it's been hard to find the time. Will you come here?'

'Maybe.'

'Christmas?' Dad said.

'Look, Dad, we haven't really thought about Christmas yet. I'm actually calling about . . . Thanks for the money you sent us through.'

'No problem at all,' he said. 'There's more where that

came from. It's just with your stepmother's haircuts, and Mirabel always wanting something new or other, I haven't been able to put much by over the last few months. But you know I'm good for it.'

'It's just . . . I mean, that's OK. But we do need it,' I said, taking a breath. 'I mean, for the renovations and everything.'

'Sure, sure. You'll get it soon enough. But you don't need much for that really. Me and Caitlin did this place up for just a couple of hundred quid, and it looks OK, doesn't it? Do you remember?'

'Yes,' I said, recalling his three-bedroom flat on the outskirts of Dublin. The woodchip wallpaper and striped carpets. The plastic shower curtain that had seen better days. 'Yes, of course. I know we can do it. But—'

'Don't you worry, Amelia. You always were one to worry, but it'll come right.'

'OK, Dad.'

'Give some thought to Christmas, won't you? We'd love to have you and Jack come and stay.'

'I will. Bye now.'

I put the phone down, unsure why I hadn't been able to say any of the things I'd planned.

I went back to the kitchen websites, and looked at some cheaper designs. They weren't the same, but there was one that looked similar, and was reasonably priced, even though it would still take up a chunk of our funds. I sent the site over to Jack, and swallowed back my disappointment.

Jack's reply came:

This one's fine with me. Jx

*

'Hello,' Jack shouted out from the front door.

'Hi, I'm in here,' I called back.

'Hey, love,' he said, coming through to the kitchen and kissing me hello. 'Are you all right? You look a bit pale.'

'I'm fine. I ordered that kitchen, and they're coming to install it at the end of the week.'

'OK, that's good.'

'Yes, I think so, and with some shelving, and this shabby-chic dresser I found on eBay, I think it'll look really nice.'

'Somewhere to display your teapot collection?' Jack teased, used to my vintage crockery obsession by now.

'Yes.'

'So, do I take it that this means no sign of the money from your dad yet?'

'It'll come through soon,' I said. 'There's just a bit of a delay – he's made the first payment, though, which is really positive.'

'Well, that's something,' Jack said, looking less than certain. 'How much was it?'

'Just a portion of it,' I said. 'But we always knew we'd be doing some of this work on the cottage on a budget.'

'How much?' Jack insisted.

'Four hundred pounds.'

'Four hundred?' Jack's eyebrows shot up. 'That's barely anything. Did he give a reason?'

'Things haven't been easy for him lately,' I said, feeling protective. 'Apparently Mirabel's been giving him and Caitlin a hard time.'

'When are they ever easy for him? Amelia, I know you're not going to like me saying it, but I think you're too soft on him.'

On Friday morning the kitchen fitters arrived, a man and woman in their forties who'd driven up in a large white van that was now parked alongside Callum's truck.

'Just through here,' I said, showing them the way.

'Right,' the woman said, sizing up the space and laying down her tools. 'Shouldn't take too long.'

'Help yourselves to tea and coffee. I'll be just across the hallway if you need anything.'

'Thanks, we'll be fine,' the man said. 'Right, Janice – let's get everything in here and get to work.'

I went back to the downstairs bathroom. That morning I'd unscrewed the pipe and finally found what was blocking the basin drain. There was a silver locket trapped in there. Inside – remarkably untouched by the water damage that had tarnished the metal – was a portrait of a man. Presumably it belonged to Eleanor. I'd polished it up and put it on the side to return to Callum.

I filled up the steamer and got to work stripping off the wallpaper, scraping so that it peeled away. The previous day I'd ordered a skip, which had arrived that morning, and I'd made a trip over to a home supplies store in Canterbury and picked out some beautiful wallpaper – white with a small green leaf print – and some other things for the room. We might not be able to afford to replace the pale green toilet and basin at the moment, but we could definitely spruce things up – I'd bought a nice wooden cabinet and a set of three shelves to go by the window. For the curtains I'd chosen some white embroidered fabric, delicate, pretty and fine enough to let plenty of light in. Once the shower was taken out, there would be much more space in there.

I put on the radio and listened to some eighties tunes as I worked. The kitchen fitters trooped past the door carrying the old units.

'*Oh, blimmin' heck!*' came a shout from the kitchen.

I dashed through to see what was going on, passing Dexter, who was standing in the hallway with his back arched, meowing. In the kitchen I was greeted with the vision of a fierce jet of water coming out from one of the pipes on the wall, soaking the floor and the cabinets surrounding it. The old cabinets had gone, apart from one, and the walls were bare behind them.

'What's going on?' I asked, panicked.

'Must've hammered through the wrong bit, I'm afraid,'

Janice said. She had one tea-towel covered hand pressed over the pipe, but it didn't seem to have any effect in stemming the flow.

'Here, hold this for a mo, would you?' she said, motioning for me to take her place. 'We'll go and get some tools from the van.'

I grabbed a fresh tea towel from the side and took over from her, pressing it onto a large gash in the pipe. They left the room, in no apparent hurry, and my jeans and top were soon completely soaked.

Callum opened the back door. 'I'm guessing there's a leak?' he said, grinning.

'No prizes,' I said, mustering up a smile in spite of it all.

He came over and looked at the source, then swiftly got underneath the sink and switched the water off. The pressure on my hand eased immediately, and the forceful jet of water slowed to a dribble.

'Only a temporary fix,' Callum said, 'but hopefully it'll stop you needing to swim out of here.'

'God,' Jack said, when he got home that evening and took a look at the kitchen with the floor covered in cloths and towels. 'What on earth happened in here?'

'It hasn't been a great day,' I said. 'We don't have any water. Or a kitchen.'

'No water?' I nodded. 'How did that happen?'

'When they were installing the new units they hammered through one of the pipes. Callum helped to stem the flow and cut off the water supply. But the place is still a swamp, as you can see.'

I'd dreamed that in a couple of days we'd have our new kitchen installed – instead, we were stuck with no running water, no flushing toilets, not even a tap to wash with.

'Emergency plumber?' Jack said.

'I'll arrange it tomorrow,' I said. 'I can't face doing any-thing else today.'

'What do we do?'

'Go out for dinner?'

'Out, out?' Jack said.

'Well, I'm not sure how much choice we have,' I said. 'Unless you know of a takeaway which will deliver here? Come on, we should get to know our neighbours. There's that little pub, the Three Kings – only about five minutes' drive away. We could road-test that – have a pint, and they must do a chilli con carne or something.'

'OK,' Jack said. 'You got me with the chilli. I'll drive.'

We got in the car and drove the short distance to the pub. What I was expecting, I suppose, was a countrified version of the Florence – a cosy, warm, welcoming local where we'd feel immediately at home. What we found, as we swung the door open, was a dozen pairs of eyes turning to look at us in a not altogether friendly way.

Jack took my hand and squeezed it, apparently sensing

my discomfort, and together we walked over to the bar. 'A ginger beer, please,' I said to the barmaid, a woman in her late forties with a stern look in her eye. 'And a pint of lager for you, Jack?' He nodded.

The barmaid poured the drinks, the whole room still silent.

'You new around here?' she said, as she passed them to us.

'We've just moved into Brambledown Cottage, down the road,' Jack explained, his voice quieter than usual.

'Oh, right. Mrs McGuire's old place. My husband said he saw a skip outside it.'

'Yes, we're doing a bit of work,' I said, picking up our drinks and giving her the money.

'I suppose you are. They all do. Used to be cheap as chips, property round here,' the barmaid continued, 'but now, what with all the Londoners moving in, place is starting to change.'

'Right. Yes,' I said awkwardly.

'Pricing our kids out of the market, you lot are,' the barmaid went on, her expression sour.

'Shall we go and sit down?' I asked Jack pointedly, picking up a menu and nodding over to a table by the window that was set safely apart from the other punters.

We made a quick move away from the bar, and I tried to ignore the stares that followed us as we sat down at our table.

'God, don't think we're going to be winning any popularity

contests around here, are we?' I whispered to Jack, putting my drink down.

'They're probably just curious.'

'Hmm, is that what it is. Mum said everyone was really friendly.' I glanced over at the old men clustered around the bar, staring mournfully into their pints, wondering who she had been talking about.

'I'm sure if you just worked a bit of your charm on them,' Jack continued.

I raised an eyebrow.

'Perhaps another pub would be more our crowd,' he said. 'And it's only been a week.'

'I know,' I said. 'We'll settle in soon enough.'

'We will. And you'll get a job before you know it.'

'I hope so. I'm still crossing my fingers that a role at Woodlands Secondary will come up. The Head there did seem really positive when we met.'

'Maybe you could do some cover lessons there in the meantime?'

'Yes, I'll contact her about that. I'm starting to miss teaching, the kids, spending time with Carly – even the marking, would you believe it?'

'I can believe it. You're a great teacher and you're not giving it up, just taking a break, that's all.'

'Yes. And we'll get used to being here, I know. The rooms will get finished, and who cares if we don't have a local cinema.' Images of how our life used to be came into my head. 'Or a pub quiz, or a cafe where I can meet my friends for coffee . . .'

A message pinged through on my phone. I got it out of my bag and checked it.

'From Suni,' I said. 'God, it's today, isn't it?' I clicked on the message and read it quickly.

> Baby Bella Graham, born at 2 p.m. today, actually on her
> due date – like Sunita she's a punctual lady! – 7 lb 2 oz.
> Mother and baby both doing really well. Nico x

Tears welled up in my eyes.

'You OK?' Jack asked gently. I nodded, and unable to talk without sobbing, passed the phone to him.

I was incredibly happy and very sad, all at the same time.

'Just got home,' Sunita said, sounding exhausted. I'd phoned her as soon as I could the next morning.

'Sorry, you must be knackered . . . I just couldn't resist calling. Congratulations, Suni! To both of you. Me and Jack are so happy for you.'

'Thank you. It took forever, and I won't tell you what it felt like, but we're so happy to meet her. She's gorgeous, Amelia.'

'I can't wait to see her.'

'Come up to London next weekend?' she said. 'Carly's coming round on Saturday.'

'I'd love to,' I replied, without hesitation. 'I can't think of anything better. See you then.'

Buoyed up by hearing my friend's voice, I felt re-energized and ready to get the kitchen sorted. I called in an emergency plumber. It was Saturday – but there was no way we'd be able to make it through the weekend without any water. The plumber baulked slightly when he saw the damage that had been done, but thankfully he was able to fix the leak in a couple of hours. We asked him for a quote on updating the pipework in both the upstairs and downstairs toilet, both of which we'd realized really needed doing.

Jack closed the door after him, then turned to me. 'So, that's one thing sorted.'

'Thank God for that,' I said. 'Everything looks better when you can fill a kettle. Fancy a tea?'

'I'd love one. Is there anything we can do in the kitchen before the fitters come back on Monday?'

'There is something, yes.' I explained about the flooring, pulling up another whole tile and showing him what lay underneath. 'Fancy getting your hands dirty?'

'Let's do it,' Jack said.

The rain poured down that afternoon, battering against the windows. But Jack and I turned up the radio to drown it out, and sustained ourselves on hot tea and flapjacks, laughing together as we ripped up the lino in the kitchen. Soon we had half a dozen black bags full of rubbish, ready for the skip. The floor was gummy with a black glue, but we could see now that it was a warm grey stone throughout.

'I'll take this lot out,' Jack said, picking up one of the bags. 'And then we can get scrubbing.'

I poured buckets of hot water and detergent and found some scourers, as Jack ferried the bin bags outside.

'You poor thing, you look like a drowned rat,' I said when he finally came back in. His dark hair clung in wet strands.

He shook his head gently so that the drops caught me, making me laugh, then looped his arms round me and kissed me in the middle of our messy, stripped-down kitchen.

We worked through the afternoon, scrubbing at the stones until the whole of the original floor was revealed. The stones worked perfectly with the dark red Aga Mrs McGuire had left, giving the place a really authentic country feel.

On Sunday Jack and I got up together, and after a breakfast of toast and tea in bed, polished the Aga and cleaned the windows and garden door until they shone, then finished stripping the patches of wallpaper so that the room was ready for repainting.

'It's going to look good, isn't it, when it's all finished?' Jack said.

'I hope so,' I said. 'I'm just hoping that the kitchen fitters don't mess anything else up when they arrive tomorrow.'

*

'Delivery for Mrs Grey?' the man said, the following Friday.

I nodded. 'It's a kitchen dresser, right?'

'Yes – an antique one. Where would you like it?'

'Over there in the kitchen. I think we're finally ready for it.'

He returned to his van and I thought back on the past week. The kitchen fitters had returned on Monday, full of apologies for the inconvenience of the leak, and worked hard until the new cabinets and sink were installed. While Jack was at work, and Callum and his cousin raked and cut back weeds in the garden, I cleaned the new units and painted the kitchen walls a pale eggshell blue.

The fridge, a red Smeg one I'd been lusting after ever since I saw it on *The Great British Bake Off*, had arrived on Wednesday and now nestled against the larder door, and I'd picked up a flower-patterned rug online which, placed under our modest table and chairs, warmed up the room and the stone floor really nicely.

In the evenings, when Jack had his head in a book or was catching up on his emails, I'd been busy at the sewing machine. I'd sewn some seat cushions in complementary pastel shades for each wooden chair, and some small cotton curtains were hand-tied on to the curtain rail above the kitchen window.

The dresser I'd snapped up on eBay for just under a hundred quid was the final piece of furniture we'd been waiting for.

'Over here,' I said as the man entered, carrying the dresser. 'In that alcove next to the Aga.'

He put the dresser down and together we shuffled it back. It looked even better than it had on the site, painted white and slightly distressed in places, with a small two-door cupboard at the base and three wooden shelves above.

I thanked him and gave him a tip, then got out the box I'd been longing to open since we arrived. One by one I unpacked my teapots, took off the bubble wrap and placed them on the dresser shelves. As I did so, I spotted something tucked away in a crack on the floor, where the newly exposed flagstones met the wall.

I reached down and tugged at it. The brown paper began to come loose and soon an envelope was in my hands, the bottom of it burnt. Sitting down at the kitchen table, I pressed the creases flat so I could read what was written on the outside – the address was almost burnt away, but the name was there: *Alfie Monroe*

I opened it and caught sight of a lock of dark hair, tied with a blue ribbon. Attached to it was a note.

I had to go away for a while, Alfie. But you won't forget about me, will you?
Yours always, Ellie

Chapter 9

Cresswell Road, London N8

Application for a place at Little Raccoons Nursery, Dalston.
For Bella Graham. D/O/B 13/9/2013. Parents: Sunita, Nico.

Saturday, 21 September

The 10.05 to London Bridge on Saturday morning. While most people might be heading in the opposite direction for their weekend's peace and relaxation, I couldn't wait to get back to the city.

I caught sight of the Shard, the pointed glass tower – a reminder of the city that had once been home. Over the two weeks I'd been away from London, I'd found myself missing the familiar streets but more than that, my friends.

The train pulled into London Bridge and I got my things

together. I stepped out into the chilly autumn air, and pulled my coat tightly around me. I bought a takeaway coffee from the platform kiosk to warm me up, then travelled overground to Dalston Junction. Sunita's home was a short walk from there – a garden flat in a row of Victorian terraces, an oasis of calm in busy East London. She opened the door to me, and her eyes lit up instantly. 'Amelia!'

She went to draw me into her usual warm hug, then remembered the baby in her sling that I was about to squash and kissed me on the cheek instead. 'Keep forgetting,' she said with a smile.

'This must be Bella.' I peered inside the fabric sling. Even with her slightly squished-up face, she was definitely adorable. 'She's gorgeous.'

'Thanks,' Sunita said proudly, turning so that I got a clearer view. 'We're pretty chuffed, I have to say. And believe me, it takes a lot to make twenty hours' worth of labour seem worthwhile. Come in, come in, and get warm.'

Carly came out of the living room and hugged me hello. 'You're here!'

'I am, for one day only,' I said, wishing it was for longer. 'I wasn't going to miss meeting Bella. Where's Nico? He was going to take some time off work, wasn't he?'

'Yes. I've just sent him out to get some supplies – most importantly, cake – for us. I think he was happy to get out of the house for a while.'

'How's he taking to fatherhood so far?' I asked.

'Good, actually,' Sunita said. 'Better than I expected. He seems to love it – he's knackered, like me. It's a pretty intense time. We knew it would be, but perhaps we didn't realize *quite* how intense.'

'And there we were thinking it was just a convenient excuse for you to have some time off work,' Carly joked.

Sunita rolled her eyes playfully. 'Hardly. I've been busier in the past few days than I've ever been before.'

'And you, Missus?' I asked Carly. 'How's the dating going? Any news on the romantic front? Good? Bad? Ugly?'

Carly gave me a thumbs-up sign, a smile breaking out on her face.

'You've met someone? Who? What's he like?'

'Not quite,' she said coyly.

'What do you mean?' I said, poking her in the arm. 'Spill.'

'I'm seeing Alex tonight, for the first time as a proper couple.'

'What?' I squealed and gave her a hug. Sunita joined in. 'What on earth happened? I thought that was all over?'

'I don't really know,' Carly said. 'Jules just changed his mind. According to Alex, he spoke to his mum about it and she somehow brought him round.'

'That's fantastic news.'

'I know.' Carly glowed. 'I still can't quite believe it.'

'Right. With so much to talk about, who fancies a cuppa?' I asked.

'Gasping for one,' Sunita said. 'Being woken up on the hour every hour will do that to you. Nico's been trying to help, but there's not much he can really do without a pair of these.' She pointed to her boobs.

'God, they're enormous,' I said, before I could stop myself. I hadn't noticed them at first but now they were all I could see – full, round, and not at all like the 34A cup Sunita had moaned about all the way through college.

'Aren't they? I wish I could hang on to them, but I have this nagging feeling that they are going to be taken off me at some point. I'll be kicking and screaming while they drag them away though.'

I made tea in Sunita's bright kitchen and then she led us through to her living room and we all sat down. 'How's it all going out there?' she asked.

'Good,' I said. 'Some of it. A lot of it's chaos. But we've got the kitchen finished and it looks gorgeous – a proper country kitchen. Here, look . . .'

I took out my iPhone and showed them pictures of the kitchen we'd made over.

'Did you make those cushions? They're so sweet,' Suni said. 'It's like something out of a magazine.'

'I do love the way it's turned out. We had to compromise a bit on the units, but they look OK now that they're in. We didn't have any running water for a little while, which was interesting.'

'How about the rest of the house?' Carly asked.

'Don't ask. Rotted window frames, ancient old carpets . . . All things considered, we'll probably be finished some time next century. But I've got someone in to help out with the garden.'

'Ooh, is he dishy, the gardener?' Sunita said. 'I've always fancied one of those.'

I laughed. 'He's nice. Easy on the eyes, I suppose. He's the owner's grandson, so the plan is to get the garden looking a bit more like it used to before it grew wild.'

'How are you managing financially? Did you put enough aside?' Carly asked.

'It's going to be tight. I reckon we can do quite a lot ourselves though.'

'Don't want to be the harbinger of doom,' Carly said, 'but that's what I thought when Ethan and I tried it.'

Carly and her ex, Ethan, had bought a period property in Dalston about ten years previously and gutted it. But after knocking two walls down they'd realized they didn't have enough money to finish the job – and after months of arguing, split up.

'I think we'll be OK,' I said, trying to stay positive. 'We're not making any structural changes.' I thought of the cottage – while we might not be knocking any walls down, every single room in the place needed work. My heart sank a little.

'Is Jack enjoying it?' Sunita rearranged her position on the sofa slightly so that she could breastfeed Bella.

'I think so. His commute hasn't been that easy.' I paused. 'It's not been entirely what either of us hoped for.'

'In what way?' Carly asked. 'You got out of our hellhole of a school, didn't you?'

'Yes, I did,' I said, taking a sip of tea. 'Although, believe it or not, I do miss it in some ways.'

'You were so brave to take the leap,' Carly said.

'Brave or stupid,' I said. 'Buying this cottage without having seen it properly was, I realize now, a kind of madness.'

'Jack went to see it that day you were ill, didn't he?' Carly said. 'When I put you to bed you were saying something about Simon Cowell and elephants. Completely out of it.'

'Yep, then. And when I went back I couldn't get inside to see all the rooms. But after talking to Jack and my mum, it sounded like a bargain, a no-brainer.'

'And it's not?' Suni asked.

'It's a wreck.'

'Jack probably didn't realize himself how much needed doing,' Carly said.

'I know,' I said. 'It's a challenge, but we'll do it. It just feels like a lot at the moment.'

Sunita was listening, but also focusing on feeding Bella at the same time.

'Why don't me and Alex come down and help you out for a weekend?'

'You and Alex?' I smiled at her. It all seemed so familiar and easy.

'I know, I'm totally jumping the gun, and I sound like a crazy person,' she said, 'but if things work out between us, I mean. We could do a bit of painting, DIY – whatever you need.'

'That would be great,' I said. 'If you're sure you don't mind giving up your weekend time? I know what it's like when term starts again.'

'Of course not. I'd love to come down and see where you're living. After all, I'm not going to be able to grab you for a quick chat in the staffroom any more. Speaking of school,' Carly went on, 'are you sure you don't want to come back? Garrett is going out of his mind thinking about how to replace you.'

'I don't think so. Although I'm not quite sure what I'm going to do now. Supply work for a while, I reckon, once the house is finished, and then one of the local schools, Woodlands, said they might be looking for a new teacher in the spring term. It seemed nice there, pretty different from St Catherine's.'

'Different how? Quiet? Organized? Not like a zoo?'

'Yes, that, more or less,' I said, laughing.

'That reminds me – I have something for you,' Carly said. 'We had a training day on Monday and I popped up to check my pigeonhole afterwards. Saw there was something in there with your name on it.'

She took a white A4 envelope out of her bag and passed it to me. My name was written in capital letters in blue biro, and the envelope was heavy.

'A secret admirer?' Sunita said, doing up her nursing bra and settling a rosy-cheeked Bella back into her arms.

'Doubt it,' I said.

'Open it, then,' Carly said.

I opened the envelope and took out the sheets of lined paper inside. I didn't need to read a word to know who it was from – my phone and wallet fell on to my lap.

Dear Miss

I heard from Shanice that you're not coming back next term. We're all gutted. And maybe me most of all because I know it's my fault – or at least part of it is. I shouldn't of nicked your stuff. It was wrong – and I'm sorry.

I had some problems last term. I still hate school – but yours was the only class

I liked. I might come back to St Catherine's — I still hate it so it's only so that Jane, my case-worker, will get off my back.

I know I never done my homework when you were teaching me, but I finished one essay over the summer. Here it is.
I hope you get this OK. Shanice gave it to her form tutor to pass on.

TREY

I opened the other sheets of paper.

If I Were Prime Minister
by Trey Donoghue

If I were PM, I'd still keep my staffy, Rocco. He'd be top dog at No. 10, with one of those harnesses with the studs on it. School would be shorter, maybe just a couple of hours a day and then we'd learn some stuff that would be more useful. I'd like it if I could learn some more stuff, like about fixing cars. I like cars, engines, anything to do with them, and I'm quite good at fixing things too. That's what people tell me, anyway.

If I was in charge of Britain then I would talk to the police, tell them to focus on the real criminals and not stop and search people who are just hanging with their friends, or walking down the street, or just because you're wearing a cap or something. That bugs me. If I was in charge then I'd have to start doing some real study and stop messing around. There you go. That's it really.

The End

When I'd read over Trey's essay I passed it on to Carly and Sunita. 'He finished something.' I smiled, feeling a wave of pride.

'Wow. You got this out of Trey? Blimey,' Carly said. 'I haven't even got a word out of him the whole time I've been teaching him.'

'I'll tell Lewis about him returning my stuff,' I said, putting my phone and wallet back in my handbag. 'He should know that Trey's done the right thing.'

'Are you OK?' Sunita said, spotting my eyes watering.

'Yes,' I said. 'Yes, I'm good.'

Bella started to wail, and the conversation came to an abrupt end as Sunita got up and starting striding around the room in an attempt to soothe her.

Nico came in through the front door. 'Hello, ladies,' he said. 'Wow, looks like I timed this perfectly.' He glanced over at his daughter and then touched her softly on the cheek. She quietened a little.

'And for the grown-ups, I come bearing treats,' he said, holding up a lemon drizzle cake from M&S.

'Thanks, Nico,' I said. 'I'll help you in the kitchen. Actually, can I ask you a quick question?'

'Sure,' Nico said.

'At the Go-Kart track, do you ever need any apprentices?'

I left London Bridge on the train as the sun was setting orange over the city. I wrote out a reply to Trey's letter, thanking him for sending my things back, and for the essay. The anger I'd felt about him stealing from me in the first place was gone now.

I added in Nico's email address, and told him to get in touch if he was interested in getting some experience at the track. Not quite cars, but a step in the right direction. Who knows, he might just give it a try.

I arrived back at the cottage just after seven, and Jack greeted me with a kiss. 'How was Sunita, and the baby?'

'Suni seems great. And Bella's lovely,' I said. 'Baby-like . . . yet surprisingly amenable to letting us have a conversation.'

'I can't wait to meet her. I called Nico and arranged to go by there after work next week. He seems really happy.'

'Yes. Suni was a bit concerned about him having a wobble just before the baby was born, but it looks like he got over it pretty quickly once Bella arrived.'

'It must be an amazing feeling, becoming a parent for the first time.'

'I guess so,' I said with a shrug. 'If it's what you want.'

'So, it was good to catch up?' Jack asked.

'More than that,' I said. I thought of the letter in my handbag. 'How have things been here?' I asked. 'Did you manage to get started on the living room?'

I felt excited at the prospect. Once we had the living room sorted, we'd have a real haven in the house. Somewhere we could be cosy, and entertain guests, even while the rest of the rooms were being finished.

'Sort of – I've made a bit of progress.'

'You did?' I said, pushing the door open to take a look. The ratty brown carpet had been pulled up at the front of the room, but other than that, it looked much the same. The fireplace still had broken tiles, and the paint on the walls was a dull grey.

'I started, but we've had a bit of a setback.'

'Really? What's that?' I went in and bent to look at the flooring. 'Floorboards look good in here. I think we could do something with them, don't you?'

'OK, so the first thing is the window frames,' Jack said. 'I got in a local joiner, but he said that as there's quite a lot of work needed, and as this place is Grade Two listed, we're going to need to get permission to replace them. Same goes for the broken banisters and our stairs. It should be doable, but it'll take a while.'

'How long did he think it would?'

'About eight weeks, he said.'

'That's a pain. Did he say anything else?'

'Well, he wasn't sure, but he was concerned there might be woodworm.'

'You're kidding,' I said. 'Surely that would have shown up on our survey?'

'I don't know why it didn't. But I think we should get someone in for a second opinion.'

'OK. So I guess we're not going to be cosying up by this fire any time soon.'

'There are a few things we need to do first,' Jack said.

'Any chance you'd be able to take a day off, help me out next week?' I asked.

'Really sorry, Amelia. I've got a work trip next week. Don't you remember me saying? I'm going to Berlin for a few days.'

'Oh yes,' I said, trying to seem nonchalant. Of course, he'd mentioned it weeks ago, but with the move it had completely slipped my mind. I realized I didn't want Jack to go away – not now, not at all. I didn't want to be on my own in the cottage. 'How long is it for again?'

'Four days.'

'Right.'

'Yes. We're going to talk to a small animation studio over there, to see if they can work together with us on *LoveKatz*, if we get funding for it. I've seen some of their work and it's amazing. Now that we're down to a skeleton staff in London we're going to need more people on board to do the work, and I have a feeling they'll be perfect.'

'Are the whole team going with you?'

'Yes – Hiro, Jason, Ben, Sadie,' Jack said. 'The timing's terrible, I know. I wish I could be here to help you sort things out, but I'll be back before you know it – and if anything comes up just call me and we can talk it through.'

'OK . . .' I started. I took a deep breath and tried to steady my nerves.

'What is it? You know I can't miss this, Amelia. I helped to arrange it, and it's a really good opportunity for us.'

'You said we'd be working on the cottage together. I thought it would be a chance for us to spend time doing something, you and me. But it hasn't felt like that at all.'

'That'll change soon, I promise,' Jack said. 'But with you at home – well, it just makes more sense. And one of us needs to be making money.'

'I know that. But you agreed to support me when I gave in my notice, and now it feels like you're taking that back. Do you think doing up the house is just a hobby for me?'

'No,' he said, shaking his head. He was getting frustrated, and so was I. 'But the cottage can wait.'

'And I suppose I can too,' I said.

Chapter 10

2 Honeysuckle Lane

Google streetview shows: cottages, parish church, post office, school and newsagent.

Wednesday, 25 September

'Amelia!' Mum said, opening the door to me the next day with a smile.

'Hi. You still got room for one more?'

'Of course. I've made the spare room up for you. Here, let me take your bag.'

I was grateful to come in out of the damp, foggy morning. I handed her the small sports bag I'd packed with essentials for my overnight stay – clothes, make-up, my iPad, a copy of *Country Homes & Interiors* and my sketchbook, so I could continue to work on ideas for the house. When the plumber told me he needed to switch off the water while he worked, I'd decided to decamp and head over to my mum's.

'Are you not feeling well?' I asked. It was unusual to see her still in her dressing gown at ten – she was usually up and dressed early.

'Bit slow this morning,' she said.

'Fair enough. I'm certainly not one to judge. I've been in overalls most of this week.'

'How are the renovations going?' she asked.

'Not bad,' I said. 'Actually, that's not completely true. Hence me being here. We've got a suspected case of woodworm and some permissions to negotiate, but we're slowly getting there. The kitchen looks good.'

'Oh lovely,' she said. 'I'm dying to see it.'

'Yes – I'd love to have you round. But when we've got things sorted out a little bit more. Is that OK?'

'Of course, I understand. Just give me the word when you're ready. It'll all get better soon, darling, I'm sure of it. It can get complicated with listed buildings, I've heard.'

'We'll get there,' I said. 'But thanks for letting me stay, really. I needed a break from the house.'

'You know you're always welcome. I thought – if you're not busy – you might like to help me out with something. I'm making some cakes for a charity bake sale tonight, and I could do with a hand. You can come along too, meet some of the locals.'

I thought back to my experience with Jack at the Three Kings pub. 'I don't know,' I said, sitting down on the sofa. 'I'm not sure I've found Hazelton that welcoming so far.'

'Oh dear,' Mum said. 'Well, you probably just haven't met the right people, that's all.'

'They don't seem to like Londoners much. Have you not found that?'

'Not at all,' Mum said, waving a hand dismissively. 'You'll be fine, Amelia. Teething problems, that's all it is.'

'If you say so. Anyway, back to these cakes. What are you planning on making?'

'A hazelnut and carrot cake, and a classic Victoria sponge.'

'Nice. Let's get to work then.'

Mum and I tied on aprons and got together the ingredients for the two cakes in her kitchen – clear wooden worktops, a brand new oven and matching polka-dot crockery.

'Did you have to do a lot of work to get the room like this?' I asked.

'No, It was like this when I moved in,' Mum said. 'I was lucky, I suppose – I think my time for big house renovations is probably over.'

'You and Dad did a bit in back in the day, didn't you?'

'When I was pregnant with you we painted the flat – your dad was longing to knock down a wall but I persuaded him to wait until you were born before we did anything major. Couldn't bear the thought of a flat full of plaster dust when you were still so young. Anyway, along you came and we never got round to any of that.'

'Sorry,' I said.

'You were worth it,' she said, smiling.

For a moment, working alongside each other, it felt as if we'd always done things like this, Mum arranging cooking equipment on the worktop as I perched on a stool. But it hadn't always been like that. I watched as Mum began to measure out ingredients. I remembered the letter Dad had sent me, the week after he left. The words were embedded in my mind.

Dear Amelia,

I'm sorry I had to go, and that I didn't get the chance to say goodbye to you properly. Know that I love you, and that this wasn't my choice.

When you were born my whole life changed – I held you in my hands and knew life would never be the same again. And it wasn't. It was so much better. Me and your mum were so happy then. But people change, and we've grown apart. We both still love you – in our different ways.

I know your mum's wanted to work for a while, but I'll never understand how or why she could take a job that would always separate our family. I want us to be together, but I realized whatever

I did, that wouldn't happen when your mum was on a plane most of the time. That's not what being a family is, in my mind. Sometimes I even wonder if she really wants to meet someone else – if we're not enough for her.

I'll be back to see you as soon as I can. I hope you are enjoying the doll's house.

Love,

Dad x

'Right. Now, where were we?' Mum said, pushing her hair back from her face and tying it with a band. 'Are you OK to grate the carrots?'

'Sure,' I said, getting down from the stool and opening the fridge.

In the early evening, when our baking was finished, Mum and I walked into Hazelton, and she led me inside the village hall, where women buzzed around stands and chattered over cakes. My stomach twisted, as if I were going into a really important interview rather than just meeting a few village locals. Hazelton was my home now, but I felt out of place. How was it that I could feel comfortable in front of a group of thirty teenagers, and yet now I felt vulnerable and shy?

'Rosie!' A woman my mum's age, in a purple pashmina,

was weaving her way over to us. 'How are you?' She gave my mum a hug before turning to me. 'And you must be Amelia. I'm Rachel.'

I shook her hand and smiled. 'Yes. Pleased to meet you.'

'You look alike, you know. It's the eyes – I've always wanted blue ones. Anyway, your mum's told me lots about you. Ever so proud of you, she is.'

I glanced at my mum, wondering if that was true. She was busying herself getting our cakes out of her bag and placing them on the central table.

'You've just moved in nearby, I hear. Brambledown Cottage?' Rachel asked warmly.

'Yes, that's right. My husband Jack and I are doing it up.'

'Oh – good luck with that. I do love a bit of home improvement.'

'It's slow going, but we'll get there. Thought I'd have a break from it all at Mum's this weekend. I'm still trying to find someone who can restore some of the original features, like the window frames; quite a few of them are rotted.'

'Ah – I know just the person. You should meet my daughter Sally. She's just bought her own place, and has run into a few hitches too. She's over here . . .'

Rachel walked me to the small kitchen, where Sally was talking to some friends.

'Sally, this is Amelia, Rosie's daughter. She's just moved here,' Rachel said.

Dressed in black skinny jeans and a red blouse, with shoulder-length dark-blonde hair, Sally stood out a bit from the flowery dresses at the bake sale. She and I must have been roughly the same age.

'Good to meet you,' I said.

'How are you settling into village life so far?' she asked kindly.

'OK,' I said. 'I haven't had much of a chance to explore. But it seems nice here.'

'It's Eleanor McGuire's place you've moved into, isn't it?' Sally said. 'Beautiful location.'

'It's stunning – nothing for miles around. I still have to pinch myself in the mornings.'

Sally laughed. 'Yes, it's lovely and peaceful out here. And I'm enjoying my lie-ins since I stopped helping Mum and Dad with the farm. I say lie-ins – I'm still up at seven, but that feels like a luxury when I was used to mucking out the animals at five or six in the morning.'

'Rachel has a farm?'

'Yes, she and my dad, Fred, run it. She didn't mention it? It's their life – there are cows and chickens, the usual, but then there's their real pride and joy – three horses – and Mum's big passion, a dozen alpacas.'

'Wow. That sounds like a lot of work.'

'It is, but they love it. Mum's been getting the alpaca wool spun – beautifully soft stuff. It was hard to leave them, knowing that they could still use an extra hand, but there are things I want to do in life that don't involve putting my hand up cows' bottoms.'

'What could possibly be more appealing than that?' I asked, smiling. I couldn't help warming to Sally and her laid-back, unpretentious manner.

'I run a bakery and cafe on the high street. I started it up last year with my husband, Dan. We specialize in wedding cakes. Got to make our own last year,' she said, beaming. 'Don't suppose you've got anything lined up?'

'Been there, done that, I'm afraid,' I said, flashing my wedding ring.

'You'll have to pop in anyway, next time you're in town. We're just next to the post office.'

'Sure. I'll do that.'

Two hours later, when the time came to leave, I had talked to most of the people in the hall, made friends with Sally and got the number of the workman she knew into the bargain. On top of all that, our cakes had gone down a storm, with only a slice left of each.

'See,' Mum said, nudging me gently. 'I told you you'd get on well with everyone. And you met Sally and her friends too – so you see, we're not all old farts around here.'

'I never thought that,' I said.

'Come on,' she said, 'let's get home. Looking at all these cakes has left me feeling famished. I think we both need a proper meal.'

After dinner, we settled down in Mum's front room with tea. 'There's a screening of *Breakfast at Tiffany*'s coming up,' she said, 'at the village hall. They bring in a projector screen first Friday of the month. Perhaps we could go along to that together? If you're interested?'

'Yes, sure,' I said. It had felt good to spend some time together. Perhaps now we could start to do that more often.

In the late-afternoon sun, something on her coffee table glinted.

I reached for it. As I lifted it, I saw it was a man's chunky silver watch. 'What this?'

'A watch,' Mum said, looking a little flustered.

'Isn't it a bit big for you?' I said, letting it dangle off my wrist.

Mum looked at me but didn't say anything for a moment. 'It belongs to a friend,' she said at last.

'Mum, are you . . . blushing?' I asked, watching a rosy glow creep up her neck and onto her face.

'Of course not,' she said dismissively.

'You are!' I said, as it dawned on me. 'Are you seeing someone?'

'I might be,' she said, 'yes.'

'Really? What, romantically?'

She nodded.

God, I thought, struck temporarily dumb. I really hadn't seen that one coming. My mum was in her *sixties*.

'You look surprised.'

'I suppose I am a bit. I thought you moved out here so you could invest time in some hobbies and—'

'Get myself ready for the old people's home? I came out here for a new start, yes. I didn't know quite what that would consist of, but it turns out it's far more exciting than I could ever have imagined.'

'Right,' I said, struggling to take it in.

'Amelia, I've fallen in love.'

The next morning, after breakfast I drove home, still trying to make sense of what my mum had said. She had the right to meet someone – of course she did. She and my dad had been separated for years, and he was with Caitlin now. It was just that Mum had been on her own for so long, I really hadn't expected it.

Callum was at work in the back garden.

'You OK out there?' I called out. Callum straightened and emerged from the long grass.

'Hi. Actually, Spencer's just driven over to the garden centre to get us some more bulbs. Would you like to come and give me a hand?'

He smiled. I knew he didn't really need a hand from a city girl who didn't know her buddleia from her begonias, but I appreciated him asking. Jack and I would be the ones looking after this garden in the long term, and we needed to know how to maintain it.

'Come on.' He beckoned me out. I put on my outdoor shoes and followed him. The early autumn sun was warm on the back of my neck and the smell of freshly cut grass filled the air, reminding me of lunchtimes on the school field back when I was a teenager.

'Help me pull these up.' Callum led me to a part of the garden where slender, twisting weeds with bell-shaped flowers were woven around the plants. 'There are some brambles round here too, so you might need these,' he said, passing me a pair of gloves.

As we worked, he talked me through what he and Spencer had done so far, and what they planned to do over the following week. 'Shouldn't be too much longer now,' he said.

I noticed the way the sun caught the golden hairs on his tanned arms, his muscles subtly defined under a pale blue T-shirt.

'What are your plans after this?' I asked.

'Who knows?' Tiny beads of sweat had begun to form on his brow and he brushed them away. 'If there isn't another job I'm thinking of taking the van, an old VW camper, and driving it down to the south of Spain. I've got some friends out there who I haven't seen in a while.'

'But what about work?' I asked, realizing as soon as I'd said it how stuffy and conventional I sounded. Had I jumped so quickly from twenty to middle-age?

'I don't need much,' Callum said, bending back down to pull up the weeds. 'I might do a bit of fruit picking or a bit of labouring on the way. Always meet some interesting people doing that.'

'Sounds like fun,' I said. I remembered the summer holidays Jack and I used to have in the south of France in campsites and hostels, time spent together in lavender fields and vineyards. Back before buying houses was all we seemed to talk about.

'You?' Callum asked.

'Oh, we'll just be here,' I said. 'I've not got a job at the moment and we're focusing on doing up the cottage.'

'You should enjoy the freedom,' Callum said. 'Sometimes a bit of time helps you see what matters.'

I shrugged. 'Maybe.'

'Won't be long, I guess, until you guys have kids, settle down properly.'

His words dissolved the feeling of freedom I had out here, in the open air. 'Not necessarily.'

'I didn't mean to assume, it's just you seem so . . .'

'*Middle-aged?*' I joked. 'Tied down? Boring?'

'Look, I didn't mean anything by it.'

'Sorry,' I said. 'I suppose it's a bit of a touchy subject. I'm not ready for all that. I'm not sure I ever will be.'

'I just thought . . .'

'Everybody does.'

'Who cares what everyone thinks?' Callum said. 'You should do what you want.'

His eyes were fixed on mine, and I felt exposed. Why was it so much easier to talk to Callum than to my own husband? With him I felt I could be myself. The outdoors was part of him, and he seemed as free as I felt trapped right now.

A shout from across the garden interrupted my thoughts. 'Got it,' Spencer called out, waving a blue carrier bag in the air. His army shorts came to just above his knees, and he had a sleeveless white T-shirt on. I could see where the brambles had caught his shins and arms, and while Callum had toasted a golden brown in the sun, his cousin's skin had turned slightly ruddy on his shoulders and cheeks.

I took off the gardening gloves, and Callum watched me. 'You don't have to go,' he said, his voice soft.

'I do.' I put the gloves down by the tools and walked back across the garden towards the house.

'Fancy some lunch?' I asked Callum and Spencer.

'You read our minds,' Callum called back.

'I'll give you a shout in ten minutes, when it's ready.'

I prepared French bread sandwiches for us all, and made a jug of lemonade to drink.

They came in, muddy and exhilarated, and dived onto the plates of ham and cheese sandwiches.

'You look like you haven't eaten in a week,' I joked, pouring out glasses of lemonade.

'Feels like it,' Spencer said. 'Tough work, gardening.'

I took a bite of my own sandwich, grateful again that I was getting help in one area of the house, at least. The doorbell rang, interrupting my thoughts.

'Expecting someone?' Spencer asked, raising an eyebrow.

'Round here? I don't even know anyone.'

I got up from the table and walked to the door, wondering who it might be. When I opened it, I found my mother standing there, a cautious smile on her face.

'Mum!' I said. In the light of what I'd learned about her love life, I couldn't help noticing her glow – youthful – and her pale yellow flowery dress, trendier than she'd normally wear.

'I thought I'd pop round. I hope you don't mind. Thought perhaps I could have a quick peek at your new kitchen?'

'OK, sure. Come in.'

'And about what I said, Amelia . . . I don't want it to come between us.'

'It won't. I'm happy for you, really.' I wanted to change the subject. 'You found the cottage OK then?'

'Oh yes, no problem. I've got a satnav now, and I've been here once before.'

'A satnav?' I said, laughing. 'And there was I thinking you were still a technophobe.'

'Not any more,' Mum said, beaming. 'I've got my own Facebook profile now, you know. Did you see my friend request?'

'I haven't checked it in a while,' I fibbed. 'Anyway, come in. Just having a bite to eat for lunch. Would you like a sandwich?'

'Oh thanks, darling, but no, I'm fine. I'm on that five-two diet and tomorrow's my day off. Got a good binge to look forward to.'

'Right,' I said. Mum had been on every diet going for years – since the divorce, I suppose. She never seemed to lose any weight, but she liked to stay on top of the latest weight-loss trends.

We walked through to the kitchen.

'Callum, Spencer, this is my mum, Rosie.'

'Hi,' Spencer said first, getting up to shake her hand. 'Nice to meet you.'

Callum hesitated for a moment. 'Rosie, hi,' he said, as if he recognized her.

Mum greeted him with a friendly kiss on the cheek. 'Hi, Callum.'

'You two know each other already?' I asked, my gaze going from one to the other of them.

'Oh, Hazelton's a very small town, sweetheart,' she said with a warm laugh. 'I would have thought you'd worked that out by now.'

Mum looked around at the kitchen and the new decor. 'You've done a wonderful job in here, Amelia. I love that dresser.' She pointed to the one in the corner with my teapots on it.

'Thanks.'

We settled down at the table, and I glanced from Callum to my mum, trying to work out what I'd missed.

'It's a marvellous place this cottage, isn't it? Bit of work to do, like you said. Must have been an awful lot for your grandmother to look after on her own,' she continued, looking at Callum.

'It was. She's better off where she is now,' he replied.

'Brought a fruit cake for you.' Mum bent down to retrieve a cake from her bag. 'From the bake sale. We sold two, didn't we, Amelia? And I couldn't resist buying one too. All for a good cause.'

'Thanks,' I said. I took the cake from her and put it on the side. 'That's a lovely thought. We'll enjoy it.'

'Don't you want to have some now?' Mum said. 'I won't have any, but you should. Perfect for dessert.'

'Sure,' I said, getting up and taking some plates out.

'How has the garden been going?' Mum asked Spencer and Callum. 'Amelia said you'd been a great help.'

'We've made some decent progress today, haven't we, Cal?' Spencer said, turning to his cousin.

'We've cleared a path to the stream and we should be able to cut back quite a lot more by sundown tonight.'

'You're working right the way through today?' Mum asked.

'We may as well pack in as much as we can while the evenings are still fairly light.'

Mum practically purred her admiration at their work ethic.

'What are you up to this afternoon?' I asked, cutting the cake.

'I've got my life drawing class this afternoon.'

'Oo-er,' Spencer said, laughing. 'You one of those passionate artistic types then, are you? Excuse for perving, if you ask me.'

'I prefer to see it as rediscovering my creativity.' Mum laughed. I turned and saw her catch Callum's eye.

I handed out cake and we ate it, my mum chatting easily with Callum and Spencer, and me watching, feeling uncomfortable for some reason.

'We'd better get back to work,' Spencer said. 'Thanks for the cake, Rosie.'

Callum got to his feet too.

'Right,' I said. 'Mum – I'll see you out.'

'OK, yes, of course. You must all be busy,' she said.

'Would you like to come back in a week or so? I'm sure Jack will be upset to have missed you, so you'll have to come back another day when he's here.'

'OK, love, of course.' She got to her feet. 'Bye, Spencer, Callum,' she said with a nod.

I walked her back to the front door.

'Just let me know when Jack's around and I'll pop back and see you.'

She gave me a kiss and a hug and headed to her car.

'Good to be home,' Jack said, giving me a hug when he got back that evening. 'I got you a couple of things,' he went on, pulling some German wine and a bag of gummi bears out of his hand luggage.

'Thank you,' I said. 'Nice to have you back.'

'What's up?' he said, pulling out a chair so that I could sit at the kitchen table. 'Has something gone wrong with the house?'

'No,' I said, shaking my head. 'Actually, some things are looking up. I've applied for permission to make the changes to the windows and stairs, and Callum took a look at the woodwork in the living room. He thinks it all looks like historic woodworm, says there's no sawdust to indicate anything going on at the moment.'

'He's sure?'

'He can't be completely, but he seemed fairly certain. When we find someone to help with the windows, we can double-check with them.'

'That's a relief,' Jack said. 'And with Carly and Alex coming next weekend, we'll be able to make some headway on the bedroom. You still look a bit stressed, though. Is it something else?'

'It's nothing really; I think I need some wine,' I said, cracking open the bottle Jack had just given me.

'It doesn't look like nothing to me.'

'It is.' I poured us both a glass. 'I mean, it's nothing I should really be worrying about. But at the same time . . .'

'Is it the house?'

'Not this time.'

'Fine,' Jack said. 'What is it, then?'

'It's Mum. She's got a . . .' What was the right word? *Boyfriend? Partner?* 'A lover.'

'Ooh,' Jack said, breaking into laughter.

'It's not funny, Jack. It's totally weird. She's got this odd glow about her.'

'Come on, Amelia. Isn't this a good thing?'

'It's not the partner part that bothers me, it's the . . . I don't know, it just seems strange. A bit icky, I guess.'

Jack took a sip of wine. 'Icky as you might find it, I hope we'll still be having sex at sixty.'

'Do you have to?' I said, covering my eyes.

'Are you sure they are? Doing it, I mean,' Jack asked.

'You are not helping. Not at all.'

'I think it's nice actually,' he said. 'Your mum's a lovely woman. She deserves a bit of fun after all these years.'

'Hmm.'

'Come on, Amelia – give it a few weeks and I'm sure you'll get used to the idea. You must have felt like this when your dad met Caitlin.'

'I didn't feel anything like this then; I don't know why.'

'Oh.'

'Mum dropped by here earlier today. I really hope her visit yesterday isn't the start of her "surprising" us. I wanted her to see this place, of course, but I hoped it would be when everything was ready.'

'She's your mum. It's natural she'd want to come and see the cottage when she lives so near. It sounds like she was trying to make amends.'

'I wish she'd just given me some space instead,' I said, taking a sip of wine and thinking back to the atmosphere in the kitchen earlier that day, when Mum was there. 'I feel as though when I was staying with her, we were just playing at being mother and daughter, everything hunky-dory, and then – bam – we were like two strangers again. And she's trying to force it – to make things OK.'

'It seems she wants to spend more time with you though. How about if we got her more involved in the house renovations?' Jack said. 'She has a bit of time on her hands these days, and she is a big fan of *Kirstie's Vintage Home*, isn't she?'

'Loves it. But no. No way. And thankfully she's not expressed any interest in helping out with the house. She's relieved enough to have finished the work on her own place.'

'You don't think you could get used to it, the idea of her having a boyfriend?'

'Don't,' I said. 'This is officially the end of this conversation. Look, we haven't seen each other all week. You've been to a glamorous European capital – let's spend the evening talking about that, not my mum's love life.'

'Ohhh-kay.'

'How were the people you met at the studio?'

'They were really inspiring. It was great to meet them and brainstorm a few ideas. I think it'll be a good match to have them on board. The studio is keen to join forces, and we're going to make a strong combined team.'

'And when will you hear from the funders about whether they approve your revised proposal?'

'Before Christmas, I hope,' Jack said. 'It would mean

everything to be working on something I care about again, not just doing bits and pieces of advertising work.'

'I know,' I said. 'I want this to happen for you, Jack. I really do.'

September drew to a close, with gusts of wind that swept up the fallen leaves and plastered them where they landed, and Callum and Spencer finished their work on the garden. There was a shift in the quality of light and air that lets you know that autumn has really arrived. Conkers littered the front garden, together with clumps of orange and golden leaves.

As I tidied in the kitchen, I heard a rap on the garden door, and through the glass saw Callum standing there. I opened it.

'Are you ready to see your new garden?' he asked.

I pulled on my boots eagerly. I'd seen the work they'd been doing over the past few weeks, of course. First thing in the morning, when I was getting dressed, I'd look out and see them weeding or cutting back brambles, returning from the garden centre and filling the dark, dull earth with bright new blooms and life. But walking round it, finished – our garden – was something I'd been looking forward to.

'Just you try and keep me away.'

I walked out with Callum, past the paved area and towards the wildflower garden. A fence made from pieces of wood and branches separated it off from the pathway, which was made of slabs of uneven stone, pieced together. 'We kept a lot of this how it was, because wildflowers flourish on quite poor soil, so we didn't want to overwork it. We've strewn wildflower seed here, so you'll see the full effects in the springtime, and the poppies in the summer – you liked them, didn't you?'

'Yes,' I said, remembering how I'd fallen in love with the garden on my very first visit. Callum had captured what I'd seen that day, a sense of nature taking over and thriving, but it had been untended and he had gently tamed it. 'It's beautiful. And I love the wooden bird table.'

'Glad you like it. Just something I knocked up. Come on, follow me.' He walked ahead down the path and led me to sections of trellis with honeysuckle and jasmine wound up on to them. 'This is going to smell incredible for you next summer,' he said. 'And there's the Japanese anemones for you to enjoy now.' He pointed to a bed of plants full of proud white blooms. It had caught my eye when I'd been looking down at the garden from my bedroom.

'Jack mentioned that the two of you had been thinking about a vegetable patch,' Callum said, 'so we've marked out this area, and got you started with a few vegetables.'

'And the space next to that is for our summer house?'

'Whenever you're ready for it.'

We walked down to the stream. The air was cooler than

the last time we'd been here together, and raindrops hung suspended on the fronds of the ferns. Leaves from the oak tree were scattered around us. 'I left things here pretty much as they were, untouched, like you said you wanted.'

'That's right. There's something special about the stream. It doesn't feel right to change it, and I don't think we could improve it even if we tried.'

'There is, you're right.' Callum said. He looked distant for a moment, and I wondered if he was thinking about his mother.

I turned and looked back at the garden. By clearing and tending the earth, Callum had created a space that I'd look out on with pleasure first thing every morning. It complemented the cottage, already overrun by nature in its wisteria overcoat.

'Thank you, Callum,' I said. 'I envy you, I really do. How you can transform things.'

I looked over at him, and his grey-green eyes were fixed on mine. 'That's funny,' he said, 'because I see that in you too.'

Chapter 11

The Bedroom

On the Mood Board

Birds and botanicals – shades of green, sand, beige, straw and fire brick, bird print wallpaper, delicate leaf prints on curtains and cushions. Liberty prints. Antique brass handles. Farrow & Ball colour swatches.

Saturday, 5 October

On Saturday morning I toasted bagels and brewed some coffee and brought breakfast to Jack in bed.

'Thanks,' he said, taking the plate gratefully. He took a sip of coffee and then put his arm round me, drawing me close. I straightened up and pulled away just a fraction, picking up my bagel.

'So Carly and Alex will be here around three,' I said. 'I

guess we probably shouldn't stay in bed all day. If we get the walls prepared this morning there should be enough time to put a first coat of paint on today.'

'Sure,' he said. 'That should be fine.'

We hadn't done a thing to the bedroom since moving in. The shabby carpet was still in place, the dark blue curtains hanging from the curtain rails blocking out light, and the drab walls, grey and stained.

'It's only half eight. Relax and let's enjoy breakfast first.'

'Yes, of course,' I said, trying to settle back down.

'What's Alex like? I can ask now that he's finally official, can't I?'

'Chilled out, kind,' I said. 'I mean, I've not met him socially before, but I spoke to him a few times at parents' evenings when I was teaching Jules. He's laid-back,' I went on, 'good for Carly, I think. You'll see for yourself when he gets here.'

'And you say his son's OK about them getting together?'

'Yes – he freaked out at first, but has accepted it now. He said if his dad had to pick one of the teachers, Carly was definitely the best choice. She's taking that as a green light.'

'I'm looking forward to meeting him. I was never that sure about Ethan.'

'Neither was I,' I admitted. 'It seemed she wasn't always able to be herself with him. Hopefully this will be different.'

We drained our coffees. I thought of how, just a few

months ago we would have let them go cold, kissing and making love, taking advantage of the weekend. But right now all I could think about was making progress on the cottage.

'I'm really looking forward to seeing Carly.'

After we'd showered, Jack and I moved the bed into the guest bedroom, so that Carly and Alex could sleep in there. We'd crash on the sofa bed in the room with the view of the apple tree – the one we planned to make our study.

'Did I tell you I spotted a fantastic vintage iron bed at that antique shop in town last week?' I said.

'Bargain or blow-out?' Jack said.

'Bargain, as it happens,' I said. 'I think it would look perfect in the bedroom, when we're done.'

'Sounds nice,' Jack said. 'As long as we don't get an antique mattress to match.'

'Don't worry, it'll fit the one we've got on that IKEA bed at the moment.'

'Let's get it then. When we're done, I mean.'

We stepped back into the bedroom, which was clear now. 'Right, where do we start?' Jack asked.

'These,' I said, going over to the curtains and unscrewing the finial at the end of the curtain rail, 'are out of here.' I pulled off the dusty navy drapes and let them pool on the floor. Replacing the finial, I went over to the other window and did the same. 'God, that's satisfying.' Golden light spilled into the room, casting squares of sun on the floor. I bundled the fabric up into my arms.

'Out with the old,' Jack said.

'Oh yes,' I said, smiling in satisfaction. 'And what do you think about the walls? Just soap them down and repaint them?'

'That should do the trick, yes,' he said, leaning in to inspect them. 'With four pairs of hands it shouldn't take too long. There are a couple of areas where the paint's cracked, though, so we'll need to smooth things back a bit first. We can do that before they get here. Are you still keen on the idea of a feature wall?'

'Definitely. That one behind our bed. I picked up some bird print wallpaper online – and no, before you look at me like that, I didn't buy the Liberty one. Or the Farrow & Ball paint.'

'I didn't say a word,' Jack said, holding his hands up and laughing. 'But that sounds good. Can I have a look?'

'Sure.' I went into the apple-tree room, where I'd been stashing the paint and wallpaper I'd bought, and brought a few things back to show Jack.

'Cool,' he said, looking at the paper. 'Swallows. I like it.'

'Great. I was thinking this off-white for the walls, with Birdwatcher's Green for detailing and trim.' I opened a tin of paint and bent to brush a small patch of the green by the radiator.

He put his arm around me. 'I like it. Right, before Carly and Alex get here, let's get this carpet ripped up.'

'All ready for the painting party!' Carly announced at the door mid-afternoon, giving me and Jack hugs hello. She strode into the hallway, holding up her navy overalls. 'We came prepared. You do remember you promised us plenty of booze for this, don't you?'

'We're exceptionally well stocked for your visit, yes,' I said, pointing to the kitchen where we'd put the wine and beer we'd bought for the occasion.

'Excellent,' Carly said. Alex appeared in the doorway with their bags from the car, and his border terrier, Pete. Pete lingered in the hallway for a moment, then seemed to smell cat on something. He started barking.

'Hi, guys,' Alex said, putting his bags down. 'Sorry about Pete. You've got a cat, haven't you?'

'Hi, Alex,' I said. 'Yes, I'm afraid we have.' I hesitated for a second, then gave him a kiss on the cheek.

He smiled. 'Good to meet you – again. Not as Jules's dad this time. And you must be Jack,' he added.

'Great to meet you,' Jack said, stepping forward and shaking Alex's hand.

'Wow, you really have moved to the middle of nowhere,' Carly said, glancing back through the open door at the fields surrounding us.

'Kind of. Although it's pretty well connected, thankfully,' I said.

'It's a beautiful part of the country,' Alex said kindly.

'So, we're finally here, at the place you've told us so much about,' Carly said. 'Can we have a poke around?'

'Sure,' Jack said. 'Right, for starters, your bedroom's upstairs – sorry, it's all a bit makeshift and there's still quite a lot of stuff in there, but it's kind of cosy.'

'Oh, that's fine,' Alex said politely.

'We'll have a proper spare bedroom for you next time, I promise,' I said.

'We're not fussy,' Carly said. 'It'll be like being students again.'

Alex took the bags up the stairs.

'This is the room we'll be working on today,' I said, opening the door to the master bedroom to show them. 'As you can see, we've been doing the destructive bits this morning.'

'We wanted to have some of it out of the way before you got here,' Jack added.

'Floorboards look good,' Alex said. 'Bit of sanding and staining and I reckon they'd polish up nicely.'

'Music to my ears,' I said. 'I've had my heart set on stripped floorboards in here, so it was great to see they're in decent condition. We've prepared the walls, so hopefully you're ready to do some painting and papering?'

'We're ready for anything,' Carly said. 'But first – I reckon we need a cuppa. Don't suppose you've got a teapot around here, have you, Amelia?'

'I suppose I can see why you're sold on the country life thing,' Carly said. 'All this floor space! Three bedrooms. And you could swing a jaguar in this kitchen. Better than your last flat, where you were tripping over each other all the time.'

'The space is great,' Jack said. 'Never thought I'd be a countryside convert, but it's starting to happen.'

After we'd had tea and I'd shown Carly and Alex the kitchen and garden, we all went upstairs to the bedroom to get started on the painting.

Carly and Alex picked up tins of paint and brushes, and Jack and I laid down newspaper. I gathered up the rolls of bird-print wallpaper and took them over to the alcove. After putting on the paste, I climbed the wooden stepladder and Jack and I worked together to put up the first strip.

'I haven't got any bubbles in it, have I?' I asked.

'Nope, it looks perfect,' Jack confirmed. We worked slowly and carefully, smoothing each sheet carefully into place.

'You planning to make anything for this room?' Carly asked.

'Some more of those hand-tied curtains, like in the kitchen, in a shade lighter than the Birdwatcher's Green. We're getting in an antique bedstead, and I found a white birdcage in the same shop that I think will look great hanging up in the corner.'

'It must be so nice to have all the time to do this,' Carly said, turning to me with a roller in her hand. 'I feel like I barely get time to think now that term's started again.'

'It certainly makes a change,' I admitted.

The four of us worked and listened to music until afternoon crept slowly into evening.

'Time to call it a day, I think,' Jack said, downing his paint roller with a satisfied smile. I glanced outside and was surprised to see that it was now pitch black. 'I don't know about you, but I'm gasping for a drink after that. Can I get you guys anything?'

'Absolutely,' Carly said.

'Let's get cleaned up,' I said. 'The bathroom's over the hall. No comments about the bright yellow decor, please . . . it's next on our list.'

Carly and Alex got changed upstairs. An hour later, we were all sitting at the kitchen table. I'd put a lasagne in the Aga to cook, and cracked open a bottle of red.

'Thanks for all your help today,' Jack said.

'You're very welcome,' Carly replied. 'It's good to be doing some manual work, actually.'

'It's pretty satisfying,' Alex added. 'In a way I wish we were staying longer. I want to see those floorboards all sanded and stained.'

'Well, you're welcome to stay . . .' I joked.

'Send us a picture when they're done,' Alex said.

'Jack,' I said, 'I've been meaning to ask you. Now that Callum and Spencer have finished work in the garden, would you mind if they helped out with some occasional jobs, like fixing things and sanding? They're short of work, and I could definitely do with the help. I know you're knackered when you get back from London.'

'Fine with me,' Jack said. 'I'm only sorry I'm not here to help more – but I can't afford to miss a day at the moment with this new project.'

'You've got a new animation coming out?' Carly asked. 'I loved *Pupz*. Appealed to my inner child a lot.'

'You worked on that?' Alex said. 'That was one of Jules's favourite films! Although he'd probably kill me for saying it.'

'Ah, thanks,' Jack said. 'It's been tricky to find a follow-up; I got a bit stuck for a while. But I think we're getting there this time.'

I topped up everyone's glasses. By the time we'd reached the bottom of our second bottle of wine, the lasagne was ready – I served everyone, and Jack helped me carry the plates to the table.

'Dig in' I said. 'So, what's new with you, Carly? How are things going at school?'

'Good. My students seem fresher after the break. The

new Head of English has started, shaken things up a bit.'

'Oh yes?'

'He's brought in a lot of new systems, and not everyone likes them. Several people have been complaining about him.'

'I'm really sorry to hear that,' I said. 'Which, as you'll know, is a complete lie. Probably shouldn't be saying all this with a parent in the room.'

'Don't worry,' Alex said, laughing. 'Now Jules has left I think that makes me an ex-parent. Or something like that.'

I smiled. 'We shouldn't just talk about work though, anyway. What else is new, C?'

'Actually, we've got some exciting news,' Carly said.

My mind skipped ahead – a proposal, a baby . . . already?

'We just booked some flights,' she finished.

'We're going out to Australia on holiday, over the Christmas break,' Alex said, with a proud smile.

'Wow!' I said. 'How long for?'

'We're planning on renting a car for a couple of weeks and travelling around,' Carly answered. 'Thought we'd swap London for some time at the beach.'

I felt envious of their freedom: the way that, unlike us, they didn't seem to be governed by how much everything was going to cost.

'With everything that's been going on – and Jules finally

accepting it – I thought it would be good for us to have some time just the two of us,' Alex said, putting his arm round Carly. 'She's been patient enough with me.'

Carly was positively glowing. 'I can't wait. I've picked out a new bikini already. This holiday I'm going to truly forget about St Catherine's for a while.'

'That's great,' I said. 'You deserve it.'

I glanced from Carly to Alex – saw the matching look of excitement and contentment on their faces.

'Are you guys getting away anywhere?' Alex asked.

'I don't think so,' I said, glancing over at Jack. 'Not this year. Money's a bit tight.'

'Of course,' Alex said. 'Moving's expensive, isn't it? And I expect you'll be wanting to save for the future,' he went on, raising his eyebrows. Then he winced. Judging by the apologetic expression she was giving me, I was pretty sure that Carly had elbowed him under the table.

'It won't be too long before we start thinking about a family, yes,' Jack said.

I turned to him, surprised, my eyes wide.

'What?' he said.

'Jack,' I said, under my breath.

'Come on, Amelia. It's true, isn't it?'

'Sorry,' Alex said. 'I didn't mean to stir things up. I should never have said anything, I just thought . . . I mean, Carly said you guys had been together a while.'

'It's OK, Alex,' I said. 'It's not your fault. More wine, anyone?'

Jack and I said goodnight to the others and went up to the study where we'd be sleeping. It must have been about two in the morning.

I closed the door behind us and turned to him. 'What happened down there?' I asked.

'I don't know.' He shrugged. 'You were the one acting weird. We've been together for years, we're married, we've moved to somewhere that would be perfect to bring up a kid. It's hardly the biggest leap of imagination to think that we might be considering having a baby, is it? Isn't that what this move was about?'

'No. And this is crazy,' I said. 'I don't know where you got that idea from. Or why you would choose to talk about it in front of friends.'

'I didn't— OK. I thought it was a fairly safe thing to say, not realizing that you, with your issues . . .'

'Issues?' I whispered. 'Just because I'm not jumping at the chance to give up our life and devote it to a baby, it means I have issues?'

'I didn't mean that,' he floundered. 'But you have to admit, there's some stuff with your mum that you've never really dealt with . . .'

'And now – in the early hours, when we have friends

staying and we've both been drinking – now is the time
you decide to bring this up? Why didn't you just raise this
at the dinner table too, and be done with it?'

He didn't reply, just took off his shoes and started getting
undressed for bed.

I tugged off my top and bra and crawled under the covers,
turning away from him.

The next morning, fragments of our conversation drifted
back.

'I've made breakfast,' Jack said, standing in the doorway.
'The others are already downstairs. Do you want to join us?'

'Hmmph . . . yes,' I said, rubbing my eyes and pulling on
my dressing gown.

I walked down the stairs a couple of steps behind Jack,
sensing a distance between us.

'Morning,' I said, as I went into the kitchen. 'Hope you
guys slept OK?'

'Fine, thanks,' Carly said, taking a bite of toast. 'You
feeling better this morning?'

'Really good, yes,' I said, as if nothing had happened. 'Bit
too much to drink last night, that's all.'

'You're not on your own there,' Alex said, putting a hand
to his head and pretending to wince, then smiling.

'How about a walk this morning?' I suggested. 'Clear our
heads a bit.'

I needed to get outside. Arguing with Jack had left a bitter taste, and even now I couldn't work out whether I'd been right or wrong to say the things I had.

'Sure,' Carly said. 'Sounds good.'

'We could take Pete for a long stroll, wear him out, and then stop for tea and cake in the village. There's a cake shop I've been wanting to try out.'

'I like the sound of that,' Alex said. 'And to be honest, I'm getting increasingly nervous that Pete's got it in for your cat.' He peered out of the kitchen window, where the border terrier was running in circles around a bemused Dexter, who was calmly washing his front paw.

'Oh, I wouldn't worry about Dexter,' Jack said. 'He can hold his own.'

'OK, so we're all agreed?' I said.

'Yes, sure,' Carly said. 'We're in no hurry to get back to the Big Smoke, believe me.'

'We want to make the most of our time here,' Alex said. 'And I think Jules would feel pretty short-changed if we came back early. I've got a sneaking suspicion that he had a "gathering" planned for last night.'

'Aha,' Jack said. 'Yeah, doubt Carly will want to be stepping over hungover ex-students back at your place.'

'Weird,' Carly said. 'Still really, very weird.'

Alex put his arm round her and drew her towards him, kissing the top of her head.

I felt a pang of jealousy. Jack and I used to be close like that.

We set out at eleven and followed a suggested route on Jack's iPhone – a three-mile circuit round the village, through woodland and fields. Pete ran ahead, with a branch the length of a broom handle in his mouth.

I walked next to Jack and waited for him to take my hand. Waited for that warm touch that would mean: you know what, let's forget about all it. I craved it. I wanted to know everything would be OK. Carly and Alex, walking ahead of us, were laughing and joking, their arms wrapped about each other. But between me and Jack it felt like there was a gulf.

'Right,' I said, as we neared the village. 'Looks like we're approaching cake o'clock.'

'Now you're talking,' Carly said, her smile bright. We walked past the clock tower and on towards the post office. Next to it was Sally's Specialities, with gingham tablecloths and towering displays of cakes in the window. 'Here we are.'

I spied Sally through the window and gave her a little wave. She waved back and beckoned us all in.

'I think I'd better tie Pete up out here,' Alex said 'With those cakes within reach, I can see him destroying your chances of settling into this village once and for all.'

As I pushed the door open, a bell rang out. 'Room for four?' I asked.

'Of course,' Sally said, wiping her hands on her apron and coming over to us. 'We always find a way.'

She rearranged some tables and chairs so that there was a table in the corner for us, even though the cafe was almost completely full.

She rested a hand gently on my shoulder. 'I'm so glad you came by,' she said sincerely. 'It's good to see you again. And we've got some great cakes for you to try this morning.'

Carly and I listened with rapt attention as Sally talked us through the cakes in the window – aside from a tiered wedding cake, there was rich chocolate Sachertorte, pear and almond and a forest fruit tart.

We put in our order, and I asked for a large pot of tea and two coffees. 'You've got a teapot collection to rival mine,' I said smiling, looking at the shelves of teapots in every colour and pattern behind the counter.

'You're a collector too?' Sally said. 'You'll have to have me round one day, I'd love to see them.'

Jack looked at me, his gaze softening for the first time that day. 'Amelia's been collecting teapots since she was twelve,' he said, 'so I'd block out a whole morning in your diary.'

Carly smiled at me, as if she too could sense the atmosphere lightening. Thank God for tea and cake.

On Sunday evening when Carly and Alex had left, Jack and I watched TV for the rest of the evening, barely speaking, then went upstairs to our bedroom. We left the windows open to let out the lingering paint fumes.

As I lay in the moonlit bedroom, wanting to cling on to the weekend and keep Jack with me for just a day more, I wondered where our marriage was really heading. I thought of the doubts I'd had lately about us. About whether we wanted the same things.

'Are we OK now?' Jack said, his voice soft. 'I mean, after this weekend? It was weird.'

'It was. But yes, we're OK.'

'Really?'

'I don't know, Jack. It's not really one where you can agree to disagree, is it?'

Jack looked at me, sadness in his eyes. 'It isn't, is it?'

'What do we do, then?' I asked, putting a hand to his stubbled cheek.

'Try and live in the moment?'

'We could try that.' Jack pulled me close and kissed me, his naked chest against mine, his arms round me. And for now, it felt like enough.

*

Jack got up to go to work that Monday as if it were any other day. As if nothing had changed over the weekend. As if the things we'd said didn't matter.

I pretended to be asleep when he got dressed in the half-darkness, but really I was watching him as he located his socks and put them on, resting gently on the end of our bed, trying not to disturb me. His familiar actions felt somehow different now.

He kissed me goodbye, a gentle flutter on my cheek, and then he left. I heard the front door close.

How could he feel that something was missing in our life when for me it was already complete? Wouldn't a child drive us further apart, rather than bringing us closer together?

I started the day at my sewing machine, running up pale green curtains. Callum and Spencer were hammering and drilling in the downstairs hallway, and fixing some of the electrics.

At midday, the iron-framed bed arrived. The delivery men brought it in, along with the fragile white birdcage I'd bought from the same shop. Callum and Spencer helped me get my Grandma Niki's antique wardrobes out of storage in the garage, and take them up to the bedroom to go either side of the window that looked out on to the garden.

By the evening, the bedroom was finished – the floorboards

were stained and polished, the curtains I'd made were in place, and I'd put a sheepskin rug on the floor. My clothes hung in one of Grandma Niki's wardrobes, Jack's in the other. I'd hung the birdcage in the corner, and some antique hatboxes were stacked on top of the wardrobes for storage. I sat on the edge of our bed and wondered when the cottage would start to feel like home.

Chapter 12

The Attic

Dimensions on estate agent's notes: 10 metres x 3 metres. Height at highest point 1.5 metres, eaves are lower. Potential for conversion subject to relevant consents.

Tuesday, 8 October

Our postman was holding out a large parcel for me. I signed for it and thanked him, then took it inside.

I opened the Jiffy bag and pulled out a stack of printed A4 sheets. I read the title on the first page: *When Murder Comes Knocking.* It was the page proofs of Sunita's latest novel. I smiled in surprise and pleasure. Resisting the temptation to start reading right away, I picked up my mobile and called her.

'How's it going, sweetie?' she said.

'Good, thanks. I just received a very exciting package, as it happens.'

'Excellent. Glad it got to you safely. Finished it in the nick of time, before Bella arrived.'

'I can't wait to read it,' I said. 'It's been agony waiting for this one.'

'You might want to check the dedication.'

I flicked to the third page and immediately caught sight of my name there.

For Amelia and Jack, in their quest for the good life

'That's lovely. Thanks, Suni.'

'I'll show you the cover when it comes in,' she said. 'Something bloody with a cross. Or a door knocker. Or a dead kitten.'

'Wow! Well, I'm sure it'll look great. How's everything been going? How's Nico?'

'I've just heard some news you'll like, actually.'

'Oh yes? I could do with some of that.'

'Nico's got a new apprentice at the Go-Kart track, and says he's very dedicated.'

'Trey! He didn't? Are you serious?'

'Yes, he came along with his caseworker the first time, and since then he's been coming on his own one evening a week and all day Saturday. Nico's getting on well with him.'

'That's great,' I said. 'I'm so pleased Nico's giving him a chance. He deserves it.'

'He's enjoying having someone to train, I think.'

'How are you doing? How's being a new mum?'

'Can't remember what it's like to have a proper night's sleep – but apart from that, we're doing great. Been spending a lot of time with the NCT people – cracked nipple chat, but it's kind of what I need at the moment.'

'And Bella? How's she getting on?'

'She's smiling a lot. Normal baby stuff, I know, but pretty amazing all the same.'

'Cute. Do you think you'll have a chance to come and visit?' I said. 'I know it's a journey for you, but it would be great to see you guys, especially Bella.'

'She's already beating us in the popularity stakes. How about during the Christmas holidays? My family never celebrates, and that always seems to mean we spend about a week with Nico's family . . . too long, even without Bella to consider. I'd much rather hang out with you guys.'

'Great,' I said. 'With any luck we'll have the cottage finished by then, so you can see what we've been up to.'

'I'm glad you called actually,' Sunita said. 'Look, I don't want to stick my oar in, but Carly did mention—'

'Ah,' I said, feeling awkward and embarrassed. 'That me and Jack had a bit of a domestic when she came to stay?'

'She didn't put it like that, but she did say it seemed a little tense. She wasn't gossiping, just worried about you.'

I sat down on a chair at the kitchen table. I guess I couldn't hide how I was feeling from other people as well as I'd hoped I could. 'It's weird, Suni. We made this huge change – moving here, me giving up my job. I thought this was it – what we needed to do. But it seems it's thrown up more questions than answers. I came here because I wanted a change in pace, in lifestyle – not to start a family. You know that.'

'Only because you told me. Did you tell Jack?'

'I guess I never said it straight out, but I thought it was a given. Jack knows I'm not the maternal kind. I've never felt that way. Dexter – yes. I can manage a cat just fine. But babies? I mean, Bella's gorgeous – but I don't feel any urge to have our own.'

'It's a tough one. That was how Nico felt at first. If it hadn't happened by accident I wonder if it would have happened at all.'

'There's no chance of any accidents here. I've never been so religious about taking the pill as I am now.'

'Have you and Jack talked much about it? Now, I mean, after what happened the other day?'

'A little bit,' I said. 'But then we just come to a stalemate. He wants one thing, I want another. I love him – of course

I do. But how do you meet in the middle on this? There is no middle.'

'I wish I had an answer for you, hon,' Sunita said. 'What can I say? I think babies are great but only if you're ready, and only if you want one. It's your choice. I hope you and Jack can find a way to work it out.'

'Me too,' I said, a lump rising to my throat. 'We've done all this, Sun. Moved here, bought this place together and invested in it – and yet there's this distance between us that there's never been before.'

I heard an electronic crackle accompanied by the baby's cry and then Sunita scrambling around. 'Sorry – baby monitor,' she said. 'It sounds like Missus has woken up. I better deal with this,' she said apologetically.

'You do that. Listen, it was good to talk to you.'

'Any time. I'm always here for you, Amelia. Now, you take care of yourself, OK?'

It was eight in the evening, and I was starting to wonder where Jack had got to. Even when his train was held up, he was never normally this late. I called his mobile.

'Hi,' he said. 'Was about to ring you. Really sorry about this, but we're up against a tight deadline this week preparing this pitch, and I'm afraid I'm not going to be able to make it back tonight.'

'At all?' I said. Jack had worked late plenty of times, but this was a first. 'Where are you going to sleep?'

'I'm not sure how much sleep we'll get, to be honest. We need to have the trailer for *LoveKatz* ready for the film company by Friday, and there's still a lot left to do. Hiro has a sofa in his office, so I'll probably crash on that.'

'Are there are few of you there?'

'Oh yes, the whole team are here. We're just ordering in some beer and pizza to see us through.'

I pictured the scene – beer, pizza, crashing on sofas in the trendy Old Street office. I felt oddly envious of Jack's work life.

'OK. Well, good luck with it. I hope you get everything done that you need to.'

'Thanks for understanding.'

'You need to do what you need to do,' I said. I was about to say goodbye, then stopped. 'Jack,' I said, 'I love you.'

'Pizza's here,' came a female voice in the background at Jack's end.

'Go on,' I said. 'You don't want to miss out on that.'

'Thanks. And— Yes, a slice of the pepperoni one, please. Sorry. Yes, Amelia, me too. I'll see you tomorrow evening.'

I put the phone down, and as I sat on my bed alone, the cottage seemed incredibly quiet.

*

Detective Sanders walked up the narrow ladder, and as he opened the hatch, it was the smell that hit him first. The metallic tang of blood mixed with the familiar trace scent of Formaldehyde. He had no choice now but to carry on up . . .

For the past hour I'd been telling myself to stop reading and go to sleep, but each chapter was more gripping than the last. All I could think about was where Detective Sanders would find the teenage girl's decapitated body.

I felt jumpy and I wished Jack was there beside me. I glanced at the alarm clock – 2 a.m. Even if he was still working, it was too late to call him.

As Detective Sanders searched in the attic of the suspect's home, I forced myself to put the manuscript down. I thought of the empty space above our bedroom. We'd never been into the attic. We'd never even taken a look up there. It must have been years since anyone had – I didn't remember Callum and Spencer clearing anything out when they moved the rest of Mrs McGuire's things. My skin prickled underneath my pyjamas, the tiny hairs on end. With the dark visions currently whirring inside my head, there was no way I was getting to sleep tonight.

A weight landed on my legs and I let out a yelp, pulling my legs back swiftly. Dexter arched his back and stared at me, eyes wide. He must have leapt off the wardrobe. I'm not sure which of us was more surprised.

'Sorry, Dex,' I said, giving him a stroke. I tried to suppress the images of what might be up in the attic: bloody knives, barbed wire, the remains of . . .

'That's it,' I announced to Dexter, who looked nonplussed. 'I'm going up.' I pulled on my dressing gown and slippers and switched on the main bedroom light.

The only way to stop imagining what was up there was to go and see for myself. I stepped out onto the landing, flicked on the light switch and glanced around. Shadows danced on the walls as I moved, but the cottage was silent. I wanted desperately to hear Jack padding up the stairs or boiling a kettle, the gravel crunching under tyres as he returned to the house. But aside from Dexter, I was on my own. I picked up a torch from our toolbox and took it with me.

I pushed the ladder against the attic hatch and checked to make sure it wouldn't slip, then rubbed my hands, a little clammy from the anxiety, on my towelling dressing gown. I got a firm grip on the wooden ladder. There would be nothing up there but dust and spiders. 'Dust and spiders,' I whispered to myself as I went up the first couple of rungs. Nothing to be scared of.

I hate confined spaces. I hate the dark. And I didn't think I'd cope well with finding decomposing body parts. But if there was something bad up in the attic, it was better that we knew about it. We didn't want to give it the chance to creep up on us in bed.

I nudged the hatch open – it needed a bit of a push and then it came free. I put it to one side and raised my whole body up and inside the dusty room. It smelled stale, and dust motes floated in the beam from my torch. If Jack was here, I knew what he'd say – forget the disembodied head, the real risk is falling right through the floorboards. I cast the torch beam around the room. It was high enough for me to stand up in the centre and the floor looked sturdy enough – I pushed on the floorboards with my hands, then I stood up.

Callum had overlooked the attic when he and Spencer came to clear the house. There were stacks of cardboard boxes, and in the corner was a black rocking horse with a faded fabric saddle. I walked over to it, and ran my hand over the worn material. I pushed it, rocking it gently. One of its ears had been nibbled away by moths.

I went back towards the ladder, and caught sight of a brown leather chest tucked away under the eaves. I went over to it, and saw that on the top, written neatly in marker pen, was the name *Eleanor McGuire*. Eleanor McGuire – Callum's grandmother's name sounded flowery and sweet. A name that chimed with the beautiful garden he had described to me. I prised open the metal clasps at the front, and lifted the lid.

As I shone the torch inside I thought I heard the sound of scratching. But then, as I leaned towards the open attic hatch – nothing. I was imagining things. I went back to the chest, and looked inside. There were exercise books with boys' names written in childish script – David McGuire, Ewan McGuire – and small school uniforms, grey with checked grey shirts. Beside them were bundles of letters, photos and postcards tied with green ribbon. I opened a red photo album and saw pictures of a good-looking young woman with dark curls, her hair falling over her shoulders. Her long dark lashes were just like Callum's. At the back was a wedding photo of the same woman dressed as a bride, the groom blond-haired and wearing glasses.

In the chest was a scrapbook, and at the back of it a folder with papers – notes and patterns on thin paper. I couldn't see what they were at first, but as I flicked through the pages, I began to understand. They were designs for cushion covers and heart-shaped lavender bags to hang in wardrobes. Scraps of fabric accompanied the patterns – gingham, flowered and plain, in pastel tones.

I wondered where the things Eleanor had once made were now. I thought back to the drab-looking sofas and armchairs we'd seen when we first moved in. The things it looked like she'd made had certainly not been hanging up, or decorating the house. I went back to the photo album. They could be seen in the early photos: pretty curtains and elegant throws. The pictures were in black and white, but I could tell they were in the same material as the pieces of fabric I now held in my hand. I could only assume they'd been boxed away, perhaps after Eleanor's husband died. There had been a lot of things still in the house, but nothing as pretty as these.

I closed the book, but didn't put it away. Tomorrow I'd tell Callum about the boxes so he could come up and clear them.

As I went to close the chest, I noticed a bronze-coloured tin box tucked away at the back, the red and teal Bluebird logo faded with age. I reached for it and tried to open it, but the lid was stuck tight. Perhaps there were sewing materials inside.

I heard it again – a definite sound this time. Scratching and scrabbling, like someone was trying to get closer to me.

As I closed the chest and latched it shut, my arms were covered in goosebumps. I took the scrapbook and tin with me and climbed back downstairs.

'Callum,' I called out to him the next morning, as he got his tools out of the van. He and Spencer had just arrived to start work at ten. 'Have you got a minute?'

'Sure,' he said. He rested his things against the wall of the house and came inside with me.

'Last night I was having a look in the attic and found a few of your grandma's things up there. I thought that you or your family might want them.'

'Oh, sorry,' he said. 'Completely forgot about the attic when we were clearing out. What kind of things?'

'Boxes mainly, a big leather chest, a rocking horse.'

'Dad's old rocking horse,' Callum said with a smile. 'I have a feeling he's fond of that – he'll be glad to hear it's still around.'

I thought about the tin I'd found with a pang of guilt. I'd tried to lever the lid off with a spoon last night, only to find it was stuck tight. I'd put it out of the way on top of our wardrobe.

'OK if I come up and see how much there is?'

We went upstairs together, and I was conscious of Callum's closeness to me. He didn't seem to notice, keeping step so our bodies were almost touching. He smelled of fresh air, of the outdoors. He put the ladder in place and I passed him a torch, then he climbed up to the attic while I stayed on the landing below, peering up through the trapdoor.

It was quiet for a moment, and I could see the beam of light moving under the roof. 'There's quite a lot, isn't there?' he called. 'Can I pass down a few boxes to you? Most of these are small enough to take in the truck today.'

'Sure, that's fine.'

I took the boxes from him and stacked them carefully on the landing. Once or twice my hand brushed his, and it sent an unexpected tingle through me.

'Christ!' Callum said, starting to laugh. I made my way back to the foot of the ladder and looked up.

'What is it?'

He looked down through the hatch. 'Did you know you've got squirrels nesting up here?'

'Oh.' I laughed, remembering the noise that had scared me half out of my wits last night. 'That's what it was. Are there many of them?'

'I don't know – only saw one, but there are a few droppings up here. You don't really want them hanging around, I'm guessing?'

'I'm not that keen, no. I might let Dexter loose.'

'Worth a go. I have a friend who got humane traps and put out crackers with Nutella on them – that did the trick. Anyway, the rocking horse, chest and a couple of other things I'll have to come back for, I'm afraid.'

'That's fine,' I said. I thought of the tin – it was too late to discreetly add it to the pile now, but I could put it with the other things when Callum came back for them. 'Whenever suits.'

'Dad and Uncle Ewan are going to be really happy to hear about this, though,' Callum said, walking back down the ladder, facing me. He closed the hatch cover and reached the landing with a small jump. 'Anything that can trigger memories for my grandma really helps. The photo album will give them something to look through and talk about together. A lot of her long-term memory is still there, and the smallest reminder can get her talking.'

'Well, I'm glad I ventured up, in that case.'

'You're a brave woman. There are massive spiders up there, you know. As well as the squirrels.'

'I think it was too dark to see them. But I'm OK with spiders, anyway.' I wasn't going to tell him how spiders compared with what I'd prepared myself to see up there.

'Right,' Callum said. 'I'll load this lot up and get the rest soon.' He walked over to the stairs, away from me.

'Callum.' I took a deep breath as he turned to face me. There was a doubt that had been nagging at me for days now. 'This is probably going to sound weird, but how do you know my mother?'

'Rosie? I'm not sure I should be the one to explain. Maybe this is something she should tell you herself.'

I stood there on the landing, frozen to the spot. I felt something – Disapproval? Envy?– that I couldn't pin down.

'If there's something to know, I'd rather hear it from you.'

'OK.' Callum shrugged nonchalantly. 'It's all quite new. But your mum's a lovely woman.'

A lovely woman?

'My dad's been single a while now. It's been over ten years since Mum died, and Rosie's the first person he's gone out with since then. It took a bit of getting used to, but she's changed Dad so much. They seem to bring out the best in each other.'

The truth hit me, and I felt instantly idiotic. 'My mum . . .' I said, relieved, 'and your dad.'

'That's right. David, my dad. One of us should have explained when she came round the other day, but I felt it was her call. Maybe she wanted to tell you on your own.'

'Your dad,' I repeated, as it sank in properly.

'She could do a whole lot worse, I promise you,' Callum said. 'We've had our ups and downs, but he's a thoroughly decent bloke.'

'You don't think it's weird, at their age?'

'No. I think Rosie's a star,' Callum said. 'They're a great match.'

Somehow, when Callum put it that way, it didn't seem like as big a deal any more.

That afternoon I painted the walls in the upstairs landing, a warm cream that set off the oak beams and flooring. It was already starting to look brighter.

As I painted, Dexter kept me company, bathing in a patch

of autumn sunlight by the window. I climbed up on to the ladder and rollered the top part of the wall, reaching up high. I lost my grip on the roller and it dropped just next to Dexter, startling him.

'Oh crap. Sorry, Dex,' I said. He was on his feet, back arched, then dashed over the paint lid, treading a trail of paint-covered paw prints across the landing. 'Dex – stop!' I called out fruitlessly, coming down the metal ladder in a hurry. His footprints led into our bedroom. When I opened the door I saw he was cowering on top of the wardrobe.

'Come down, Dex,' I coaxed. I had to clean those paws or he'd cover the whole house in paint.

With a flying leap, he came towards me, sending the Bluebird tin from the attic crashing to the floor. It hit the floorboards with a smack, the contents spilling out.

Dexter looked at me, trying to work out what he'd done wrong. I bundled him up in my arms and cleaned his paws off in the bathroom with some white spirit, which he complained about with loud meows, then wiped the paint from our newly stained floorboards.

Back in the bedroom, I picked the tin up, relieved there was only a tiny dent on it from the fall.

On the floor lay a pink bonnet. I bent to pick it up. The crocheted fabric was soft, and it looked as if it had barely been worn. Scattered beside it were photos, face down, and on the back of one a name was written: Sarah. I turned it over to see the face of a small baby with a bow in her hair.

Chapter 13

The Bathroom

On the Mood Board

Wooden cabinets to match the beams, floorboards stripped and varnished, free-standing tub, Victorian-style bath/shower mixers, large gilt-framed mirror.

Thursday, 10 October

In the morning I drove into town, bought some new fabric for throws, and then went into the antique shop. The bell rang out as I entered.

'Morning,' the woman behind the counter greeted me. 'Anything in particular you're looking for, love?'

'Just browsing this morning,' I replied.

It felt good to be out of the house. Jack had got back at around seven thirty the night before, so tired from his all-nighter working that he'd fallen into bed after a quick dinner, with barely a word. There was nothing wrong with him working hard, of course – but given the way things had been I couldn't help but wonder if it had been an excuse to get some space.

I ran my hand over an antique wooden towel rail and checked the price. It was reasonable. In the corner I glimpsed a dark wood bathroom cabinet and a gilt mirror that would look perfect alongside it in the bathroom.

'Could you pack a few things up for me?' I asked the shopkeeper. 'The rail, the cabinet and the mirror?'

'Of course,' she said. 'Nice choices. That mirror in particular is a real find. Why don't you have a browse downstairs while I get this lot ready for you?'

Downstairs in the shop were shelves of bric-a-brac and treasures. To my right was a row of glass medicine bottles in shades of green and blue. I picked out a dozen of them in different sizes. They would look nice on the bathroom windowsill, with flowers inside.

Back at the cottage, I checked in on Callum, who was sanding the floorboards in the living room. 'Everything OK in here?'

'Fine,' he said. 'Making progress.'

'Can I get you a cuppa?'

'Go on then.'

He switched the sander back on, and I turned and walked towards the kitchen. I boiled the kettle and filled the cups, added milk and sugar and carried one through to Callum. He took it gratefully. 'What are you working on this afternoon?'

'The bathroom,' I said. 'I bought some bits and pieces in town this morning. Here, let me show you.' I went out into the hall and picked up the things I'd collected.

'Really nice,' he said. 'It's going to look good. So you're not tempted to do anything more drastic?'

'Oh yes.' I smiled. 'I'll be doing that too. That whole grisly primrose yellow suite is going – sorry to your grandma, but there's just no way I'll ever get used to that. I'm going to look for a new bath this afternoon. I've got my heart set on one of those free-standing ones – you know, with the little claw feet?'

'Those are brilliant,' Callum said, sitting up straighter. 'I've seen them in a few cottages round here. There's a great bathroom shop in Canterbury – let me find you the site . . . They work with a lot of properties of this period and know what suits them.' He got out his iPhone and searched for it.

'Here you go,' he said, passing it to me.

I flicked across a couple of screens – porcelain basins and antique taps. They were gorgeous. I noted down the URL.

'Thanks. I think you might have found exactly what we're looking for.'

I went into the kitchen and got out my laptop, returning to the bathroom shop site. I scrolled through the free-standing tubs until I found one that was just right. I saw the price tag and bit my lip. It was far more than Jack and I had budgeted for.

A bath was an essential though, wasn't it?

I hesitated for a moment, then picked up my phone to make the order.

'Are you hungry?' I asked Jack. 'I was going to make a chicken pie.'

'Yes, sounds good,' he replied. 'Sorry I was such a zombie last night; I really needed to catch up on sleep.'

'Don't worry, it's fine. I know you needed to meet that deadline, and it's not often you're out at work that late.'

'It was a rare situation. So what did you get up to today?'

'This and that,' I said, thinking guiltily about what I'd done that morning without running it past Jack first. 'I bought a few things for the bathroom.'

'You did? What, towel rails and stuff?'

'Not quite. You remember that gorgeous free-standing bath at Arcadia Cottage – the claw-foot one that we both really liked? And the porcelain sink with Victorian-style taps?'

Jack looked at me, surprised. 'You haven't . . .?'

'What? I found a really good shop in Canterbury selling some similar stuff. We got a discount for buying a few things at once. We need a bathroom, Jack.'

'I know that – but still. I thought we were going to choose all the bigger things together. How much did it all cost?'

'Not *that* much. Like I said, there was a discount. It worked out at just over a thousand pounds.'

'A thousand? I would really have liked to have a say in that. Don't you think we might have looked at the house spreadsheet first, to see how we're getting on?'

Jack had a point. It had been a little while since I'd opened it.

'I suppose so,' I said. 'I haven't actually looked at it for a while.' There was no point cutting corners on a bathroom – it was an important part of the house.

'Shall we sit down and have a look at it now?' Jack said. I could tell he was trying to stay calm.

'OK,' I said. 'But you agreed I could make certain decisions on my own, if you were busy with work. And you were.'

'I was thinking more about cushions and place mats than entire bathroom suites.'

Jack opened his laptop and clicked to open the Excel spreadsheet that held all our financial details in it, and then opened up our joint account online banking page.

The figure that had looked like more than enough when we started out had dwindled considerably.

'Right,' He said, running his eyes over the columns. 'Given that we still have the living and dining rooms, spare bedroom, study and the wood restoration to organize, this doesn't look great, does it?'

'We've got options,' I said. I thought of the large white bath, the basin that would create a lovely country ambience. I didn't want to cancel the orders. 'There are things we can do.'

'And you know where we need to start, don't you?'

'Amelia!' My dad came over bright and clear on the phone first thing the next morning.

'Hello, Dad.'

'Hi, sweetheart. How are you doing over there?'

'Good, thanks.'

'And the cottage?'

'It's coming along. We've almost finished the bedroom and kitchen now, and have tamed a jungle in the back garden.'

'You've never shied away from a bit of hard graft, have you?'

'I suppose not,' I said. 'Anyway, how are you? How's everything going?'

'Life is good, can't complain. Picked up a couple of jobs

this past fortnight doing the wiring for a new development of flats in the centre of town.'

'That's great.' That meant he would have some money coming in, surely. I readied myself to ask him about repaying our loan.

'Amelia, I'm really glad you called actually. Caitlin and I were hoping you might be able to help us out with something. Bit of a favour.'

Not money again, I prayed inwardly. Please don't ask that, Dad.

I steeled myself. 'Sure. What is it you need help with?

'It's Mirabel.'

'Mirabel?'

'She's not listening to us, Amelia, and we're desperate for a break. Could she come and stay with you for a week or so?'

'I don't know,' I said, glancing at the plaster dust that covered every surface, the unfinished walls of our hall. 'We're still doing the cottage up – we're not really ready for people to come and stay yet.'

'Mira's only a kid. She'll be fine on the sofa.'

'Couldn't it wait a month or two?'

'I'm not sure. I'm worried about her, and Caitlin is too. She did well in her GCSEs, well enough to stay on at college, but she says she doesn't want to – she's missed the start of term now. She's a free spirit, like me, and I know she'll find her way in the end, but your stepmother's panicking about it. Mirabel's out every night with this guy Jesse, drinking and God knows what else. We thought a change of scene might help. She hasn't stopped talking about the last time she came to stay with you.'

'That was different.' The last time, a year ago, we were living in east London with dozens of clothes shops and gigs to keep her entertained. She'd loved that. 'We're in the country now. There's not going to be much for her to do.'

'She'll be fine,' Dad insisted. 'And it'll give Caitlin and me a chance to get back on track – you know how I hate arguing. This house is full of it at the moment.'

I paused, trying to find another way to let my dad know what a bad idea this was.

'You're all right with the idea, aren't you?' he asked again.

I took a deep breath, but the strength I needed to refuse him faltered. 'OK, Dad. Mirabel can stay. But while she's here, I'm going to need her to help out.'

Later that evening Jack and I were lying in bed. I was looking through the interiors book Carly had bought me, and Jack was checking messages on his phone.

'You're annoyed with me, aren't you?' I said. 'I'll understand if you are.'

'No, I'm not,' he said, putting his phone down and turning to look at me. 'I'm just . . . I don't know, I'm a little frustrated with the situation I guess.'

'Because of the money,' I said, recalling how I'd bottled out of asking my dad what I'd intended to.

'Not really. Well, not only that. It's just – you're tough, Amelia. You're straightforward and honest with most people in your life, and yet with your dad . . . I don't know – it seems like you let him just walk right over you. Instead of getting back the money you need, we've now got Mirabel coming to stay.'

'Do you not want her to stay?'

'It's not that – she's your sister, Amelia. It's up to you. But do you want her staying here? When this place is still a building site? I don't get the impression you do. From what you told me it didn't exactly sound as though it was your decision.'

'I wasn't keen at first, you're right. But that was selfish. If Dad needs a break then I want to help. Once she's here, I'm sure it'll be absolutely fine.'

'As long as you're all right with it, I am,' Jack said. 'I don't want to argue.'

'I know. And I don't want that either,' I said. I closed the book and put it on the side. 'I'm just tired, Jack.'

'So am I.'

*

'Hello there!' It was good to hear Carly's voice, familiar and comforting.

'Hi,' I said, settling down on my bed and cradling the phone in my hand. 'I'm glad to catch you – thought you might have more interesting things to do on a Saturday evening.'

'Not tonight, no. Alex and Jules are having some bonding time at the cinema.'

'How is the planning for your trip to Australia going?'

'Good, thanks. Alex has been in touch with his cousin in Melbourne, so we'll have a place to crash there, and I've got a friend in Sydney, by Bondi. She's offered us her spare room for the days that we're there.'

'Sounds amazing,' I said. 'I'm a bit envious, I must say.

'Well, if you will leave me in this big city all on my own, I have to make plans to keep myself entertained. So what's new in your world?' Carly asked.

'My mum's in love.'

'Really?'

'I know. And there you were thinking you might have missed the boat at twenty-nine.'

'How do you feel about it?'

'It's strange. But OK, I guess. Anyway, talking about my family, Mirabel's coming to stay in a couple of weeks.'

'Mirabel the mentalist,' Carly said, laughing. 'How are you going to keep her entertained for a whole week?'

'She'll be OK,' I said. 'She's going to help us out with the house.'

'Mirabel? The same Mirabel who came to stay with you last summer?'

'She's sixteen now. I'm sure she'll be a bit more mature this time.'

'If you say so,' Carly said sceptically. 'Have you forgotten about her shoplifting excursion last year?'

'I think that was a one-off,' I said, recalling the incident at Claire's Accessories vividly. Thank God the police had let her off with a caution. 'Or if not, I'm sure she's over that stuff by now.'

'Good luck,' Carly said. 'I think you might need it.'

'God, don't say that. There have been enough unexpected things to deal with in the cottage.'

'How are things there?'

'Fine,' I said.

'Fine, really fine – or pretend fine?'

'Really fine,' I said, my head feeling foggy. 'Or perhaps not entirely. I don't know, Carly.'

'What is it?'

'Jack and I aren't getting on that well. It's little things, but they've all been building up – the house, my family, money . . .'

'I thought you were OK for money for the renovations?'

'So did I . . . but I think I've probably been splashing out a bit more than I should have. But I want to make this place perfect, and I thought he did too. I can't remember the last time we had any fun together, Carls.'

'Doing up a house does put a lot of strain on you.'

'I know, and I was prepared for that. I thought we were strong, but I feel it's been a while since we brought out the best in each other. I mean, you saw how it was between us the other night.'

'It did seem like you might have a few things to discuss.'

'But we're not. We're barely talking about the things that really matter.'

There was something else, of course. Something that was getting to be too big to ignore. Something I couldn't admit to Carly, and that I'd barely started to admit to myself. When I fell asleep at night, it wasn't always Jack I thought about.

'You'll work it out,' Carly said, her voice lifting a fraction, becoming more upbeat. 'You have to. You're Amelia and Jack – you're meant to be together.'

Meant to be together. That was what I'd always assumed too.

A week later Jack opened the door to the bathroom fitters, who were delivering the bath and basin. He stood back as they went upstairs to the room. We'd spent the previous day preparing the floorboards so that everything was ready.

'I'm sure you'll feel differently when they're all plumbed in,' I said, standing with him in the hallway.

'Maybe I will. But it's not the bath, Amelia. You know that.'

I heard the bathroom fitters knock into something, and had a sudden urge to go up and see what was going on. After what had happened with the kitchen, I didn't want to take any chances.

'I know, it's the money,' I said. 'But we can work to a budget on the other rooms. The kitchen and bathroom were always going to be the big expense.'

Jack's gaze drifted towards the floor, then he looked at me again. 'Do you really still believe that's what's going on?' he said.

I looked at him, trying to find the words to answer.

'It's not just about the cottage.'

'Then what is it?'

'I just feel we're not on the same page at the moment,' Jack said. 'About anything.'

'We talk.'

'Yes. But we're not really communicating with each other – about the house, about money, about what we really want from life.'

'I've told you where I stand.'

'Yes – and that's exactly how it felt, Amelia. You've made your decision, and that's that. End of story.'

His eyes were unusually stern.

'It's not like that,' I said. 'But can't we just live in the moment for a while, like we said? Until we have the cottage finished, at least.' I reached out to put my hand on his, but he didn't respond.

'Until we have the cottage finished . . . I don't know.' He shook his head. 'It feels as though we're building a house, but not a home.'

I heard something clatter upstairs, and I moved to go up. Jack put a hand on my shoulder. 'Amelia. Are you even listening to me?'

'Yes, I am. It's just . . . You remember what happened last time with the leak.'

'I couldn't care less about that right now,' Jack said. 'I'm trying to tell you I'm not happy. And I can't see myself being happy if things carry on the way they are.'

A lump formed in my throat. Somewhere, deep down, his words resonated, chiming with my own feelings. I might have been able to hide from those, but I couldn't ignore Jack's words.

'I want us to want the same things, but I don't know if we do any more,' Jack said.

'We do,' I said feebly. It pained me not to be able to say it with more certainty, not to know the right answer.

There was silence between us for a moment.

'I think we need a break,' Jack said.

'A break?' I asked, my voice faint.

'Yes, from each other. Amelia, I'm going to move out for a while.'

PART THREE

Winter

Chapter 14

The Spare Bedroom – Starting

Before: Dark room with dirty windows. Striped wallpaper. Green carpet with worn patches. Heavy velvet drapes in red.

Monday, 21 October

From: Amelia@gmail.com
To: Jack@nextgenerationanimations.com

Hi, Jack:

I don't really understand what just happened, or what's happening to us. I know you said you needed space to think, but did you really have to leave the cottage? Can't we talk?

Amelia x

From: Jack@nextgenerationanimations.com

To: Amelia@gmail.com

Hi, Amelia.

I can't help thinking your mind – part of you – has been somewhere else lately. I don't know where it is, but it's not in bed with me at night. That closeness . . . I don't know, I feel as if the woman I fell in love with has disappeared.

I thought we could get past anything. After all these years together. But maybe we can't. We've both admitted that having a baby isn't something we can meet in the middle on and I've realized that matters to me more than I thought.

I'm staying in London with Hiro for a while. I can't see another way – it didn't feel we were being honest with each other. Maybe with some time and distance we can start to be.

Jack

Saturday, 26 October

The oak in the back garden had lost its leaves completely, as had the apple tree. The spindly branches wove up into a white winter sky. I'd scraped frost off the windscreen of our car when I went to pick Mirabel up from Gatwick that morning.

'God, if Dad had told me you were all the way out here, I'd never have agreed to come,' Mirabel said, swiftly dumping her things on the floor of the spare bedroom and checking her hair in the mirror. Black out of a bottle, it fell past her shoulders in shiny waves. Her eyes, grass-green and piercing, were hooded by shadow-heavy lids.

A week on from Jack leaving, my ears were still ringing from the shock. I felt numb. I'd sat with him that Sunday in the bedroom, watched him pack his bags with clothes and essentials, neither of us saying a word. I'd wanted to tell him to stop, that there was a way round this, that we could fix things. But I hadn't said a word. Instead I'd walked with him to the front door, and watched him leave.

Mirabel had shown her displeasure that we weren't heading towards London this time during the car ride.

'This is where we live now, simple as that,' I said firmly.

'It's in the middle of nowhere. And this room is a dump.'

'That's exactly what you're going to be helping with.'

She didn't seem to hear me, or at least didn't register what I was saying. She pulled back the curtains and caught sight of Spencer and Callum out on the patio having a tea break.

'Ooh, but perhaps things are looking up. Who are they?' She let out a quiet wolf whistle.

'Their names are Spencer and Callum. They're helping us out with some of the work.'

'They definitely look like the most interesting thing to do around here.'

'To "do"? Did you really just say that?'

Mirabel tilted her head and shrugged.

'I thought you had a boyfriend, anyway?'

'Is that what Dad told you?' She threw me a cutting look. 'Argh, drives me crazy when he talks about me behind my back. I'm not with anyone, OK? Jesse and I broke up. Mum and Dad don't know – I couldn't deal with them being smug about it. I knew how badly they wanted me to dump him.'

'Sorry things didn't work out.'

'I'm not,' Mirabel replied flippantly. 'I was getting bored with him anyway. I'm too young to be tied down.'

'Fair enough. Sounds like perhaps it was a good time for a trip like this.'

'I thought it would be fun to visit you. But that was when I thought we'd be going out on the town together like last time, with Jack and his friends. Not stuck in a rural backwater. Where is he, anyway?'

'Jack's away. He's staying in London for a few days with a friend.'

'Great. So it's going to be even more boring around here. Did you two fall out?'

I flinched, unsettled by the way she'd seen right through me. 'No,' I lied. 'He just has a lot on at work. Anyway, your stay is going to be a bit different this time. Did Dad tell you what you'd be doing while you were over here?'

'What do you mean, doing? I'm here for a break, to have

a holiday. I brought some stuff with me to chill out with.'
She unpacked some things from her bag – an iPad, magazines and a copy of a *Fifty Shades of Grey* knock-off. I averted
my eyes from the handcuffs on the front cover. Christ, I
thought. She's only sixteen.

'You're not here to chill out, no. I need some help with
doing up the cottage.'

'You are kidding,' Mirabel said, her finely arched and
pencilled eyebrows rising.

'Nope, I'm definitely not.'

'Me? What a nightmare.' Mirabel sighed.

'Hardly,' I said. 'A bit of painting, that's all. I'll show you
what I mean.'

'I bought this nautical print wallpaper for the two side
walls of the spare bedroom,' I said, unrolling part of it to
reveal a blue anchor print on a white background. 'What
do you think?'

'Cute,' she said. 'And you'll have the other two walls,
what, painted white?'

'Yes, that was what I was thinking,' I said, running my
fingers over the tired red-and-green striped wallpaper that
had bubbled in places. 'I've got some fabric to run up pale
blue curtains, and then I'd like to set up a little table in the
corner, so that when people aren't staying I can have my
sewing machine in here.'

'You still into that stuff?'

'You could say that.' I smiled. 'I think it's got worse with age, actually. I'm going to make a few cushion covers too. So, do you think you could help with the painting and wallpapering?'

'Sure.' Mirabel shrugged. 'It should be easy enough. But I'm not starting today – it's the weekend,' she said stubbornly.

'That's fine. Today we can have a wander into the village and then tomorrow we'll start work.'

'The village,' she said. 'Wow. That sounds unmissable. I can't believe Mum and Dad didn't say a word to me about the manual labour they've contracted me out for.'

'Dad was happy enough to agree to it, so take it up with him if you want.'

'Maybe I will,' she said. 'And if I really do only have one day of rest, I'm going to get on with enjoying it. You don't mind if I go and get to know the guys downstairs, do you?'

In the afternoon I took Mirabel into the village to show her around. We crossed the village green in the direction of the high street. A brass band was playing on the bandstand, the notes ringing out in the crisp, cool air, and a small crowd had gathered next to it. Brown and yellow leaves lay across the path, and the flowers that had bloomed so brightly in the summer had all but gone now. I was grateful for my thick woollen scarf.

'There aren't many shops, are there?' Mirabel said, eyeing the newsagent and post office.

'Good thing,' I said, 'because I doubt you've got much money to spend in them. But you're very lucky that you've got a big sister who's going to treat you to some cake.'

I led her past the flower shop and into Sally's. It was warm, and a welcome escape from the chill in the air outside.

'Hi, Amelia,' Sally said with a smile. 'Come in and get warmed up, you two. Good to see you again. Pot of Earl Grey, is it?'

'Yes, thanks,' I said. 'What do you fancy eating, Mirabel? This is my sister, by the way. Mirabel, this is Sally – she's a cake-making genius.'

'Hi, Sally,' Mirabel said, taking off her duffel coat and putting it on the back of her wooden chair. 'Nothing for me, thanks – I'm on a diet.' She shrugged her slim shoulders.

A couple of older ladies in the cafe swung round in their seats, aghast. Sally looked at Mirabel as if she'd just let loose the foulest of swear words.

'Not in here you're not,' she said firmly. 'That word doesn't exist between these four walls. What will you have?'

A tiny smile spread from the corners of Mirabel's full lips. 'A Bakewell tart it is then.'

Mirabel and I drank our tea at a table near the door.

Sally brought over the treats. Out of the window I saw an elderly woman in a navy coat and white woollen hat walking past, holding on to the arm of a man in his twenties. Her green eyes gazed straight ahead. Her face, fine-featured, and her white hair in a pleat were familiar – it was Mrs McGuire. Eleanor.

When I'd first seen her in the window of Brambledown Cottage she'd had that same expression on her face, as if she was only partly present. I thought of the bonnet and photos I'd seen, then tidied back into the tin and put away.

'Why are you staring at that old lady?' Mirabel said.

'She used to live in our cottage. She's Callum's grandmother.'

'Do you know her?'

'No,' I said, thinking of the things of hers that I had in my possession and should give back. I shook my head. 'No, not at all.'

Mirabel was tucking into the Bakewell tart hungrily.

'You know you don't need to be on a diet, don't you?' I said.

She tilted her head and shook it. 'I do. I feel fat. Jesse used to say it to me sometimes.'

'Charming. You're best rid of him then. Feeling fat doesn't mean that you are. If anything, you could do with putting on a bit of weight.'

Sally walked back across the cafe and pulled up a chair

with us. 'How long are you staying, Mirabel?' she asked.

'A week. My sister here's trying to rope me into some manual labour in the cottage.'

'A bit of light painting and decorating,' I corrected her.

'Ah, the grand cottage makeover.' Sally smiled. 'Well if you get a spare moment, you should pop over to my parents' farm – they've got horses and alpacas. They love having visitors.'

'That sounds OK,' Mirabel said. 'I quite like horses.'

I met Sally's eyes and smiled appreciatively.

'We'd like that.'

When we got back to the house that afternoon, I bumped into Spencer standing in the hallway. It was usually Callum I chatted to, and now it was almost as if I was seeing Spencer for the first time. I noticed his slightly lopsided smile.

'Hi,' I said. 'Everything going OK?'

'Yes,' he said quickly. 'We've nearly finished the dining room flooring now, and we've got the living room ready for when you're ready to begin staining.'

'Great. We'll need to change the window frames first, but once that work is out of the way we'll get to it. Should be really cosy. Thanks for all your help, I'm so grateful that you to have been able to stay on.'

'It's nothing,' Spencer said. 'We've enjoyed it.'

He hovered awkwardly in the doorway, not saying

anything, just shifting from one trainer-clad foot to the other.

'Anything else you wanted to talk to me about?' I ventured.

'There is, actually.' His bright blue eyes met mine.

'Go ahead then.'

'It's about your sister.'

'Mirabel? Sure. What about her?'

'There's a band playing in the village tonight, and with no friends here I thought she might enjoy it.'

'OK, sure. Fine with me, if she wants to,' I said. 'It would be good for her to see a bit of village life while she's here.'

'Great,' Spencer said, his whole posture lifting and straightening.

'I'll give her a shout.'

I found Mirabel in her room stretched out on the bed reading a magazine, dressed in jeans and one of my favourite tops, a bright red one with black trim. Her hair hung in damp strands, leaving a patch of darkness on the sheets and on the shoulders of my top

'Are you coming to tell me the Wi-Fi's back up again?' she asked, hopeful.

'Sorry, not yet. Don't know what's up with it today. But if you're bored, I've got some good news. Spencer's just asked me if you want to go out this evening – there's a gig in town. He's downstairs now. I said it was fine with me.'

'Spencer,' she said, looking slightly interested. 'The fit one?'

'Depends what you mean,' I said, feeling awkward. 'He's the younger one, lighter hair.'

'Not the fit one,' Mirabel said, turning back through her magazine and flicking through it.

'Don't be harsh,' I said. 'He's a perfectly nice guy. It's not like he's asking for your hand in marriage.'

'OK, I'll talk to him.' She got to her feet, taller than me now. I noticed she wasn't wearing a bra under the top she'd borrowed without asking. Better to choose my battles, though.

A few moments later I could hear Mirabel's laughter drifting up the stairwell, and the buzz of chatter coming from the kitchen.

'I said yes,' Mirabel said, putting her head round my bedroom door. 'We're going out in half an hour. I can wear this, right?' she said, pointing to the top.

'OK. But check with me next time, would you?'

'Fine.' She pouted, and turned to leave the room.

'Mirabel.'

She turned back to look at me.

'Maybe don't mention this to Dad and Caitlin. I don't want them to think I'm letting you run wild.'

'Do you really think I tell Dad anything about my life?' Mirabel said dismissively. 'He wouldn't let me do anything if I did.'

I would have liked it if Dad had cared what I was up to when I was a teenager. It wasn't that I'd kept anything from him, but I'd only seen him a few times a year, when he came over to England, usually with Caitlin, once she was on the scene.

'You couldn't lend me twenty quid, could you?' Mirabel said. 'Just in case I have to get a cab at the end of the night.'

'OK,' I said, getting a crisp note out of my wallet. 'Be back by midnight, OK?'

'I feel like Cinders,' Mirabel said, taking the money with a cheeky grin. 'Thanks.'

At that moment I saw my father in my little sister. The charm that I couldn't stand up against.

'You'll be good, won't you?'

'Are you sure you won't join us?' Spencer said, downstairs in the hallway that evening. 'Callum's coming along for a drink too.' Mirabel was standing beside him, putting her black fake-fur-trimmed coat on.

'You should come along, Amelia,' Callum said, his voice warm and husky. He was dressed in his work jeans and a long-sleeved navy top. 'It'll be fun. They're a great band.'

His grey-green eyes rested on mine, and I felt my cheeks grow hot. I could go out. There was no reason not to.

'Oh, she won't,' Mirabel said. 'I can tell she's moping around at the moment, with Jack away.'

And there, in an instant, the moment passed.

'You have a good time. Mirabel's right: I feel like a night in tonight.'

'OK,' Callum said. 'Have a good evening.'

'Thanks. Midnight, remember!' I called out after Mirabel, as she disappeared into the darkness.

I closed the door after the three of them and stood for a moment, facing the empty hall. I went to the downstairs toilet, then washed my hands and looked at myself in the mirror. I looked tired and felt old.

What would Jack be doing right now? Was he with friends, or alone somewhere, like me? Was he distracting himself, ignoring the divide that was growing between us, or thinking how we might bridge it? I wondered about the woman he worked with: Sadie, with her fresh graduate eagerness, sleek bob and trendy trainers. Was I the only one wondering if there could be another life out there for me?

By the side of the basin, I saw the locket I'd found in the drain and had meant to give to Callum to return to his grandmother. I opened it again and looked inside: a hand-some man with dark hair and brooding dark eyes. Her husband? I thought back to the wedding photo up in the attic: the bride, Eleanor, next to her groom, fair-haired and wearing glasses.

The man in the locket was someone different altogether.

Chapter 15

The Spare Bedroom – Finishing

On the Mood Board

Nautical theme, white cushions with anchor print, fluffy white rug. Driftwood picture frames. Navy and white pouffe. Swatches – colours of sand, watery shallows and stormy grey seas.

Sunday, 27 October

Mirabel appeared in the kitchen doorway, fresh from her bath, her make-up smudged.

'Good night?' I was pretty sure I'd heard the door go at one or two in the morning, after the curfew I'd set her, but I didn't feel like having an argument. 'You've got panda eyes, by the way.'

'It was, actually,' she said, rubbing at the make-up under

her eyes. 'Considering we're in the arse-end of nowhere, I mean.'

I rolled my eyes. 'Let's get some breakfast. I've been up for hours and my stomach's starting to rumble. You got on well with Spencer?' I asked. I hoped she had at least been kind to him.

'I got on better with Callum. But then I already knew that would happen.'

I tried not to feel anything, but a smidgen of jealousy wrestled its way into my consciousness.

'The gig was OK – a bit lame really,' Mirabel continued. 'Then I went on to a club.'

'There's a club in the village?'

'There are clubs everywhere, if you know where to look.'

She slouched down in a wooden chair and unwrapped her hair from a towel turban, letting it fall loose around her shoulders. 'What's for breakfast?'

'Whatever you're making. There's bread and cereal on the worktop. Coffee's just brewed. I'd love a cup, thanks.'

She went over to the side to get a mug, dragging her slipper-clad heels.

My phone rang, and I picked it up from the kitchen table. Mum. Mirabel spotted the name on the display and for a moment looked nervous.

'Hi, Mum.'

'Hello, love. I don't want to interfere, but has Mirabel told you anything about last night?'

'What about last night?'

'About what she was doing.'

'Doing? Yes, a bit. She's just surfaced. Mine's milk, no sugar, Mira.' Mirabel pushed the plunger in the cafetière and poured out two cups.

'I expect she will have needed a lie-in.'

'What are you on about?'

'I just had the neighbours round, telling me about a teenage girl causing a disturbance in town. Something about her running around with some local boys, drinking out on the village green and then scrawling graffiti on the railway bridge. I didn't want to believe it was Mirabel, but from the description – well, it has to be.'

'Oh God,' I said. I looked at Mirabel again – her pale skin – yep, she was definitely hungover. 'You're certain?'

'I can only tell you what I heard. And I don't want this to sound like I'm judging your sister – I know she can be a lovely girl, but she's your responsibility for the time being and I thought you should know. I'm afraid people are gossiping – and of course I've done my best to put them straight – but, love, this seems to be rubbing off a bit on you, too.'

'OK, Mum. Look, don't worry. Leave it with me – I'll sort it out.'

I put the phone down and looked at Mirabel, whose eyes flicked up this time and caught me watching.

'What?' she said, widening her eyes confrontationally.

I sat down at the table with her. 'That was my mum. Apparently there are a few stories flying around town about what you got up to last night. Do you want to put me straight?'

'Oh, for God's sake,' Mirabel huffed. 'So Rosie's called up, trying to get me into trouble? I thought she was all right, your mum.'

'She's looking out for me and Jack, that's all,' I said. 'Mirabel – what happened last night?'

'Not much,' she said. 'We saw the band, I met a few people, then I came home, just like I told you. I'm sixteen, Amelia. I'm not your kid sister any more. You can trust me.'

'I hope that's true but from what Mum said, I'm really wondering.'

My phone buzzed with a text. Spencer.

Hi, A. I hope Mirabel got home OK. Tried to make her get a cab home, but she insisted on staying out. There was no persuading her, I'm afraid. Really sorry. Spence

Mirabel hadn't just disregarded my rules, she'd ignored Spencer and Callum's attempts to get her home safely too.

'I knew I shouldn't have let you out. Who were the guys you stayed out with?'

'Just . . . No one, OK? Look, I don't have to stay here, you know,' Mirabel snapped.

'Fine,' I said, my patience running out. 'Mirabel – you're free to go. There's the door.' I pointed to it. 'Good luck getting to the airport and paying for a new flight.'

'Come on,' she said. 'This isn't fair.'

'While you're here, you'll live by my rules. And that means no getting drunk, and it also means pulling your weight. I want to see the spare bedroom painted – today.'

'This is worse than being at home.'

'I don't care. Do you want me to call Dad and your mum right now and tell them what's going on?'

'No,' she said, an expression of genuine panic on her face. 'Please don't do that.'

'You know what, Mirabel, you're getting off lightly here. You'll be lucky if no one goes to the police about what happened, and I guess they still might. You may as well do something positive for once. I'll show you what I want you to do, and then I don't want to hear from you again until that room's finished.'

As Mirabel got on with her work in the spare room, I resisted the temptation to look in on her. Instead, I sat down at my sewing table with the pale blue fabric I'd ordered online for the spare-room curtains. Seeing Eleanor McGuire in town the day before had reminded me of something.

I got out the scrapbook I'd found in the attic and took another look through it, using her patterns as inspiration. As I worked, the comforting hum of the sewing machine silencing the thoughts I wanted to forget, I imagined how she must have done the same thing once, perhaps in the very same room. Maybe with Sarah, the girl in the photo.

When the curtains were finished, I started on cushion covers. I'd picked up some cheap cushions at one of the charity shops in town – they were new enough but the patterns were dowdy. I unfolded the nautical-print fabric I'd bought and cut it into squares. I used the remnants of the fabric to make decorative lavender bags in heart shapes. I could use the lavender I'd collected from the garden when we moved in. I made some for the house, and then one each for Suni, Carly and Mum.

'It's done,' Mirabel bellowed out, entering the room, paintbrush in hand.

'The room?'

'Like I said. It's done. I've finished.'

'Really?'

'Come and have a look if you don't believe me.'

I followed her out, wondering what I might find when I got to the spare bedroom. Spilled paint maybe, wallpaper pasted to the wall with huge bubbles underneath. While I'd carefully talked her through how to do the wallpaper, I wasn't at all confident that she'd been listening. Perhaps sending Mirabel to do this when she was still so angry with me had been a bad idea.

'Look,' she said, motioning into the room with the brush.

I peeked in. The front and back walls were rollered a pristine white, with not a drip in sight, and the side ones were transformed from the tired stripy wallpaper that had been up there and were now covered in smart nautical print, white anchors on a blue background.

'Wow,' I said, stepping forward to get a better look. 'This isn't bad.'

Mirabel shrugged, as if it were nothing. 'It wasn't hard,' she said. 'I guess you thought I'd mess this up too.'

'I'll be honest, I'm impressed.'

'I did up my room and Mum's study at home, so I knew what I was doing.'

'I appreciate you doing it,' I said. 'Get yourself washed up and I'll put the kettle on.'

Downstairs, Mirabel pulled out a seat and watched me as I got our tea ready. 'Does this mean I'm off the hook?' she said.

I mulled it over for a minute. While I'd been pleasantly surprised that she'd finished the room, she'd only done the minimum I'd expected of her. She wasn't even part-way towards making up for her bad behaviour the previous night.

'Not yet,' I said, putting our mugs on the table with some biscuits. 'I've got something else in mind for you this coming week.'

'Tell me it's something that involves me not being cooped up here in this stupid cottage,' she said, flicking her hair over her shoulder.'

'Yes,' I said. 'That's exactly what it is.'

'That's something.'

I smiled to myself. A phone call or two tomorrow ought to do it.

'And if you're feeling that cooped up, how about dinner out tonight?'

'How come?'

'Why not? You're my sister and I barely get to see you. Plus, you've worked hard today. Do I need another reason?'

She looked at me, and a smile crept on to her lips. 'All right.'

I drove into town with Mirabel, parking up on a side street. We walked together to a small Italian restaurant my mum had mentioned to me.

About twenty minutes after we'd arrived, the waiter brought us our orders – 'Here you go, *signorinas*,' he said with a wink. 'Carbonara for you,' he said, passing the plate to Mirabel, 'and crab linguine for you. Excellent choices.'

'Thanks,' we both said.

I looked across at Mirabel. 'It's actually kind of fun having you around, you know.'

'Really? I got the impression you only agreed to it because Dad pushed you into it.'

'It wasn't like that . . .' I said. 'OK, a bit – only because of the timing, but you're always welcome here.'

'It's been good to get away. Mum and Dad have been driving me mad lately. I know they want me to get a job, or some work experience or something, but I don't know what I want to do with my life yet.' She took a forkful of pasta, but hesitated before putting it in her mouth. 'Was Dad strict with you when you were a teenager?'

'No, not really,' I said. 'I didn't see him that much back then. He and Mum had only just separated, so they were giving each other a bit of space. Mum was travelling a lot, and Grandma Niki didn't really know what I got up to. When I did chat to him, he was always quite laid-back – he certainly didn't lay down any laws. He'd just met your mum; he was starting a new life, I guess.'

'That must have been weird,' Mirabel said. 'It's not as though I like him being on my back all the time, but if he wasn't there – well, that would be worse, I think.'

'There were times when I would have liked to talk to him more.'

'I suppose he was busy with my mum, setting up home

and stuff,' Mirabel said flippantly, taking another a forkful of pasta.

'I guess so. He deserved a new start anyway, after the way Mum pushed him out.'

'What do you mean?'

'I get the sense he didn't have any choice but to go. Back then, Mum was putting herself first.'

'What gave you that idea?' Mirabel said.

'I heard them, the night Dad left. It didn't sound as if it was his choice to leave – or if it was, it was something Mum had driven him to. She wanted to be an air hostess even though she knew it was likely to put a strain on the family.'

Mirabel raised her eyebrows. 'That's not how my mum tells it.'

'She's probably just being nice,' I said. I called the waiter over and ordered a glass of red wine and a top-up of lemonade for Mirabel.

We ate in silence for a while, until Mirabel spoke up, 'Mum said she feels awful about the way Dad left your mum. She never thought he'd really go through with it – leave her with you still quite young.'

'Oh, she's got that wrong,' I said. 'That's not why Dad left. He didn't meet Caitlin until about a year later.'

'Is that what he told you?' Mirabel said, her voice unusually soft.

I put down my fork. My chest felt tight. 'He wouldn't lie to me.'

'OK, then.'

Would he? There was the loan, still unpaid; the visit to the UK he'd been promising to make for the past few years; the celebratory graduation dinner that, eight years on, I was still waiting for. I'd never thought of them as lies before – just slight bending of the truth that kept the cogs of our relationship moving smoothly.

'There was probably fault on both sides,' I said. 'I can't see how Mum is blameless in all this . . .'

'Maybe it doesn't matter; they've both moved on now. Callum told me about her and his dad.'

'Oh yes. That,' I said. I still hadn't quite got my head round the idea of my mum being in love.

'I really don't see the problem,' Mirabel said, shrugging. 'Dad's always saying she deserves to find someone else, someone who can treat her better than he did.'

The story I had always believed about my family life and my parents' break-up butted up awkwardly against what Mirabel had told me. My sister was only sixteen. How could she possibly know more about my family than I did?

'Did he really say that?'

'Yes,' Mirabel said, nodding. 'He said he couldn't help falling in love with Mum, but he wishes he could have done it without making such a mess of things.'

The words sank in, and my chest began to tighten. Had I really got it wrong all this time?

I was distracted by the chatter of two women at a table about five feet away from us. I recognized them from the village bake sale I'd gone to with Mum.

'That's her,' I heard one of them say. 'Not much of a role model, the sister, is she?' They didn't seem to be making any effort at all to lower their voices.

I felt a rush of heat come to my cheeks.

'You're not going to let those idiots bother you, are you?' Mirabel said, noting my discomfort.

'No. Of course not. We've got nothing to feel bad about.'

'I heard she was running riot in the streets. About three in the morning it was.' The words echoed out in the restaurant, which had fallen quiet. 'Not the sort of thing you'd see from the locals. It's Rosie I'm embarrassed for really. It's her reputation that's taken the knock.'

'Oh God, what a pair of idiots,' Mirabel said, laughing.

'They are, aren't they?' I said, glancing over at the other table. Now I looked more closely, they were just two bored women in their sixties, who clearly had nothing better to talk about.

'Nothing like being a local celebrity,' Mirabel called out boldly. She alerted the attention of most of the people in the restaurant, and all eyes were now on her. 'And I'm fine

with that. Yes, I did go out and get pissed, and yes, I probably should have behaved a bit better.'

I bit my lip as Mirabel continued, trying to gauge if and
when I should step in and say something. She turned and
gave me a nod. 'Relax,' she mouthed silently.

'But don't drag my sister or her mum into this. They've
got nothing at all to feel bad about. As it happens, they are
two brilliant women you'd be lucky to have as your friends
– not that you'll get that chance any more.'

I felt a swell of pride for my little sister. The two women
muttered something to each other, and then picked up
their handbags to leave without saying a word in reply.
Mirabel and I looked at each other and burst into laughter.
I covered her small hand with mine, and gave it a squeeze
in thanks.

'Bravo!' came a male voice from the corner. I looked up
to see Sally and her husband having dinner, and Sally gave
me a little wave. I hadn't seen them when we came in. Her
husband called over. 'Had that coming to them for a long
time, those two.'

On Monday morning Mirabel and I set out early in the car,
and drove down to a flea market on the Kent coast.

With takeaway coffees in hand, we joined the shop owners
and traders browsing the stalls and car boots, picking out
bargains – I chose a 1920s desk lamp and a Persian rug, and

Mirabel picked out a flowered set of crockery and some sparkly costume jewellery for herself.

When we'd reached our budget, we packed everything away in the car and stopped for lunch at a cafe overlooking the sea. We ate our bacon and egg sandwiches looking out at the sunlit waves crashing onto the shore. After lunch I bought us both ice creams and we strolled along the beach, collecting seashells and pebbles.

'This'll look good on the side table,' Mirabel said, picking up a piece of driftwood from where it lay half-hidden on the sand.

'It's perfect. Let's take it.'

'It's nice to get out here, get some fresh air, isn't it?'

'Really nice, I said, pushing back a few strands of my hair, damp with the sea air, that had blown in my face.'

'Are you missing him a lot?' Mirabel asked, her green eyes fixed on me.

'Jack?'

She nodded.

'Yes. But sometimes even people who care about each other need some time apart.'

When we got back to the house, we arranged our finds in the newly decorated spare room.

'Well, I think we're almost done,' I said to Mirabel, hanging a picture on the white wall.

Mirabel's eyes moved across the room and a smile spread over her face. She looked from the pictures on the wall – seaside scenes, beach huts and piers – to the blue and white cushions I'd sewn strewn on top of the new pale blue bedspread. The cushions had a small boat print on them, and matched the curtains I'd hung up at the window.

Two of the blue glass bottles I'd picked up at the antique shop in town were on the sill, with a Japanese anemone in each. A desk, with distressed white paint, was in the corner, with Mirabel's driftwood find next to my sewing machine. A basket full of fabrics sat just underneath.

'So, would you be happy to stay in here tonight, do you think?'

Mirabel smiled at me, her eyes bright. 'I suppose so. It'll do.'

Chapter 16

The Hallway

On the Mood Board

White walls, bright and airy entrance to the house, large mirror facing door to enhance feeling of space, framed prints on walls. Classic books on a small shelf. Large vase filled with cornflowers

Tuesday, 29 October

I sat down in the kitchen and had breakfast, the conversation I'd had with Mirabel about Mum and Dad running through my head. I'd assumed at first that what she'd told me couldn't be true – but as I thought about it, the pieces fell into place. I'd never before questioned what Dad told me, but if he'd really left me and Mum, let us both down, then he had reason enough to lie to me. After all these years, and me supposedly an adult, I'd been punishing my mum. When she told me she was in love I'd still, somehow, thought she didn't deserve that happiness. Hurt can make you blind to the truth, I suppose. But things were starting to look clearer now.

I picked up my mobile and called her.

'Hi, Amelia. How are things?'

'Good, thanks.'

'Is your sister OK?'

'Mirabel's fine, yes. She's not up yet, but I'm going to drop her in Canterbury later – she wants to go shopping.'

'There's plenty to keep her busy there. You could take her to—'

'Listen, Mum,' I interrupted her. There was one way I could start to put things right again between us. 'I was actually calling about something else.'

'Oh yes?'

'I was hoping I might be able to meet him.'

'Who, love?'

'David. The man who's put the smile back on your face. What do you say?'

'I think that could be arranged,' she said, and I could hear the bubble of excitement in her voice.

On the way to Mum's house I dropped in at a shop in the next village – the Better Hearth. I'd seen a fireplace in the window and once inside the shop I saw that it was even more stunning up close – it would look perfect in the dining room. Then I looked at the price. It would put us into the red for sure. *Perhaps* – then I stopped myself. I remembered Jack – what he'd said before was right. We didn't have the money. We could work with the fireplace that was already there.

I drove on and pulled up outside Mum's house. As I waited for her to answer the doorbell, I straightened my skirt. She smiled as she greeted me. In the hall behind her was a man, average height, with wire-framed glasses and a full head of grey hair. He smiled at me cautiously as I stepped inside.

'This is David,' Mum said, pointing to him. 'David, this is Amelia.'

'Your mother's told me a lot about you,' he said, shaking my hand. 'It's nice to finally meet.'

Here he was – Mum's lover, Callum's dad, and the most ordinary-looking man I'd ever seen.

'You too,' I said, hanging up my coat.

'Well, I'll put the kettle on,' Mum said, scurrying off to the kitchen and leaving David and me standing in the hallway.

'This is strange,' I said. 'Me living in your mother's house, and you and Mum going out together.'

'Oh, you get used to coincidences here in Hazelton,' he said with a smile. 'It might not look that small at first, but believe me, it really is.'

'Shall we sit down?' I said, leading the way through to the living room. 'Callum told me your mum's finally settled in the new house. Is that right?

'Yes. As settled as she can be,' David said, with a weary shrug of his shoulders.

'I'm sorry. It must be hard.'

'This is going to sound unkind,' David said, 'and we've only just met, but there's something to be said for people going quickly. Watching one of the people you love most in the world fade away is a akin to heartbreak.'

'I can imagine. From what Callum's told me, it sounds like she was a wonderful mother and grandmother. Is, I mean,' I corrected myself awkwardly.

'That part of her is still there. We catch glimpses of it now and then, when something triggers her memory.'

'Did Callum show you the things we found in the attic? He thought they might be useful for that.'

'He did, and I have most of them at home with me now. Thank you for that. Fragments of the past can really help to bring back the woman we all love,' David said with a smile. 'The attic – I used to be terrified of going up there when we were kids. Not that I was afraid of a few spiders, mind you – it was just always too dark to see. Even if you took a torch there were more dark corners than you could light up.'

'One of my more adventurous moments. There are squirrels up there too – I've caught one already. Callum recommended a few things and they seem to have worked.'

'I'm still embarrassed the cottage was left in such a mess for you.'

'Oh, don't worry about it,' I said, waving away his concern. 'It seems like a long time ago really – we've created plenty of our own chaos since then.'

My mum came in with a tray of tea and cake. 'Tea's up,' she said. 'So, what have I missed?'

'We were just talking about how strange it is, the cottage going from David's family to ours.'

'At least you know it's in safe hands now,' Mum said, touching David's arm gently. 'Well, I'm assuming that.' She looked at me questioningly. 'That's if Mirabel hasn't done any damage?'

'Believe it or not, she's actually made some home improvements,' I said. 'My wayward teenage half-sister,' I explained, turning to David. 'Dad sent her over here to straighten her out a bit and give him and my stepmum a proper break.'

'A handful, is she?' David asked, the warmth in his expression showing that he'd had experience and come out the other side.

'You could say that,' I replied. 'But actually Mirabel's been working hard to make up for it. She's decorated the spare bedroom.'

'Well, I am impressed,' Mum said.

'I was too. She's done a terrific job, actually. It's now a lovely, relaxing haven that guests won't want to leave. Which was always the plan, although given this week . . .'

'Are you thinking you don't want it to be *too* inviting now?' She laughed warmly.

'I'm not sure how long I can keep her under control.'

'It's a tricky age, isn't it? Sixteen.'

'I guess so,' I said. 'Although I don't remember rebelling that much.'

'I think your memory's a little selective there,' Mum said tenderly. 'Anyway, what have you got planned for her this week? Another room to paint?'

'No,' I said. 'I've got something different in mind, actually. You know your friend Rachel?'

'Yes. What about her?'

'Could I have her phone number? Sally mentioned that her parents have been struggling to stay on top of the day-to-day running of the farm since she left to start her cake shop. So I was wondering if they might appreciate another pair of hands.'

'You're not suggesting . . . ?' Mum said.

'It'll be good for her, don't you think? Just a couple of

days of getting her hands dirty. I don't think she's even been on a farm before.'

'How are you going to persuade her to go there?'

'I'm not going to give her any choice.'

'Sounds like a great idea,' David said. 'Me and my brother used to love spending time with animals when we were teenagers. Kept us out of trouble.'

'That's what I'm hoping. Did your sister go too?' I asked, thinking of the photo I'd seen.

'My sister?'

'Sarah.'

'I don't have a sister,' David said, shaking his head. 'Just me and Ewan. Poor Mum, I think she would have liked a girl really, but we muddled on OK.'

I tried to think of a way to change the subject. It had been silly of me to make assumptions. 'So, David, do you still work or are you retired now?'

'I'm retired, supposedly. I do like to be busy though, so I'm still doing the odd bit of work at the opticians when they need me.'

'He's a workaholic even now,' Mum joked.

'I'm much better than I was. Rosie was a godsend. A reminder that there's something better out there that's worth finishing work for. I haven't had that, not since Callum and Alice's mother died.'

I thought of the long years that Mum had been single

and felt bad that I'd never encouraged her to find happiness.

'How did you meet?' I asked.

'A mutual friend,' David said with a cheeky smile. I saw his resemblance to Callum then, the sparkle in his eyes. 'Emma who runs the local art class. When we both popped along to see the end-of-term exhibition she introduced us. I think she had an inkling we might get along.'

'She got that one right,' Mum said. She sounded younger, flirtatious almost. It would have bothered me a month ago, but it didn't now.

'I'd seen your mother about a couple of times, as it happens. I would have loved to have had the courage to talk to her then.'

She looked in my direction. 'It gets a bit harder as you get older, working out who's already taken, and you don't want to tread on any toes in a place like Hazelton.'

'You wouldn't hear the end of it,' David said, 'if you chatted up a married man in the newsagent's. You're happily settled, aren't you, Amelia?'

I paused for a moment. 'Jack and I are married, yes.' I thought of the happy memories we had together – the times we had shared as a couple over the years, things we'd supported each other through. I didn't know how things had gone so wrong, so quickly. 'It can take its toll on you as a couple, doing up a house,' I continued. 'The truth is, we're working a few things out at the moment. He's moved in with a friend in London for a while.'

Mum looked concerned. 'I'm sorry to hear that, love.'

'I hope things get better soon,' David said. 'It can't be ups all the time, can it?'

David, like Callum, had a way of making you feel that everything would be OK.

'I'd better be getting on my way,' David said, getting slowly to his feet. 'It's about time I went to Mum's for tea. But it was a real pleasure to meet you, Amelia. And I hope I'll see you again soon.'

'Yes, I'm sure we'll meet again,' I said. I got to my feet and gave him a hug goodbye.

Mum led him out to the front door. When she came back, she sat down next to me.

'David seems really nice,' I said.

'I'm glad you think so. What you see is what you get with him,' Mum said. 'He's very caring, and he looks after me.'

'You deserve that, Mum.'

She looked at me, as if seeing me for the first time.

'You never gave me the whole story about Dad leaving, did you?'

She moved a little, crossing her legs. 'The whole story?'

'Mirabel told me about what happened back then with Caitlin. It wasn't you who broke up our family, was it? It was him.'

A faint flush came onto my mother's chest, just visible at the neck of her white blouse and beneath her silver moonstone pendant.

'Nothing in love is ever straightforward, sweetheart. I'm sure I made mistakes.'

'You never let on that he'd betrayed you – us. Your job was never the problem – him falling in love with someone else was.'

My mum took a deep breath before she spoke. 'In terms of what your father did, well, I thought it was best to let you make up your own mind. Him leaving was to do with our marriage, it had nothing to do with his love for you, so I didn't see the good of dragging you into all that.'

'You kept it from me,' I said. 'The truth. About Caitlin, about him. You never said a word about the way he let us down.'

'I'm sorry.'

'No,' I said, feeling a wave of guilt for misjudging her all this time. 'Don't be sorry. You did the right thing. You could have driven a wedge between me and Dad, but you chose not to. You were strong enough to let me see for myself what kind of man he was. I just feel bad that it's taken me so long.'

Mum gave a nod, and I saw some of the strain lift from her face. 'I suppose so.'

'All these years, I thought it was your fault that I grew

up without a dad and had to live with my grandparents most of the time. I thought you flying around the world was what had destroyed everything for us – you'd put your ambition first.'

'No, love,' Mum said, shaking her head. 'It was never like that. I only took the job because it was the best-paid one I could get. I wanted you to have all the things you needed.'

'I understand that now.' Her eyes met mine, and I put my hand over hers. There was still time to make things right.

When I got back to the cottage from Mum's, the only noise was Callum and Spencer drilling in the living room, putting up the bookshelves I'd asked for. Mirabel must still be in Canterbury, shopping. She hadn't called yet to ask me to pick her up.

Talking to David had brought back thoughts of Jack, of how bad I'd let things get without even acknowledging it. I opened my laptop and started a new email.

Hi, Jack.

How are you doing? It's strange not having you here.

I'm fine. Mirabel is still here. I'm surviving the visit, just about. It's been quite colourful, to say the least. Remember last time when she came to stay and we ended up talking to the police in Claire's Accessories, where she'd nicked some hair bobbles? Rumour has it she's upgraded to underage drinking and graffiti . . . not sure Hazelton knows quite what's hit it. Anyway, she's been helping out with the house, and is going to help out on a farm for a few days.

The cottage is coming along, step by step. We got the permissions through today, for the work in the hallway.

I miss you, Jack.
Amelia x

I sent the email and waited for a moment. Then refreshed the page, as if it would make a reply magically appear, in a moment.

Then I closed my computer.

'Fancy a tea break?' Callum asked, putting his head around the door of the kitchen. 'Spencer's had to head off early today, and I could do with some company.'

'Sure,' I said, putting my sketchbook to one side. Callum flicked the kettle on and got us out a couple of mugs.

'What's that you're working on?' he asked.

'It's a mood board for the living room,' I said. 'Images and ideas for how I want it to look, some of the things I want to buy – like this armchair. But then the other things, like the chestnuts, are more about what I imagine us doing there, the kind of atmosphere we want in the room.'

I was still talking about us, we – Jack and me. Even though he'd barely looked at my plans for the house and, with how things stood now, there weren't any guarantees we'd even be living here together.

He poured out the tea and milk and brought them over. 'Do you mind if I take a look?' he asked, nodding at the sketchbook.

'Of course.' I passed it to him.

Callum looked over the images with interest. 'It's good to see this stuff, so that I have a sense of your overall vision and can keep it in mind when we're working. My grandma was creative like you,' he said, turning the pages. 'Before she got ill, I mean. There was the garden, of course, and she was always making little things for the house, clothes for me and Alice. My granddad loved it about her. He doted on her.'

'Were you close to him, your granddad?'

'In a way. He was a quiet man. He and my grandma didn't always get along, but he was kind. Dad got along better with his mum from what I can work out.'

'I met your dad this morning,' I said. 'He's lovely.'

'So, will he do?' Callum asked with a smile.

'Yes.' I laughed. 'He definitely will. Mum seems really happy. I don't know why I found it so hard to get my head round the idea at first.'

'Oh, I don't know – it took me a few days too, to be honest.' Callum closed the book and moved it aside. 'For so many years our parents are focused on us, and then suddenly they start getting on with their own lives. It shouldn't be allowed really.'

'I think that was it. Perhaps I'm not quite as grown-up as I thought I was. That and the fact I think I'm only just starting to understand what happened between my parents when they broke up.'

'I guess marriage isn't always easy,' Callum said, taking a sip of tea. Then, as if realizing what he'd said, he shook his head. 'Sorry, I mean, what do I know about it?'

'No, you're right.' I thought of Jack, wondered when exactly it was we'd stopped talking to each other properly, honestly. 'It's not easy.'

Later that afternoon, I got a reply to my email.

Hi, Amelia.

It's good to hear from you. I'm glad Mirabel is keeping you entertained at the cottage, even if she is wreaking havoc on the village.

Things are fine here. I'm crashing on Hiro's sofa. It isn't the comfiest, but it's five minutes from the office so I have a pretty good commute. He's been a very generous host, and is instructing me in the fine art of noodle-making. He says if I stay long enough he'll teach me how to make sushi too. I'm hoping that won't happen – not because I don't like raw fish, but – well, you know.

I often think of you (of course I do) and how things are going at the cottage. Sometimes I wonder how we let certain things, stupid things like what kind of bath we were getting, drive a wedge between us. But then I remind myself there are bigger things at the heart of this.

Last weekend I went for a roast at Nico and Suni's, and holding Bella reminded me of that. I don't want to pressure you into anything you don't want, Amelia. I'd never do that. But I can't just hope I'll change my mind either, because I don't think I will.

Give Dexter a stroke from me.
Jack

'Hi, Suni. It's me. Is now a good time?'

'It's an excellent time,' Suni said. I could hear her putting the kettle on. 'Bella's out for the count, and I've been looking for an excuse to open these biscuits.'

'What kind?'

'Double-chocolate chip.'

I went over to the biscuit tin and took out a couple of ginger nuts myself. 'I'm going to join you, in cookie solidarity.'

'We saw Jack the other day. He came over.'

'I know. He mentioned it. How did he seem?'

'OK. Distracted, I guess, which isn't surprising. I think Bella took his mind off things a bit. Amelia, he told me he's staying in London at the moment – why didn't you mention what was going on?'

'I don't know.' There'd been half a dozen times when I'd gone to pick up the phone to call Sunita or Carly and then stopped. 'Maybe because it would make it seem more real.'

'How's it been?'

'Strange. But I've got Mirabel staying at the moment which keeps me busy.'

'Have you had a chance to think about things? I got the impression Jack had been doing a lot of that.'

'I suppose. I don't know, Suni. I haven't really wanted to think about it.'

'But Amelia – look, I know it's not my business, but this is your marriage. It's serious. What are you going to do? Just give up without even trying?'

'Of course I'm going to try,' I said as her words hit home. 'It's just . . . I don't know what I want right now, Suni.'

'Is there someone else involved?' she asked gently.

For a moment I felt frustrated with her for even suggesting it. But my annoyance wasn't really for her, it was for me. All her question had done was force me to confront what I'd been trying to hide from myself.

'Nothing's happened. Jack needed space to think about our future, and since we moved into this cottage these four walls have seen us bickering more than we ever have before. But yes, I suppose there is someone. I don't know what's going on, but I'm attracted to him. I feel happy when I'm with him.'

'Right,' Suni said. I could hear her taking a deep breath. 'I wasn't really expecting that.'

'Nor was I, believe me.'

'And what – is he interested? Can you imagine having a relationship with this guy?'

'Maybe. I don't know. Like I said, nothing's happened yet and I haven't thought that far ahead. But when I'm with him I feel something I haven't felt in a little while. Relaxed. Free.'

'So this man is offering you a way out.'

'What do you mean?'

'Nothing. Just that I guess maybe Jack's become bound up in all the stress of the cottage, and now you can't separate him from that.'

'I don't think you can reduce it down to that.'

'Sorry. I don't know – maybe this guy you've met is the one for you. The truth is that as much as I'd like to, I can't be completely objective. I love you, but I also love Jack.'

'So do I,' I said, tears welling up. 'It's not like you can just stop loving someone overnight.'

That evening I walked into the bathroom in my blue towelling dressing gown and sat down on the simple wicker chair next to the bath. I ran the tap and poured lavender bath foam under the stream of water.

The clawfoot tub was now in place in the centre of the

room, with a fluffy white bathmat beside it, the fabric soft under my feet. Fresh white towels were folded neatly in piles on the wooden dresser, with one on the antique towel rail, ready to use. The floorboards were stained to a deep chestnut, and the walls were painted in a simple white that set off the timber beams and posts. I'd draped the small window with light muslin curtains, and the sun shone through the coloured glass of the bottles I'd arranged on the sill, casting blue and green patches of light onto the floor. At last, this bathroom was the haven Jack and I had dreamed of.

I looked over at the bathroom cabinet I'd left clear for his things. I'd bought this bath because Jack and I had loved the one we saw in Arcadia Cottage, because we'd joked how it would be big enough for two. I slipped the towelling robe off and dipped a hand into the water to test the temperature. I'd been so sure that the bath would make our lives complete – and yet now there was no one to share it with, no one to laugh with or talk to. Jack had gone.

I climbed in.

Chapter 17

Rachel and Fred's Farm

Livestock

Chickens:	eight
Cows:	five
Horses:	three
Alpacas:	six

Wednesday, 30 October

'Rachel, hi,' I said, when I got through on the phone. 'It's Amelia, Rosie's daughter. I know this is out of the blue, but I have a bit of a favour to ask. It's to do with your farm.'

'Would you like to visit?' Rachel said warmly. 'You're welcome any time.'

'Actually, I was wondering if you might let my sister, Mirabel, help out for a couple of days.'

'We'd love to have her!' Rachel said. 'It would be great to have a hand around the place, and we can teach her a few things about farm life as we go. Just bring her round. We've got a few things here she can borrow: waterproof trousers, wellies – that sort of thing.'

'That's brilliant. I really appreciate it. We'll be round at ten.'

Mirabel was sleeping soundly when I looked in on her in the spare room. 'Wake up, sleepyhead,' I said, gently shaking her.

'*Mmmmhgruuunahhh*,' she muttered, turning to face me and rubbing her eyes.

'Big day ahead,' I said.

'Where are we going?' she asked, propping herself up on her elbow.

'Get some jeans on, and I'll explain on the way.'

After a quick cup of tea in the kitchen, I drove Mirabel over to Rachel and her husband's place, fifteen minutes away from our cottage. On the journey she was silent, gazing out of the window, and I listened to the local news on the radio. We pulled up outside the farm.

'No way,' Mirabel said, looking across the courtyard and towards the stables. 'There's absolutely no way you're sending me in there.'

'That's a shame,' I shrugged, 'because they're expecting you.'

Rachel, dressed in jeans and an Aran jumper, came out of the farmhouse as if on cue. 'Hello,' she said cheerfully. We got out of the car and she walked up to Mirabel and shook her hand. The smell of manure was hard to ignore, and Mirabel's hand went up to her nose, covering it. 'You must be our angel of a helper.'

'That's Mirabel,' I said with a smile, ignoring the grimace my sister was making at me. 'Thanks for agreeing to this, Rachel.'

'It's a pleasure – and as I said on the phone, we're so grateful for the help.'

I could sense Mirabel's desperation to escape. Rachel motioned for her to come into the house. 'Let's get started then. I've got some clothes for you, and then I can introduce you to the animals.'

Mirabel shot daggers at me as Rachel gently led her away by the arm.

'Sorry,' I mouthed. Then, out loud, 'See you later!'

'Fred'll drop her back when we're done,' Rachel said.

'Thanks so much Rachel,' I said. 'See you later. Call if you need anything.'

Back at the cottage, I looked up from the sewing machine at a knock on the spare bedroom door.

'Sorry to disturb you,' the joiner said, putting his head around the door. A man in his sixties, with grey hair and ill-fitting clothes, he'd become a familiar presence in the cottage over the past few days. 'But I wanted to tell you that I'm all done downstairs now. Would you like to come and have a look?'

'Great.' I got up from the desk. 'Of course. How have you found it?'

'Not bad. Quite a typical job for this area, I'd say – these old cottages all have similar issues, so I had most of the materials at the workshop. The banister spindles were the trickiest part to source.'

We reached the top of the staircase and he bent down to touch the new ones he'd put in. 'Quite an unusual design, this one.' He ran a finger over the acorn engraving that spiralled down the wood. 'Beautiful though.'

He had also repaired the steps that I'd got in the habit of skipping over so that I didn't put my foot through them. 'I was thinking of carpeting these stairs,' I said, 'but actually they look nice how they are, don't they?'

'I'd leave them be,' the joiner said, 'but that's just me. I always like things done the traditional way. Bit of a boring old fart, the wife says.' He laughed.

We walked down to the living room, where I'd seen him working on the window frames over the past few days. 'Replaced almost all of these,' he said. 'Normally I like to keep some of the old wood in place, but I'm afraid yours were just too far gone. It's made a big difference though, I think, to how the whole room looks.'

I looked at the living room, our living room – it was barely recognizable from the day that Jack and I had moved in and found it full of Mrs McGuire's clutter. Now the windows were clean and sparkling, with smart new wooden frames that fitted in with the style of the cottage perfectly. The floor was all ready for a rug to be fitted – I had in mind an oatmeal-coloured one I'd seen in a shop.

I went over to the windows and peered at the frames more closely. The colour match of the wood was really good. 'They look great,' I said. 'Just what we'd hoped for. Thank you.'

I was painting the hallway later that day when my phone rang. Still wearing my paint-spattered overalls, I walked through into the kitchen to answer it.

'Amelia!' Dad's voice, playful and warm. My reaction was normally instinctive – an immediate smile and a comfortable feeling of being reconnected with him. But today I didn't feel that. I just felt numb.

'Dad, hi.'

'Hey there, darling. How are things? How's your sister coping at boot camp?' he asked, with a laugh in his voice.

'Really well,' I said, holding back the full story. I realized that my loyalties had shifted. 'She's helping out on a friend's farm today.'

'Well I'll be damned. How did you manage that – chloroform?'

'She's been helping out with a few things, actually. I think she's grown up a lot, Dad.'

'Do you? We certainly haven't seen any of that.'

'She's becoming more responsible,' I said. 'Not sure I'd say she was quite there yet, but she's only sixteen after all.'

'She's not bad. But thanks for letting us have a break, eh. She was really giving us a headache!'

'Dad,' I said, steeling myself. The thoughts and emotions that had been whirring in my head and stomach for days were fighting their way to the surface now that I could hear my father's voice. 'There's something I've been wanting to talk to you about.'

'Sure. There's no need to sound all serious, sweetheart.'

'Maybe there is.'

'OK. Well, fire away then.'

'Daughters aren't there for you to pick up and put down when it suits you. That goes for Mirabel, and it goes for me too.'

'What's all this about, Amelia? What's brought this on?'

I breathed deeply and tried to keep my voice steady. 'Let's just say I've had a wake-up call.'

'Has your mum said something to you?'

'No. In fact, you should be grateful to her – she's never said a word against you.'

The other end of the line fell silent. It was the only time it had ever happened in a conversation with my dad.

'I'm sorry you feel that way, Amelia. I've always tried to be there for you, but obviously sometimes it's difficult living further away like this. But you're always welcome to visit, you know that, and I try to get you things to show that I care.'

'I don't want jewellery and I don't want empty promises. Not any more. I want honesty from you.'

'I've always been honest with you, sweetheart.'

'Have you?' I said, a trace of venom creeping into my voice. 'Really, truly – have you?'

He fell silent again.

'What's all this about? Everyone makes mistakes, sweetheart. I can't undo the things that I might have done wrong.'

'No, you can't. I understand that. I love you, Dad, and what went on with Mum is in the past now. But I need things to change between you and me, here and now. '

'OK. What is it that you want?'

'I've always respected you, and I now need you to respect me. Where I want to start is with the loan. I don't want empty promises. Jack and I lent you that money in good faith, and now we need it back. When can you pay us?'

'It's been tricky,' he said. 'I'll see what I can do.'

'I want a date.'

I heard him draw in his breath.

'Sure,' he said at last. 'By Christmas. I'll have it in your bank account by then.'

'You swear?'

'Yes. I won't let you down this time,' he promised.

'Fine. I'm trusting you on this,' I said.

'OK. Bye, Amelia.'

After saying goodbye, I pressed the disconnect button on my phone and put it down on the side.

I breathed deeply and sat down. Then, slowly, a smile crept on to my face. I'd done it. I'd finally done it. From now on, I was going to be in control.

At just gone six, I heard the door knocker downstairs and went to answer it.

Mirabel was standing on the doorstep with a man with a grey beard, who I vaguely recognized from the village.

'Hi, you must be Fred. I'm Amelia,' I said, putting out my hand for him to shake.

'Pleasure to meet you,' Fred said. 'But I won't be shaking hands if it's all the same.' He held up his mud-covered ones. 'Thanks for lending us Mirabel for the day. Absolute star, she's been.'

'Thank you. I'm pleased to hear it,' I said, trying to catch my sister's eye, but she was staring at the floor.

Fred said goodbye to Mirabel and walked back towards his muddy Range Rover.

'God, that was *awful*,' she said as soon as front door was closed.

'What did they do to you?' I asked, feeling the tiniest hint of satisfaction that Fred and Rachel hadn't gone too easy on her.

'First I had to muck out the horses. All this dung, it was gross.' She lifted her checked shirt and sniffed and it. 'Seriously – I still smell of it. It was completely disgusting. Go on, have a smell if you don't believe me.'

'I'll take your word for it. Give me those clothes and I'll stick them in the wash.'

Mirabel sighed. 'Then, when I'd done the mucking out, I had to brush the horses.'

'That doesn't sound too bad.' I said.

'Actually, that part was OK. They're going to be in a county show at the weekend, and Rachel wants them to look their best.'

'Did you get to see the alpacas?'

'Yes. They're pretty actually, but really shy. Whenever you get close to them they just run away.'

'Well, maybe once they get used to you. Perhaps tomorrow when—'

'I'm not going back there tomorrow,' Mirabel pronounced.

'Oh really?' I said nonchalantly. 'That's interesting.'

'You can't make me.'

'I know I can't.' I shrugged. 'But I also know Rachel and Fred will be pretty disappointed if you don't go back.'

Mirabel sighed and then stomped up the stairs to her room.

Chapter 18

The Living Room

On the Mood Board

Period fireplace with a fire lit, cream rug, wicker basket overflowing with logs. Cosy red sofa with cushions. Antique armchair. Curtains in gold and red.

Thursday, 31 October

I fiddled with the thermostat in the kitchen. We'd barely had the heating on since investing in a new boiler, but today we were going to need it. There was a fine frost on the hedges and trees outside, and hailstones were rattling against the windowpanes. In my pyjamas, dressing gown and furry slippers I was shivering in the kitchen. I heard the boiler flare up and the heating click in, then pressed my hand against the radiator, impatient to feel it heating up.

Mirabel came in with one of my woolly jumpers on over her nightie and leggings. 'Flipping freezing in this cottage.'

'I know. I've just put the heating on. Fancy tea and some crumpets to help us warm up?'

'Yes, please.'

I put the kettle on and took a blue and white polka-dot teapot off the dresser.

After Mirabel's attitude the night before, I was surprised to see that she was up early of her own accord.

'You'll soon get warmed up, working with the animals,' I said, testing the waters.

'I suppose so.'

'You're OK about going to the farm again today, then?'

'Yes. Nothing better to do around here, anyway.'

'Fine. Well, I'll give you a lift in an hour or so.'

'Actually, do you think . . . I mean, Rachel said I could help get the horses ready on Saturday for that show, if there's time before my flight . . . Would that be OK?'

I hid my smile. 'I think we could probably manage that, yes.'

When I'd dropped Mirabel at the farm, I came back to the cottage. In the living room, Spencer was crouched down with a hammer in his hand, fixing a piece of skirting board.

'Hi,' he said, glancing up at me. 'This skirting's come loose. Thought I'd tidy it up a bit.'

'Thanks,' I said. 'That seems to be the way with this place – you fix one thing and then find another.'

'I know what you mean. I love old houses though, don't you? I wouldn't swap mine.'

'I've had my moments of doubt. But I'm a convert now, I have to say.' I glanced back out into the hallway, in case I'd missed Callum somehow. 'Is, er . . .'

'Callum around?'

'Yes,' I said, unconsciously smoothing down my hair. 'I was hoping to talk to him about something.'

'He'll be back in a sec. He's just out in the garden on the phone.'

'Oh. Right,' I said, nodding.

'I sent him out there.' Spencer smiled and rolled his eyes heavenward. 'Got sick of hearing all that romantic stuff.'

My breath caught. 'Romantic?'

'Don't worry, it's not interfering with his work. It'd take more than a new woman on the scene to shake Callum's focus. I say new, but actually I think there's some history with this one.'

'Oh yes?' I asked, trying to sound like I didn't care.

'Spanish girl. I think she's the reason he's planning to travel out there.'

Spain. Of course. The trip Callum had told me about. The

one I'd thought showed just how carefree and spontaneous he was, without ties to anyone, anywhere.

'Right,' I said. My stomach twisted. Of course there would be a woman in Callum's life. Why had I assumed there wasn't?

Sensing a presence behind me, I turned to see him in the doorway, his mobile still in his hand.

'You're not listening to Spencer's gossip, I hope?' he said with a smile.

I made my excuses and left the room quickly, heading upstairs to my bedroom. Sitting down on my bed, I thought about what Spencer had just told me. I felt like a complete and utter fool. Embarrassment crept up onto my cheeks, which burnt red-hot.

And yet at the same time I felt oddly relieved.

All this time I'd thought there might be something between me and Callum – I'd convinced myself I'd felt some chemistry there, that the attraction I felt towards him was reciprocated. Yet while I'd been thinking about him, he'd been thinking about someone else entirely. His talk of Spain had seemed like a hippy, bohemian escape – a symbol of the freedom that my life no longer contained any trace of. But that was a story I'd invented – his plan to travel was dictated by love and caring, as much as my life was.

Or at least as much as my life had once been. Those priorities had fallen to the bottom of my list lately, and I'd let that happen. In my quest for happiness and a perfect home, I'd all but disregarded what I already had – my love for Jack and his for me. I'd allowed myself to picture what another man could offer, the alternate self I might be if I wasn't a wife, a homeowner . . . or, as Jack seemed to see me, a mum-in-waiting.

I'd been cold and selfish, and it was no surprise he'd ended up stepping away from me. I wouldn't blame him if he never wanted to come back. But I knew now what I needed – more than that, I wanted him.

Was there still time? If there was a chance of saving this relationship I had to try – and it was down to me to make the first move. I got out my laptop and started typing an email.

Dear Jack,

Do you remember how things used to be between us? I've been thinking, and I'd really like to get back to how we were . . .

Later that afternoon I went to pick up Mirabel from the farm.

'She's worked really hard today,' Rachel told me, as we all stood together in the courtyard.

Mirabel scuffed the toe of her welly on the ground. 'It was quite fun,' she said, quietly. 'I learned a lot, actually.'

'With just two days to get the horses ready for the show

it's been great to have your help, Mirabel,' Rachel added, putting her arm round her. 'I think Dora and Brodie are going to miss you when you go.'

Mirabel glanced up and smiled.

'Mirabel mentioned that you had the show on Saturday – we should have time for her to go with you before I take her to the airport. If you're sure that's OK?'

'Of course,' Rachel said. 'It's great fun, and only right she should get to see the horses perform after everything she's done here.'

'Great,' Mirabel said. 'I can't wait.'

'Right,' I said, giving her a gentle nudge. 'I think it's about time the two of us got back home and had some dinner, don't you?'

She nodded.

'See you tomorrow, Rachel,' she said.

'See you – and thanks again.'

Rachel waved us off as we drove away in my car.

'So you enjoyed it?' I asked.

'A bit,' Mirabel said, taking off her hair elastic and shaking out her ponytail. She raked her dark hair with her hands. 'Tomorrow Rachel's going to run through the preparations with me so that we're all ready for Saturday. She told me something else today too – Dora's pregnant. She'd going to have a foal.'

'How lovely.'

'She promised she'd send pictures, so I can see it when I'm back in Ireland. I sort of wish I could be here when it's born. Do you think when it's here you could show it to me on Facetime?'

'Sure,' I said.

'What's for dinner tonight?'

'I thought we could have shepherd's pie. Sound OK to you?'

'Definitely. I'm absolutely starving.'

We listened to Magic FM in the car as we drove home, singing along to the tunes together. Back at the cottage, Mirabel went upstairs to get showered and changed.

Callum stepped out into the hall as I was hanging up my coat.

'Hi. Spencer and I have just finished in the living room. Looks like you're going to have your cottage back to yourself soon.' He paused. 'You and Jack will, I mean,' he added awkwardly.

It was hardly surprising that he'd picked up on the fact that my husband had gone from being a regular presence at the cottage to not being there at all.

'Great,' I said brightly. 'Show me. I've been looking forward to seeing it.'

So this was it, I thought. Callum's last day at the cottage.

He led me into the living room. Walking by his side, I felt

none of the chemistry I'd sensed before – something invisible that had seemed to bind me and him, even when we were no more than strangers. Since finding out about the girl he was seeing in Spain, any imagined connection I'd had with him had faded away. At thirty years old, I'd had a proper schoolgirl crush, and now – thank God – it was over.

'We stripped the floorboards, sanded and stained them like you asked, and the walls are ready for the new wallpaper.'

'It looks good,' I said, surveying the room. It looked so much bigger and lighter without the old carpet. It was somewhere I could actually imagine snuggling down in the evening now, on our sofa, or hosting guests.

'I can't thank you and Spencer enough for all you've done. We're up to date on the money, aren't we?'

'Yes, that's sorted, thanks,' Callum said warmly. 'We've really enjoyed working here. Especially in the garden – my grandma would love how it is now.'

'Thanks again,' I said, giving him a hug goodbye. He pulled back after a moment, and his grey-green eyes met mine with an intense gaze.

For a split second I wondered. If maybe, after all, there was something between us.

'I have a feeling you're going to be very happy here, Amelia.'

*

On the way to the airport on Saturday, Mirabel filled me in on her morning.

'It was incredible to see Dora win, after looking after her all week.'

'It sounds like it was a great day.'

'Rachel said she was sure it was due to all the care I took of her.'

'You do seem to have a flair for it. You know what, I bet there are all kinds of NVQ courses you can do in animal care. Is that something you might be interested in?'

'Maybe,' she said. 'It would be better than the stuff we learned at school, I bet.'

'I'll look into it for you,' I said. 'Send you a few links through.'

'OK. Thanks.'

I pulled into the short-stay car park. 'Right. Here we are. You all ready?'

'Yep,' she said, getting out.

We walked towards the departures lounge, Mirabel wheeling her suitcase and me carrying her shoulder bag.

'You'll be OK, won't you, getting home?' I said.

'Of course I will. What are you getting all worried about? Mum's already called to say she can pick me up from the airport.'

'OK. Right. Well, have a safe journey then. Be good.'

'Thanks for having me,' she said with a curtsey, a parody

of the polite girl we both knew she wasn't. 'And for all the slave-driving.' She smiled. 'But seriously, good luck with the house. And say hello to Jack for me.' She touched my arm, gentle in a way I hadn't seen before. 'I hope he comes home soon.'

I took a deep breath. I didn't want to cry in front of Mirabel, not now. I was supposed to be the strong one.

'Come back and stay again,' I said. 'We've got a gorgeous spare room for guests these days.'

She gave me a squeeze and then picked up her bags. 'See you later, sis.'

She walked away without a backward glance. Striding towards the check-in desk, Mirabel was more of a woman than when she'd arrived.

When I got back to the cottage the carpet fitters were there, putting the oatmeal carpet down in the living room. Already the whole room looked different – intimate and cosy.

I brought in the remainder of the furniture from storage – Grandma Niki's walnut drinks cabinet and side table, the armchairs I'd picked up cheap in an eBay auction – and, with help from one of the fitters, our sofa from home.

When the fitters had left I put some music on and draped the sofa with the warm red fabric throw I'd made. Singing, I hung up the matching curtains, put our books on the bookshelves and arranged our ornaments on the furniture and windowsills. I took out the wedding photo of me and Jack by Clifton Suspension Bridge, and put it in the centre of the mantelpiece.

I sat back on the sofa and took it all in. The living room was finally finished. Everything was right.

And yet nothing was right at all.

Chapter 19

The Study

On the Mood Board

Cream and green-apple wallpaper to complement the view into the front garden. Re-carpet in oatmeal or cream. Antique wooden desk and chair facing outwards. Swatches of organic colours – greens and browns.

Saturday, 30 November

November had brought with it a deepening chill, and it seemed as if every time I looked out of our windows, the frost on the oak tree and hedges was brighter and thicker. Wandering through the garden that morning, with a cup of hot chocolate in my hand, I felt I should be in an advert for country life. But at the same time I felt like a fraud. Our country idyll was just mine now.

Back inside, the cottage was blissfully warm, especially now I'd got the woodburning stove in the dining room going. I'd bought an Advent calendar ready for the start of the new month, and begun collecting holly and evergreens from the garden ready to make Christmas decorations. The golden early autumn days when Jack and I had first moved into the cottage, and when everything was still simple between us, seemed a long time ago. It felt almost normal now, just me in the cottage, alone.

We'd been using the smallest room upstairs, with the view of the apple tree, as a bit of a dumping ground since we first moved in. All the pieces of furniture that didn't have a home, and the paintings that weren't our favourites, and the lever-arch files full of papers that we'd never known where to put them, were in there, piled on top of each other, so that the little room was a microcosm of the chaos the whole cottage had been in when we'd first arrived.

Today I had time to tackle it. I brought in the steamer and began stripping down the dark wallpaper – a nicotine-stained William Morris design that must have been there since David and his brother were children. Below it was a layer of rosebud paper. By the door I saw dates and heights marked in pencil – Ewan and David's names were still legible. I ran my finger over them. It seemed a shame to cover them up.

The rolls of apple-print wallpaper I'd got discounted in

town were in the corner of the room. This room was where I'd put my sewing machine – I'd have all the space I wanted to make cushions and even dresses now. Dexter meowed in the doorway, and rubbed himself up against the frame.

Not that I'd have as much free time for things like that – I was working a bit now and hopefully would be able to do even more in the new year. I'd recently covered a few English classes at Woodlands Secondary, and enjoyed every minute of them. The teenagers were bright and enthusiastic and had read all of the set texts – they even listened without me having to shout when I asked them questions, and participated dutifully in the activities I gave them. It felt like another world – I was finally able to use some of the techniques and plans I'd learned at college, rather than just disciplining pupils all the time. While I missed some of my students from St Catherine's, the change was refreshing.

Charlotte Jacobs had called me earlier in the week asking if I could do some more supply work in the new year, and confirming that they'd be interviewing for a new English teaching post in the spring.

'Your CV's right at the top of my pile,' she'd told me on the phone. 'I do hope we'll be seeing you, Amelia.'

While I'd needed a break, not teaching had left me feeling like part of me was missing – I couldn't wait to get started again. There was something else I'd been mulling over too.

From the window, I could see Rachel and Fred's farm. I thought again of the change in Mirabel, and wondered what might happen if only I could get some of Class 10E here: Trey, Paul, Shanice and the other students who never got out of the city, not even for a single day. Was there a way that I could bring some of them down here and show them something different? The country, albeit just in books and films, had given me an escape when I was a kid. Perhaps the real thing could do even more? Perhaps the less troubled teenagers at Woodlands Secondary would benefit from placements of a few days too?

I put down the steamer and decided to drive over to Rachel and Fred's farm. There was something I wanted to ask them.

Back at the cottage, I sat on the window seat in the spare bedroom and dialled St Catherine's.

'Is that Lewis Garrett?' I asked, when a familiar male voice picked up.

'Speaking.'

'Hi, Lewis, it's Amelia. Amelia Grey.'

'Hello, Amelia. It's good to hear from you again.'

'Yes, I suppose I wasn't really expecting to be calling,' I said with a laugh. 'Is everything going well?'

'It is,' he said. 'I hope you know by now how sorry we were to lose you.'

'Thank you.'

'I have some good news to pass on, actually.'

'Don't tell me – you haven't seen Paul O'Reilly for detention since I left?'

'Oh, I'm afraid not. He's in here every week, like before. Mr Kilfern's not having any more luck with him. Trey Donoghue's back in class, though, and seems to have pulled his socks up a bit since last term.'

'That's wonderful,' I said, feeling a glow as I pictured Trey's formerly empty desk by the window, with him seated in it once more.

'But actually the good news is to do with Isabel Humphries. I'm delighted to be able to tell you that she's recovering well, is currently in remission, and should be returning to work with us in the spring term.'

A smile broke out on my face. Isabel's chemotherapy had worked!

'That's fantastic news.'

'We're all delighted,' Lewis said. 'She looks better. Much better.'

'Please give her my love.'

'Of course I will. Was there something in particular you were calling about?'

'I had an idea I wanted to run past you, actually. Something to give the pupils a break, particularly those who don't often get the chance to get out of the city.'

'Oh, yes?' Lewis said, curious.

'There's a farm near where I live. It wouldn't take long for me to bring a few of the teenagers down on a coach, maybe once a term. They could spend the day helping out – get a break from the city, do something different. The farm owners would be happy to talk them through what happens, and if they can lend a hand with some of the work, well, all the better.'

'Hmm . . . I rather like the idea,' Lewis said, mulling it over. 'Let me discuss it with a few people, and I'll get back to you. But I don't see why not.'

I got back to working in the apple-tree room. By midday the walls were ready to be re-papered, and I'd sugar-soaped the window frame and skirting so that it was all prepared for a fresh coat of wood paint.

I took a break and went down into the kitchen to make myself some lunch. I buttered some bread and took out some ham and some fresh salad from the fridge. Next year, I thought to myself, there might be vegetables from our very own vegetable patch. It would feel good to get out there and start growing things.

Apart from the dining room, the cottage makeover was now nearly complete.

My mobile rang.

'Hi, Mum,' I answered.

'Hello, darling,' she said. I could hear right away that something was wrong.

'What's up?'

'I'm at home and Callum and David are here with me. We've just had a call from Eleanor's neighbour to say that she's gone missing.'

I could hear Callum and his father in the background, talking to each other.

'Oh no, that's awful,' I said.

'Yes. Something must have spooked her. Apparently the neighbour saw her wandering up the road in her nightdress about an hour ago. We've taken the car out for a drive around but there was no sign – David's been in touch with her other neighbours and one thought they saw her heading back home, so we've been back and forth today.'

'Poor Eleanor,' I said, thinking of the frail woman I'd seen on the high street from Sally's cafe. The winter chill had intensified over the past few weeks and the weatherman said there was a frost coming – these weren't the conditions for a pensioner to be wandering around the village in her night clothes for hours on her own.

'Is there anything I can do?'

'That's why I'm calling,' Mum said. 'This is a long shot, I know. We wondered if there was a chance she might have walked back to the cottage on autopilot. You know how cats can be? Not comparing her to a cat, but you know what I mean . . . Would you be able to give the place a quick check, just so that we can eliminate it from the search before we get the police involved?'

'Of course,' I said. 'I'll have a look right now.'

I thought of the morning's painting – to air the house I'd left the front door and ground-floor windows open. As Eleanor knew the house so well, it was more than possible she could have found her way in without me even realizing.

'Mrs McGuire,' I called out softly, opening the door to the downstairs toilet, and then crossing the hallway to check the living room. The space was bare, and it was immediately clear that the room was empty – I wasn't going to find her in there.

I climbed the stairs, continuing to call her name. I thought of how disorientating it would be for her – to arrive back at her familiar home, at the cottage, but find that everything had changed, her bedroom furniture no longer crammed into the ground-floor rooms, all her things gone.

I looked into the rooms hurriedly, worried about leaving her alone and bewildered for any longer than was necessary – after the walk down from her bungalow she might already be suffering from the cold. I checked the room I'd been painting – nothing. The house was empty.

There was one last option – I glanced up at the attic. But no – Callum had said she couldn't even get up the main staircase these days.

I headed back downstairs and called Mum back. 'I'm sorry. I've searched the house but there's no sign of her.'

'Thanks for looking, love. It was just an idea. And I suppose we were all hoping it might be the answer, given that your place is safe and warm. But it was only a silly hunch.'

'It was worth trying,' I said. 'Well, good luck tracking her down, and if there's anything else I can do, just let me know.'

I hung up, and looked over at the sandwich I'd started to make. My hunger had disappeared. I tore the bread into pieces. The birds would want it.

I put on a thick wool cardigan and opened the back door, and an icy blast entered the kitchen. I pulled the sleeves over my hands and looked out over the garden. As I put the bread out on the bird table I saw a flash of white in the distance, down by the stream. It disappeared as quickly as I caught sight of it. I stepped further out into the garden and made my way down the paving-stone path that led to the stream. After a few steps I spotted the white-clad figure again, and this time I could see her properly – a woman of Eleanor's age, her white hair loose, pacing up and down by the side of the water.

'Mrs McGuire?' I called out. She seemed lost in her own world and didn't look up – but I could tell it was her. The features, so much like her son's and grandson's, were unmistakeable.

'Mrs McGuire,' I tried again. This time she tilted her head towards me and there was a glimmer of recognition in her bright green eyes. Not of me – but of her own name. She smiled at me.

'The garden,' she said softly as I drew nearer.

'Here,' I said, taking off my thick wool cardigan and passing it to her. 'Put this on. You must be cold out here.'

She shook her head, then reluctantly put her arms into the sleeves and pulled it around her. 'I was cold. But the garden,' she said, with a faint smile, 'is pretty this time of year, isn't it? I've always taken good care of it.'

I saw now that her feet were clad only in slippers, and her pale white legs, with veins showing through the paper-thin skin, had a blue tinge.

'It's a lovely garden,' I said. 'Beautiful. Shall we go inside?' I asked, holding out my hand.

'No,' she replied stubbornly. 'I came here to be by the stream.'

I offered my hand again, and this time she seemed to have forgotten her reasons for wanting to stay, and took it, walking slowly with me towards the warmth of the cottage.

'I'll get you a cup of tea,' I said. 'And some cake. And then I'm going to call David and he can come and get you. You've had everyone worried, you know. Your family care about you a lot.'

'Too much,' she muttered. 'For the liar I am.'

After the slow walk, we arrived at the kitchen. Her eyes came to rest on the one feature from her time at the cottage – the Aga in the corner, and she seemed comforted by its familiarity.

I put the kettle on, thankful that the other, newer features in the kitchen didn't seem to have alarmed her.

'I'm just going to call your son and let him know you're OK.'

'If you have to,' she said, sitting down at the table.

I called Mum and told her that Eleanor was fine, and that she was inside now, getting warmed up. I heard the relieved responses of David and Callum in the background.

'You came back to the cottage,' I said, putting her tea down in front of her. She eyed it suspiciously.

'I came for her things,' she said. 'I need to find them. She took my hand in hers and looked me directly in the eye. 'You know.'

'The tin?' I asked tentatively.

'That's where I put them. Yes.'

'OK.' I walked over to the back door and locked it. 'Promise me you'll stay right here, Eleanor? And have your tea? Then I'll bring them to you.'

'You will?' she said, her eyes pleading.

'I'll be back in a minute,' I said. I left the kitchen and

went upstairs to my bedroom. I found the tin right away, the tarnished bronze gleaming out from my shelf.

I took it downstairs and passed it to Eleanor, who hadn't moved from her spot at the table.

'Sarah,' she said, taking the tin from me. 'Sarah's things.' Her eyes filled with tears as she opened the box and took out the photograph of a baby girl. She lifted the bonnet out next, pressing the soft fabric against her face for a moment and then holding it close to her chest.

I sat opposite her, feeling as if I was intruding on a deeply intimate moment.

'Was Sarah . . .?' I started.

'I didn't want to let her go,' she insisted, looking at me as if I'd accused her of something. 'I had to.'

'I know,' I said. It seemed to reassure her. She put the photo down on the table and looked at me again.

'I don't want them to find out,' she said. 'That's why I came here, why I came back. I don't want them to know. My boys. All these years I've never told them about Sarah. It would be too much. Too much hurt, to have them find out now.'

Her gaze was focused and she seemed lucid – not the scared shadow of a woman I'd found down by the stream just a few moments ago.

'What happened?' I asked gently.

Her eyes filled with tears again but she brushed them away roughly.

'It was during the war. I was too young to know better. I could have coped though, I know I could. I wanted her so much, my little girl.'

I thought back to my conversation with David. Pieces were starting to fall into place now.

'You gave her away?' I asked, as softly as I could.

'I didn't want to. But I had to, you see. My mother said it wouldn't do. Even if I could cope, she said people would judge me. It wouldn't be something I could hide. I was just a girl really, when I met Alfie. My first time out at a local dance, and he swept me off my feet – literally. I'd saved for weeks to buy that dress, emerald-green it was, and my sister Marie helped me do my hair. My parents wouldn't normally have let us go out unchaperoned, but the dance had been organized by the church and they didn't see the harm in it.

'I danced with Alfie all night. He was from out of town, passing through. He never told me what his job was, and well, I never asked. It didn't seem to matter. We just clicked, you see, laughing and joking together, and didn't talk much about anything serious at all. Alfie asked to see me again the next weekend, to go to the pictures, and I'd never had a man ask me that before. It didn't feel right lying to my parents, but Marie told me I shouldn't miss my chance.

She'd seen Alfie, of course – and she was as caught up by his dark eyes and hair as I was. The grin, and those beautiful dimples he had.

'I'm not a bad girl, you know.'

'I'd never have thought that,' I said.

'But I suppose I did get swept up. It would never have crossed my mind that he'd be married. He didn't wear a ring, and of course no one much in my village knew him. He had a house in town. I don't know if it was his or a friend's. Two months later, I realized what had happened.'

'Did you tell him?'

'Yes. I thought he'd be happy about it – and you know what? For a moment I think he was. He told me he wanted me to have it – the baby – her, Sarah. We could have found a way.'

'He never told you he was married?'

'No. But when a friend of my father's saw us together – it was inevitable really, we weren't as careful as we should have been – my parents started to ask questions about him. They found out what I hadn't really wanted to know, or believe. That weekend was the worst of my life. My parents told me I couldn't see Alfie again. I met him one last time; he came to my bedroom window at night so we could talk. He told me he was sorry for lying to me, that he would leave his wife. Perhaps I was naive, but I would have gone with him. Only I knew my parents would never forgive me. That was the last time I saw him. He left his address.'

'And then?'

'It was my mother who noticed me beginning to show. She was horrified, of course she was. Didn't dare tell my dad; he went to his grave never knowing. Probably for the best. She sent me away to stay with an aunt in Plymouth, and I had the baby there.'

'Did you ever tell Alfie what happened?'

'I wrote him a letter. Hoping he'd tell me I couldn't give the baby away. That I didn't have to do what they told me. But I never heard back. Broke my heart. Not sure it ever really got fixed.'

'But you had your sons . . .'

'And I couldn't have loved them more. But there was always a piece of me missing. There still is. The pain of giving her away . . . my firstborn. I'll never forget it.'

Behind the white hair and creased skin, I saw the flash of a teenaged Eleanor, scared and alone, with no choice but to go through with the course of action her mother had put to her.

'I'm sorry. You never . . .'

'I never saw her again, and the boys – they don't know about her. I don't want them to know this about their mother – to think she was heartless enough to give away a sister of theirs. You'll help me, won't you, please?' Eleanor implored me, pointing to the tin.

Could I really help hide the truth from David and his brother?

'Please,' she repeated. This woman, clinging to threads of the world she knew, trying to keep control. I had to do what I could to help her retain that hold, before she lost it completely.

'What do you want to do?' I said.

'The garden,' she replied, looking out of the kitchen window towards the stretch of green behind the house. 'David and Ewan had such a lovely childhood out there. Callum and Alice too. Always playing, enjoying summers in the fresh air.'

'It's a perfect garden for children.'

'Sarah never had the chance. They took her away. To Cornwall, I think.'

'Would you like us to put her things somewhere in the garden?' I asked.

'By the stream,' she said, resolute. 'So she can be near the water.'

'Shall we go now?' I asked. 'David is on his way, and I know you'll want to do it before he gets here.'

'Yes,' Eleanor said.

I persuaded her to put on my navy duffel coat and a hat, and some proper shoes, so she'd be warmer.

We took the tin and went down to the end of the garden, I stopped at the shed to get a trowel to take with us.

'Here?' I said, pointing to a spot by the water's edge.

Eleanor looked around her carefully, as if there was something in particular she was trying to remember. 'By the tree,' she said, pointing to the gnarled oak a few feet from where we were standing. I followed her lead, and when she stopped, I bent down with the trowel and dug a hole in the soft, wet earth. She watched as I removed the mud, until we had a hole the size of the tin and about a foot deep.

She passed me the tin, and I put it deep inside.

'I love you, Sarah,' she said quietly. 'And I always will.'

I reached up to take her hand and this time she squeezed it.

I put the earth back on top of the tin until the spot was covered again. There was barely a sign that we'd ever been there.

From the end of the garden I heard the faint ring of the doorbell far in the distance. 'That will be David and Callum here for you,' I said.

'Well, it's time to go then, isn't it?' she said, as if she was no longer sure what we were doing down there by the stream at all.

'Mum!' David said, as I opened the door with Eleanor beside me. The tension in his forehead disappeared in an instant.

He drew his mother into a warm hug, her tiny frame looking even more fragile cradled in his strong arms.

'You had us all so worried.'

Callum looked on, relief evident on his smiling face. 'Thank God,' he said. 'Well, thank *you*, Amelia. We were going out of our minds.'

'Glad to be able to help,' I said. 'I almost didn't spot her, down at the bottom of the garden.'

'In the garden, Grandma?' Callum said. 'In your night-dress? You could have got pneumonia.' He shook his head at her.

'I'm tougher than you think,' Eleanor said. 'And I won't be bossed around by the likes of you, Callum.'

As she said her grandson's name, entirely lucid for a moment, we all stopped. David's eyes misted over with unshed tears. Callum put a hand gently and discreetly on his father's shoulder.

'I came back,' Eleanor said, 'because I left something here. And this lady helped me find it.'

Callum looked at me, expecting further explanation. I shrugged as if there was nothing more to tell.

'Can't remember what it was now,' Eleanor said, 'but it was nice to see the stream again.'

'Dad, I'll let the police know to call off the search,' Callum said. 'Do you want to get Gran in the car?'

'I'll get myself in the car, thank you very much,' Eleanor

said, pulling the cardigan I'd lent her more tightly round her. 'Tired of being bossed around by you lot.'

'Take care,' I said. She held my gaze for a moment, then looked away. 'I like it here,' she said.

Even with the wallpaper stripped back and the old carpets torn up, a new kitchen fitted and radiators changed, it was still the cottage she knew. She seemed to feel at home.

'Eleanor, I have something of yours. Wait here a moment.' I went to the downstairs bathroom and picked up the locket that had been lying on the side. Back in the hallway, I passed it to her. Her fingers closed around it.

'Thank you, dear,' she said. I thought I saw a glint of recognition in her eye.

She walked ahead with Mum as Callum spoke to the police on his mobile. I caught David by the elbow as he went to leave.

'Just a thought,' I said, 'but would you and your family like to come for Christmas? Eleanor seems to feel at home here, and you and Callum are part of our family now.'

David smiled. 'Thank you. I think we'd all like that very much.'

I thought I'd heard the car drive away, but a couple of minutes later the doorbell rang again. *Mum*, I thought. She must have forgotten something.

When I saw who it was, it felt like my heart stopped for

a fraction of a second. That face, the person who made me feel complete. The man who I knew, right then, meant home for me.

'Hi, Amelia,' he said.

'Jack. Come in.'

I suppose I should have known he'd come back at some point, that we'd talk again. But having him back here, so close, after six weeks apart, brought all my emotions to the surface.

I'd been willing him to come back, and yet now he was here, I didn't know what to say. How I could undo everything I'd done wrong and make things right between us again?

I led him through to the living room and we sat down together on our old sofa.

'It looks pretty different in here,' he said, smiling.

'Yes. Everything except this,' I said, running a hand over the worn fabric of our sofa.

We hadn't had the money to upgrade it, but I didn't care – it was a reminder of Addison Road, and of where we'd come from.

'I've missed you,' Jack said.

'I've missed you too.'

His hand brushed my cheek gently, noticing the tears I hadn't been able to hold back.

'So what do we do now?' I said.

'I don't know. But I know that I can't be without you, Amelia. I miss this. I miss being us. I love you.'

I thought back over the past few months – the upheaval of moving, the disagreements about our future, and the way I had doubted Jack – and myself. Somewhere in all of that, the intimacy of just being us, Amelia and Jack, had been lost. We'd once wanted nothing more than time to be the two of us – and now I wanted that again.

'I love you too,' I said. 'And I'm sorry. For everything. For not putting you – us – first.'

'It wasn't just you. I promised I'd help with the cottage, and when it came to it you did so much on your own. I never really thought work would take over like it did.'

'Did you get it?' I asked. 'The commission?'

'The funders loved it. We'll start the project in the new year.'

'Congratulations.'

'Thank you,' Jack said. 'I haven't really been able to enjoy it yet, to be honest, with all this going on.'

'How was it, staying in London?'

'The truth?' Jack said, a wry smile on his face. 'I think my days of sofa-surfing are probably behind me.'

'But you were never tempted to come home?'

'Are you kidding?' Jack laughed. 'I was *always* tempted to come back here. But I didn't want to gloss over what went wrong, Amelia. And I still don't want to. There was something we both needed to work through.'

'It was pretty lonely here,' I admitted. 'I missed your silly jokes, and the way you wake me up in the morning with a kiss.'

'I missed everything about you. Even your obsession with bathroom fittings. I even missed your pyjamas. Can you believe that?'

'I knew you liked them really.'

He reached out and ran his fingers gently down the line of my jaw, coming to rest on my mouth.

I placed my hand on his arm. That touch of him. I'd missed it so much.

'Amelia, do you think we could have another chance at being you and me?'

'I'm willing to try if you are.'

Chapter 20

Making a House a Home

Monday, 2 December

'Chestnut?' Jack asked, passing me a plate of them, freshly toasted.

The fire crackled in front of us, and I took one, breaking open the tough exterior to reveal the pale, fleshy contents inside. I bit into it hungrily. Snow was falling outside.

Sally and her husband Dan had just left the house. We'd had them round for dinner, and wound up the evening drinking wine here in the living room.

We'd done it. The beamed ceiling, the clean windows, the new rugs that made this the cosiest room in the house, and our favourite one to spend time in. But far more importantly than that, Jack was back home again.

A Christmas tree stood in the corner, the tip nearly touching the ceiling, a tiny angel balanced on the top.

'It feels like home now, doesn't it?' Jack said, turning to me, his face warmly coloured by the glow of the fire.

'It does. Well, almost.'

He looked at me. 'You think we need to do more work on the place? I thought you said that we were finally finished? Just a few changes to the dining room, right?'

I shrugged and smiled at him. Over these past few weeks, something inside me had shifted. Perhaps it was that after all the ups and downs of the year I felt closer to Jack, and more in love with him than ever. Maybe it was finally understanding what my mother had gone through in order to bring me up, and realizing she was a better parent than I'd ever thought. Or perhaps it was seeing Eleanor, getting a glimpse of the pain she still had inside over not being able to be a mother to every child she'd given birth to. My ideas weren't set any more. I didn't need me and Jack to remain just the way we were. I wasn't scared of change any more. Rather than being a project drawing to a tidy conclusion, finishing the cottage felt like the start of something for the two of us.

'It's just that we've got a spare room upstairs,' I continued, 'and I'm not sure we need a study after all. And the garden . . . it seems too good now, not to share.'

'What are you saying?' he asked, narrowing his eyes at me.

'The room upstairs, with the view of the apple tree,' I

said. In an instant I imagined how the cottage would be. Full of laughter, and chaos, and mud – and it wasn't such a bad image after all. 'It would make a lovely nursery, wouldn't it?'

Jack took my hand and squeezed it tight, a wide smile spreading across his face. 'Are you sure you're ready? We can wait, if you want.'

'Nothing can be harder work than doing up this cottage, can it?'

'You want to bet?'

'I'm ready for the challenge.'

Jack took me into his arms and kissed me. In that kiss I felt the blending of our past and present and a glimpse – just a glimpse – of our future.

Chapter 21

The Dining Room

On the Mood Board

Large oak table from Heal's, wooden chairs, branches draped in fairy lights, fireplace with Christmas cards on the mantelpiece, Persian rug on the floor, dark red curtains, mistletoe.

Wednesday, 25 December

The dining room was the last room in the cottage that we finished, and Jack and I had done it with my mum's help. The two of us had hacked away at the green-tiled seventies fireplace to reveal the original brick one behind it. I'd sewn the red drape curtains and reupholstered the window seat, and Jack had papered the walls in a cream and red paper that matched the soft furnishings.

But it was Mum who noticed that just a couple of weeks before Christmas we still didn't have a dining table or any chairs, only the cheap kitchen table we'd brought with us from Addison Road. As a surprise, she bought us a beautiful oak table from Heal's, with matching chairs, that she knew Jack and I had fallen for. It was a very generous Christmas present, and one we were making use of today.

Eleanor was seated at the head of the table, closest to the fire that kept the room toasty. To her left was David, and opposite him my mum. Then came me and Jack, with Sunita, Nico and baby Bella next to us. A funny sort of family really, but just the right one for me.

In the centre of the table were decorations made from holly and the evergreens from the garden, wound into candle holders and left as sprigs. Red candles bathed the room in a warm light.

Mum passed me a plate piled high with pigs in blankets, and smiled. 'Your Grandma Niki would be pleased to see you serving these. They were her favourite.'

'Most of this stuff is from her recipes,' I said, looking out over the Christmas spread, our dining table heaving with turkey, roast potatoes and bread sauce.

'She was a great cook, my mum,' Mum said to David. 'Taught us all a thing or two.'

'Seconds for me, please,' Eleanor called out from the head of the table, banging her fork against her plate.

With her family around her, in what was once her home, Eleanor bore barely any resemblance to the woman I'd seen lost at the bottom of the garden. Back then her skin had been translucent and her eyes empty and she'd seemed adrift. Today she was wearing a smart red top and had her hair neatly combed and there was a glow in her cheeks. 'Delicious, this is,' she said.

'Seems like today's a good day,' David said to me quietly, with a smile. 'The cottage looks wonderful. I think that's cheered her up.'

My dad had called me that morning to wish us a happy Christmas, and to let me know that he'd paid our loan back in full. It was too late to use it on the house, but we had something else in mind for it now. He invited Jack and me to stay with him in the new year, and this time I'd said yes.

Mirabel had snatched the phone off him to tell me about the NVQ course she'd signed up for, a foundation in animal care. She wanted to get some more experience on farms over the next year and then planned to start the following September.

Callum wasn't here today – when December had rolled round he'd driven to Spain. He'd left some presents under the tree for all of us to open though, and said he'd be back next summer to see how the garden was doing. 'Perhaps we could talk again then about the summer house,' he'd said. With the permanent job I'd had confirmed at Woodlands

Secondary starting in the spring, we might actually be able to afford it this year.

As for Carly and Alex, my Facebook timeline was full of pictures of the two of them sunbathing on Bondi and eating oysters in Sydney fish market. Carly looked tanned and happy, and Alex was relaxed beside her in board shorts. It seemed now as if they'd always been together.

Bella gurgled from her place on Sunita's lap. 'I think she's enjoying her first Christmas,' Nico said, tickling his daughter under her chin. 'Hopefully next year she'll be able to eat a bit more.'

'She loves the fairy lights,' Sunita said. 'She's been staring at them for ages.'

'You guys have done so much with this place,' Nico added.

'I guess we have, haven't we?' I replied.

Jack caught my eye and smiled. 'It feels like home now,' he said.

I thought of the plans we'd made, and realized it was finally true.

Hello!

Abby, here. I hope you enjoyed reading about Amelia and Jack's adventures in home renovation! In case you're inspired to take on the challenge yourself, I've got a few ideas to get you started.

As always, I'd love to hear about your own home make-over triumphs (or catastrophes!) Here are the ways you can contact me . . .

www.abbyclements.co.uk

Twitter: @abbycbooks

Pinterest: /abbycbooks

Lots of love,
Abby x

Create Your Own Mood Board

In the book, Amelia plans how she wants her house to look by using a mood board. Here are a few tips on how to get started making your own!

1. A mood board is a collection of colours, textures, images and shapes that will help you plan how you want a space to look before you begin decorating. Professional interior designers use them to create a feel for a room, and to check that everything from the furniture to the fittings look good together.

2. You can make a mood board either on the computer, or scrapbook-style on paper. Work how you feel most comfortable.

3. Begin by brainstorming images that make you happy, and that you want to be incorporated into your space. These can be anything from colours and patterns to images of people, places or things you love. For example, if you want your bedroom to have the feel of retro Hollywood, find some pictures of vintage fashion, beautiful houses, or stills of old films and add them to the board to inspire you!

4. Remember your mood board doesn't have to be flat – fabrics, textures, bobbles and buttons make great additions.

5. Be realistic – we'd all love to have an unlimited budget, but your mood board will be most useful if it's a practical tool. Use the board to brainstorm the most cost-friendly ways to get the look you love.

Good luck! x

Fifteen Facts about Abby Clements

Where were you born? In north London

What's your favourite tipple? Rum and ginger beer

What superpower would you want? To know what male family members really want for Christmas

Dog or cat? Dog all the way – particularly dressed in antlers or silly outfits (sorry, dogs)

What keeps you sane? Friends who've known me since I was in school, when I wore huge red glasses and my mum cut my fringe

What scares you? I can't swim in the sea without thinking of great white sharks

Beaches or adventure? Both. Just not at the same time, thanks (see above)

What's your holiday read? *The Villa* by Rosanna Ley

What is the best present you've ever received? A silver necklace with a fox, from my boyfriend. The chain also has a little silver hat on it, so at certain points of the day the fox can be wearing the hat. Hours of entertainment for a writer with deadlines to meet

What have you learned about yourself as you've got older? That I'm more cheerful after my first coffee of the day

What would people be surprised to discover about you? Quite how grumpy I can be before that

Sweet or savoury? I love chocolatey things

What is your favourite way to travel? Buses – I can't resist snooping in people's first floor windows . . .

What's your comfort food? Macaroni cheese, or gnocchi. Yum. I can't resist carbs

Night in or night out? summer – night out, winter – night in by the fire

Acknowledgements

As always, thanks go to my brilliant editor Jo, whose creativity, skill and kind encouragement has been essential in shaping this novel from the very start, and to my agent Caroline Hardman, for her practical support, keen editorial eye and unwavering sense of humour.

To the team at Quercus – Kathryn Taussig for her efficiency and flair on the editorial side, Georgina Difford for working magic with schedules, Caroline Butler for her endless smart marketing ideas, Alice Hill, my publicist, for her dedication and energy. Thanks also to Mark Thwaite, David North, Daniel Fraser – and to Jenny Richards for creating another beautiful cover.

To my friends and family, in particular those who shared their experiences of renovation projects – Donna, Tracey, Sophie and Vicki. This novel is based on none of these real stories, but the resilience shown in the face of burst pipes, no stairs and crumbling walls was an inspiration all the same.

I'm grateful to my partner James for supporting me every day, especially when deadlines approach, and for always making me laugh. J, I look forward (with just the tiniest bit of trepidation) to the day we make over a house for ourselves.

Lots of love,
Abby xxx

Meet Me Under
the Mistletoe

Vivien's Heavenly
Ice Cream Shop

Take a break from painting

& curl up with another

scrumptiously sweet tale

from

Abby Clements